A BIG STORM

KNOCKED IT OVER

A BIG STORM
KNOCKED IT OVER

a novel

LAURIE COLWIN

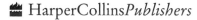 HarperCollins*Publishers*

Designed by Jessica Shatan

Library of Congress Cataloging-in-Publication Data
Colwin, Laurie.
   A big storm knocked it over / Laurie Colwin. — 1st ed.
      p.   cm.

   1. Women—United States—Fiction.   I. Title.
PS3553.04783B53   1993
813'.54—dc20   92-56219

To Harriet Shapiro,
Franny Taliaferro,
and Julie Devlin

Surely, of all things in the world the rarest is a civilized man at peace with himself.

—GONTRAN DE PONSCINS, *Kabloona*

PART I

CHAPTER 1

Jane Louise Parker sat at her drawing board looking out her office window. The late September light was hazy and warm, but the breeze—the window was open a crack—was slightly chill. This was what the Chinese called "pneumonia weather." Jane Louise knew this from having designed the interior of a book entitled *Magic Needles: The Story of Acupuncture in the West*. She yawned.

Two weeks ago she had stood up in front of a judge and had been transformed from Jane Louise Meyers into Jane Louise Parker and become the lawful wedded wife of Teddy Parker, named Theodore Cornelius for his father and great-grandfather. After wedding cake and champagne they had gone off to Maine for a week and then returned to the apartment they had shared for a year. Now they were married and back at work.

Back at work! Jane Louise had occupied this office longer than she had known her own husband. She had lived in this office for more years than she had lived at her present address. In some ways this office was her true home. She had come to it a comparatively young woman, and in not so long she would kiss her thirties good-bye.

In this very chair she had agonized over love affairs gone wrong and wondered, as she had stared out of this selfsame window, if she would ever meet and fall in love with someone she might care to marry. At this drawing table she had realized that she had fallen in love with Teddy and had spent hours daydreaming about him.

Then, after one short ceremony in the formal room of a rented mansion, she had been reclassified as a married woman.

She could not stop looking at the plain band Teddy had bought for her at an antique store. His parents' marriage had been short-lived and acrimonious, while Jane Louise's mother's hand was tiny. Therefore no family rings would have done. Besides, Teddy's mother favored white gold, and Jane Louise's mother preferred pink, whereas Jane Louise liked gold that was almost green. She was gazing at her hand when she heard a noise in the doorway and there, staring at her, was her boss, the art director, Sven Michaelson.

"Nuptial radiance," he said. "Covered like a veil."

Sven was compact and well made, like a good canoe. He had short-cropped silver hair and light, cold-blue eyes. His clothes were very beautiful and expensive. It was said that he had two real interests in this world, besides running the art department of a prominent publishing house: poker and fucking. There were numerous stories about him. His mother was a Dane. His father had been something of a shady character in show business. He was half Jewish, half flinty Scandinavian, and it was said that the art departments of major New York publishing companies were littered with his victims. When once confronted with this reputation by Jane Louise, Sven said: "I don't discriminate against editorial."

He was married to his third wife, with whom he had produced

his fourth child. His secretary, Adele Lewitkin, claimed that Sven's motto was "A family for every decade."

There was no question about it: Sven exuded a kind of louche, creepy charm, a sex appeal devoid of such frills as affection or love. You looked at Sven and saw that action, plain and simple, was the name of his game.

For years he had been nosing around Jane Louise, of whom he liked to say that he had seen her grow from a callow girl into a ripe peach. And one night, four years ago, Sven had made his move.

They had both worked late, and Sven had come into her office. Only her drafter's lamp had been on, throwing a cone of light onto her desk. The rest of the room was a dark, velvet brown.

As Jane Louise bent over her work, her hair, which was shiny brown, shoulder length, and very straight, had parted. Sven had leaned over and placed his lips on the back of her neck. The electric jolt she had felt was as good as a dire warning.

It was sort of depressing to spend your first day back at your office as a married woman being scrutinized by a man whose interest in you was almost exclusively carnal. Sven seemed unable to take his eyes off Jane Louise.

"Married," he said, settling into a chair. "Let's have a look at you to see how you've *changed*."

"Why don't you shut up, Sven?" Jane Louise suggested.

"My sweet girl," said Sven, taking a little cigar out of a leather case. "You can't imagine how I pined for your return." He crossed his legs, revealing blue-and-white-striped socks. He had many pairs of these sent to him from Paris by Anik, the beautiful product of his second marriage. He was still tan from having spent his vacation in Martha's Vineyard with his present wife, Edwina; their little son, Piers; as well as his twins—Allard and Desdemona—from his first marriage, and Anik.

"Ah, Jane," he said. "I feel almost grandfatherly, watching you turn from a scrawny chicken into . . . " His voice trailed off.

"A married hen," Jane Louise said.

"Oh, sweetheart," he said, crooning. "A wedding ring only adds to a woman's basic appeal. I mean, of course, if she is basically appealing."

"Listen," Jane Louise said, almost pleading. "This is my first day back. My desk is piled with work. Don't sit around here being provocative."

"In that case," Sven said, "I'll wait until your desk is clear."

Jane Louise gave him a look.

"Never mind, Janey," he said, flicking his ashes into her potted orange tree. "I must say marriage looks wonderful on you."

In the ladies' room Jane Louise wondered if this was true. She felt she looked as she had always looked, but then she had never been married before and had no idea what was supposed to happen. She was tall and skinny, pale with the kind of paleness that is prone to blush, and her eyes were blue. She wore plain, trim clothes: She liked her skirts short and her sweaters large. For jewelry she wore a large gold man's watch that had belonged to her late father—she had snagged it before her older sister, Nora, got it first—and she wore a Navajo silver bracelet with one round turquoise, and a plain brass bracelet, both presents from Teddy.

She peered into the mirror. Had she changed? Was there now some new creature named Jane Louise Parker who was older, wiser, more grown-up? Did married people look and smell different?

Back in her office she picked up the telephone and dialed up her closest friend and former college roommate, Edie Steinhaus. Edie was a caterer and pastry chef. It was she who had made Jane

Louise's pink wedding cake, festooned with sugar violets and roses.

"Hello," Jane Louise said. "Is this Miss or Mr. Edith Steinhaus?"

"Oh, hello, darling," said Edie.

"I have just returned from a voyage to another planet," Jane Louise said. "I am a stranger in your country. I wonder if you could help me out."

"I can't," said Edie. "I am on a voyage to another reality. I am now rolling little round watercress sandwiches in chopped parsley. The Teagarden christening is this afternoon."

"Gee," said Jane Louise. "Wouldn't I just love to roll little sandwiches in chopped parsley. Who *are* the Teagardens?"

"Oh, how quickly you forget," Edie said. "Haven't you heard chapter and verse? Besides, the question is, Who *were* the Teagardens? They used to be extremely rich and vulgar, but they acquired an old master painting, and now they're less extremely rich and refined."

"Oh, isn't money heaven?" said Jane Louise.

"They have a baby called Dudley. Or maybe that's their dog," Edie said. "This christening is straight out of *House and Garden* in the fifties—the British edition."

"No cake in the shape of a teddy bear?"

"We're having the traditional simnel cake with bachelor's buttons and forget-me-nots."

"Those must be hell to make," Jane Louise said.

"Fortunately," said Edie, "it's all the rage amongst these people to use real flowers. Mrs. Teagarden told me."

"Don't they wilt?" Jane Louise said.

"No one hangs around that long," Edie said. "How's Teddy?"

"He seems exactly the same," Jane Louise said. "Here we are, married, and everything is exactly like it was before. Although, as

Sven pointed out to me, now I have to get divorced if I want to be single again."

"What a sweetheart," Edie said. "He thinks of everything. Did he send you a wedding present?"

"A bottle of vintage champagne," Jane Louise said. "Extremely appropriate."

"Well, call me a million more times," Edie said. "But not after one-thirty, because I'll be in Mrs. Teagarden's replica of the kitchen in an English stately home of the nineteen-thirties."

Edie came from a distinguished family. Both of her awful brothers had political ambitions. She was the only girl and the black sheep in a family of lawyers. When she had gone off to study at Paris's most esteemed cooking school, her parents could only bring themselves to say: "Our daughter is studying in France." Jane Louise hated Edie's brothers and her parents, too, and when Jane Louise pointed out their awfulness to Edie, whom she loved with all her heart, Edie lowered her eyes and said, "Thank you for hating my family for me."

Like Jane Louise she was tall and skinny. She had a mop of frizzy hair and a passion for vintage clothing and things made by people in dim little shops the size of pincushions. She was a clothes rack to hang wonderful garments on, another of the many things about her of which her parents did not approve.

"By the way," Jane Louise said. "Before you rush off, if you're rolling those little sandwiches around, what is Mokie doing?"

Mokie was Edie's partner. It was not known to her family that he was also her lover and that they had lived together for several years. His name was Morris Talbot Frazier. He was tall and thin. He was also beautiful and black—the color of coffee. They had met at school in Paris and had come home together to start their catering business. He wore small horn-rimmed glasses and spoke perfect French.

"Mokie's chatting up the victims," Edie said. "Those Teagardens are extremely nervous. Mo says it's like catering for whippets."

"There's a new angle," Jane Louise said. "Parties for dogs."

"Next we have the Norris memorial service," Edie said.

"Catered funerals," Jane Louise said. "What will they think of next?"

"The old guy gave a couple of mil to the library, so this is not a funeral as you or I know them," Edie said. "This is a public function."

"Public function," Jane Louise said. "Just like my wedding. Gosh, I'm lucky I got you for a caterer. Have I told you what a work of art our cake was? I was so sad to cut it."

"Your mother felt there wasn't enough of it," Edie said.

"My mother feels there's not enough of anything," Jane Louise said. "Do you think in the old days people got married and two weeks later had to go to a conference in Seattle?"

"Is Teddy going away?"

"I was going to go with him, but I'm too tired."

"Maybe you're pregs," said Edie.

"Give a girl five minutes," Jane Louise said. "Besides, didn't we swear we would try to coordinate this?"

"We did, and we will," Edie said. "Go back to work. I'm sure we'll speak several hundred more times today." And she hung up.

CHAPTER 2

Being newly married made Jane Louise feel weird. She felt peculiar when people came in to congratulate her, as if her clothing was too itchy and didn't fit. She suddenly became shy and at a loss for words. It seemed odd to her that people would congratulate you for being able to sleep with your boyfriend legally. But to her office colleagues marriage was about matched towels with monograms, wedding presents sent from all over, and eventually the creation of a nice little family. It was not, except to Sven, about the marriage bed. But then, who knew what marriage really meant to Sven? According to her secretary, Adele, a veritable encyclopedia on the subject, Sven liked being married because it gave him a reason to feel guilty about adultery.

Jane Louise did not believe that Sven felt guilty about anything, but Adele's theory was rather more complicated. She said that Sven did not feel guilt in the sense of feeling bad about something. Guilt to him was like a seasoning in cooking—hot peppers or chili powder—that put an edge on his philandering, without which he would have been bored.

It was odd to feel so uncomfortable at work. Her office had always been like a friend. She had spent the crucial hours of her girlhood in this place, and even though she was hardly a girl when she got married, she felt that she had crossed some border.

Her door was open, and through it stepped Adele, a compact young woman with bright yellow hair, long pink nails, and a fondness for outfits—clothes that actually matched. She was engaged to her boyfriend, Phil, who had given her a little diamond engagement ring. She came from an enormous family of telephone company workers, nurses, and taxicab drivers. On the subject of Sven she was brilliant. Her only other interest was her engagement and pending wedding, for which elaborate plans had been made.

She had been invited to Jane Louise and Teddy's wedding and had been puzzled by it, Jane Louise could see. It was so plain, so not like a wedding. But she loved Jane Louise, and she admired her. Adele felt that Jane Louise came from some loftier artistic territory in which people wore what looked like a sundress—and not even a white one—to their wedding, with no hat, no veil, and only the tiniest little bouquet of flowers, which the bride actually had to be reminded to throw. Adele, of course, had caught it, but then Jane Louise had thrown it right at her.

"So hi!" Adele said as she entered. She was more than ten years younger than Jane Louise and seemed a veritable baby. "I see Sven's been in to check you out."

"For signs of wear," Jane Louise said.

"I'm so glad I don't register with him," said Adele. "It would creep me out to get the once-over from him. You're his type."

Jane Louise considered this. Sven's wife, Edwina, was a strawberry blond. The mother of Allard and Desdemona had been a reddish blond, and the Swede, mother of Anik, had also been blond. Jane Louise mentioned this.

"He marries out of type," said Adele.

Jane Louise made a mental note to remember to tell this to Teddy. She thought Adele was a genius, but Teddy said she was only a genius on the subject of Sven.

Jane Louise noticed that Adele, too, peered at her, as if for signs of wear. She focused on Jane Louise's wedding band, and her face relaxed. Here was an identifiable and correct piece of wedding protocol! Adele sat at her desk at lunchtime and read such magazines as *Modern Engagements* (which Jane Louise originally had thought was a literary magazine) and *Today's Bride*. Or she set out with Phil-the-Fiancé and went shopping for towels and matching shower curtains, place mats, and napkins. She and Phil were going to be married in two years, but they shopped assiduously for specials and sales (YOUR MONOGRAM EMBROIDERED FREE WITH THE PURCHASE OF TWO BATH SHEETS!), and the stuff was hauled away and stored at Adele's grandmother's house.

All this made Jane Louise feel very tender toward Adele. She did not begrudge Adele any of it: She wanted *someone* to want it.

She and Teddy had simply merged their possessions and were now thinking about buying a sideboard. Jane Louise had never bought a piece of furniture with another person in her life. It seemed to her an act of almost exotic intimacy. After all, anyone can sleep with anyone, but few people not closely connected purchase furniture in common.

Dita Neville was Jane Louise's next visitor. Jane Louise was dreading her. She breezed into the office trailing cigarette smoke and wearing the sort of clothes girls might have worn in French convent schools in the forties. No one could identify where she got these clothes which, as Edie pointed out, were killingly lovely. Today she was wearing a heavy white shirt, a knife-pleated black serge skirt, heavy black stockings, and flat suede shoes like ballet slippers. Her stripey, tawny hair was cut asymmetrically. She was older than Jane Louise, and they had been close friends, but recently Dita had faded out of her life.

When Dita first came to the firm she had created a minor stir: She was extremely glamorous. No one else in the office carried a burled-walnut cigarette case with a twenty-two-carat-gold clasp. No one else had lunch with people whose title was Princess. She seemed to know everyone: old film directors, movie stars, wild Southern boys who wrote dirty novels, elephant trainers who wrote poetry. At the moment she was publishing a novel entitled *Dream of the Biker's Girl,* by a woman who had ridden with the Hell's Angels and came to the office in full biker regalia. Undeterred, Dita, wearing sober gray and real pearls, took her out to lunch at the fancy women's club of which her mother was a member.

She was small and wiry, like a wildcat. She stalked about like a cat, too. Her stride was nervous and taut. At the moment she was married to her third husband, the reportage photographer Nick Samuelovich, an overlifesized, blond man. Handsome. Her first husband had been a charmless, appropriate stockbroker. This had pleased and then displeased her mother, who was horrified by divorce. Next she married a poet from a very old family but left him for Nick, who had carried her off to Cambodia.

Dita had taken Jane Louise up with a vengeance, and Jane Louise had been somewhat dazzled. Together they had gone to the movies at lunchtime armed with huge sandwiches from the local delicatessen. When Nick was out of town, Dita and Jane Louise camped out at the cozy Samuelovich flat in Greenwich Village, where they talked and gossiped endlessly. Dita had given Jane Louise access to her private life: In front of Jane Louise she felt free to cry, rant, let down her public face, and display what seemed to Jane Louise a boiling vat of emotion. In public Dita was perfect: a clubwoman who used dirty language, a freewheeling, freethinking maverick from an impeccable background, the person you could count on to get all the jokes and nuances. Their friendship prospered over the years, but around the time that Jane Louise first met Teddy, Dita began to withdraw. She no longer came into Jane Louise's office to yak. Their midday movie dates were over. Dita was never home in the evening anymore, and Jane Louise had known in her heart of hearts that Dita would never make it to her wedding.

And she hadn't. It turned out that the birthday party for Nick's old father was the same day, even though it was not his official birthday. And although a smaller party would be given for the old man on his actual birthday, Dita said it was imperative that she attend both. If it had not been Nick's father's birthday, Jane Louise had suspected, it would have been something else.

"Hello, sweetie," Dita said. "I'm so sorry about your wedding. Those ghastly White Russians."

Jane Louise knew this voice. Its tone did not encourage conversation. It made breezy, unchallengeable statements.

Dita thrust onto Jane Louise's desk a large box covered in shiny black paper and done up with an enormous silk bow—pink.

"Open it, please," said Dita.

Jane Louise obeyed. Inside a nest of bright pink tissue was a large sprigware pitcher—a Georgian water jug from an antique shop Jane Louise had never so much as dared to browse in.

"Oh," said Jane Louise. "I love it!" She felt she would have to clench her teeth to prevent herself from bursting into tears.

"Sprigware," Dita said. "To go with your nice white ironstone. I felt a little decoration would be a good thing."

"Oh, it's wonderful," Jane Louise said.

"And do you suppose your old man will like it?" Dita said.

For a moment Jane Louise thought she was referring to her father, long deceased, but Dita meant Teddy.

"It's just the sort of thing he'd like," Jane Louise said.

"Now, sweetie," said Dita, clearing away the tissue paper and tapping an unfiltered cigarette on her case to pack it down, "let's get serious."

For an instant Jane Louise wondered if she and Dita were going to talk about why they seemed no longer to be friends. Sven had once warned Jane Louise that Dita would be a dangerous person to know. Jane Louise had had dangerous boyfriends, but in her experience, women had never been the enemy.

"Can we change the lettering on *Dream of the Biker's Girl?*" Dita said. She blew a smoke ring. "The author hates it. I can't think why, but she feels it isn't *raunchy* enough."

"What isn't *raunchy* enough?" asked a voice from the hallway, and in strolled Sven. He stared at Dita. "An infiltrator from editorial."

"Oh, hello, Sven," Dita said. Her voice was perfectly formal.

"You never come down here anymore," Sven said. He leaned over and filched a cigarette from the open walnut case, brushing Dita's arm. He took the lighter out of Dita's hand and lit his cigarette with it. Jane Louise held her breath. "You don't mind, I'm sure," he said.

"It's heaven to be able to smoke in peace," Dita said to Jane Louise as if Sven were mere dust on the window ledge. "Upstairs you can hardly light up without two editorial assistants coming in to give you a health lecture."

Throughout this interchange Sven gazed at Dita. If this made her nervous, she did not show it. It made Jane Louise sort of hysterical, however. She longed to get them out of her office.

"Listen," she said to Sven. "Why don't you go out and smoke that thing in the hall?"

Sven feigned hurt. "You don't make *her* smoke in the hall," he said.

"She's here on company business," Jane Louise said.

Sven crushed out his cigarette. "Well, Josita," he said, using Dita's real name. "We all missed you at Janey's nice wedding. We were all sure you'd barge in at the last minute."

"Nick's papa—" began Dita.

"Oh, yes. Nick's thousand-year-old papa," Sven said. "Well, girls, I'll vanish. I'll just grab another smoke as a keepsake." He took another cigarette and put it behind his ear. As he turned to leave his eyes met Dita's. It was perfectly clear to Jane Louise that they either had slept together or were going to.

CHAPTER 3

Teddy liked a real dinner: It made him feel adult. Jane Louise, who was a very good cook, felt that on the first business day of married life you ought to feed your husband his favorite meal.

He was not home when Jane Louise walked in, which gave her a few minutes to get acclimated. Although they had shared this apartment for a year, in some ways she was still not used to it. She had never lived with anyone before, and the fact that she shared this dwelling with a man amazed her.

The kitchen was as they had left it, the coffee cups washed and set neatly on a tea towel. She and Teddy were both neat: Jane Louise had the tidy habits of a designer whose tools are always clean and put away in the right place. Teddy was a plant chemist. His firm invented nonpoisonous alternatives to such toxic products as pesticides and household products. His mind was orderly, and order banished bad, chaotic thoughts.

The household they had created in their own image was more bare than cluttered. The couch, which they both loved, was elegant and uncomfortable. It had belonged to Teddy's grandmother and was made of mahogany in the Empire style. When Teddy inherited it it had been covered with crumbling black horsehair, and Jane Louise had had it recovered in green-and-yellow stripes. She loved it because it was beautiful, and Teddy loved it because it rooted him in his history.

There were times when Jane Louise was quite enraptured by that history, at least on Teddy's mother's side—generation after generation of stable New Englanders. She herself had been dragged around as a child and could never really say she was from anywhere, whereas Teddy had grown up in the country, in the house his mother had inherited from her mother. His best friend, Peter Peering, had been his friend since he was born. Otherwise Teddy's life had been something of a mess. His parents had been bitterly divorced when he was three and had never had a kind word for each other since.

The least happy part of planning the wedding had been the contemplation of Teddy's parents in the same room. After all these years they still hated each other, and Eleanor loathed Cornelius's second wife, Martine. But in the end they had stayed in separate corners, and Edie and Mokie had served as runners between them, making sure everyone was calm.

Teddy's father was a Brit, with a stiff white mustache and the bearing of a naval man. He had been in the British navy during the war and had spent the years after it doing something for a company his family had long had an interest in. Later he became a wine merchant, which he was quite good at, and had married Martine, a big, soft woman from Bermuda who had produced Teddy's three half-sisters.

Once upon a time Teddy's parents had had a wedding and thought they might be happy. Teddy had a photo of this event: Eleanor, looking the same, except younger and interested in looking pretty, and Cornelius, in his dress uniform, looking as if his only interest were in having his photo taken. In spite of his fractured boyhood, Teddy had turned out to be level and even tempered, even if he was not an easy read.

What was it about marriage, Jane Louise wondered, sitting down on the couch's hard, striped, unavailable surface, that made it seem so strange to her? It was not a bit strange to Adele and Phil-the-Fiancé. They were schooling themselves in it, buying towels and hampers, shopping for china patterns, and saving their money in a joint account. Adele and Phil had known each other for ten years, since they were babies.

Whereas, Jane Louise reflected, she and Teddy were barely acquainted. They had met two years ago, courted for one year, lived together for another, and here they were, virtual strangers in each other's lives, married forever.

Suddenly Jane Louise was very tired. She grabbed a pillow off the chair, stuck it underneath her head, and closed her eyes, wondering about her own parents.

Her mother, Lilly, had remarried after Jane Louise's father, Francis, had died. She was happily married now in a way she had never been happily married to Jane Louise's father, who was charming but never made enough money, and to whom the things of the world didn't seem to mean much.

Her new husband, Charlie Platt, was rich and settled. He had always been rich and settled. Together they had bought a sizable town house just for themselves and either gave or went to parties almost constantly. Lilly had a passion for social life. If she was not invited to a party, she gave one. She and Charlie were on the boards of hospitals, halfway houses, and foundations to study rare diseases, and they went to balls that raised money for the opera, the Artists League, or the Print Society. Her closet was the size of Jane Louise's bathroom.

Her father had been dead for ten years. He would never see his daughter's husband and would never see her children, if she ever had any. At the thought of this, tears sprang out of her eyes. For a minute she could not stop crying. Then she turned on her side and fell into a dreamless sleep from which she was awakened by Teddy.

"You must have been really wiped to fall asleep on that thing," Teddy said.

"I just suddenly felt as if someone had pulled the plug," Jane Louise said. "All my energy went. I'm starving. Let's make dinner."

Teddy made the salad, and Jane Louise grilled the chops, just like dolls in a dollhouse. The kitchen rang with the sound of the two of them.

"My mother called," Teddy said. "She's going off to see her friend Nancy Aldrich in Boston and she wants to know if we want to use the house."

"Do we?" Jane Louise asked.

"It's up to you," said Teddy. "The leaves have turned, and we could bundle up and go canoeing."

The idea of bundling up and going canoeing on Marshall Pond—actually a lake—where Teddy's grandmother, mother, and Teddy himself had learned to swim seemed like heaven to Jane Louise, and being married to Teddy gave her access to it.

"I love lamb chops," Teddy said. Jane Louise looked at him. Was this a conversation between married people? It seemed to her that they had been much freer three weeks ago, before they were married.

"I bought them because you love them, you twit," she said. "Isn't marriage weird?"

"It's probably less weird when you do it in your early twenties," Teddy said. "Like Beth and Peter."

"Yes, but mostly, unlike Beth and Peter, when you get married in your early twenties, by the time you're our age you've already been divorced and remarried."

"I think my dressing is delicious," Teddy said.

"Curry," said Jane Louise, tasting it.

After dinner Jane Louise attempted to curl up on Teddy's lap. Her legs were too long, so they sat with their legs intertwined. "I don't feel at all like myself," she said. "Do you think something's wrong with me?"

"I think we just got married," Teddy said. "We're not kids, so it's more serious."

Jane Louise gazed into the eyes of her husband, a serious person if there ever was one. His eyes were hazel. It was often not easy to know what he was thinking or feeling. On the other hand, he was easy to make comfortable, and his wants were not many. Furthermore, although he had had a series of long-term relationships with women, he had put in time living alone and could fend for himself. He did not eat out of cans.

Thus, when Jane Louise was sick she could expect more than a piece of toast. Teddy did not much like cooking: He seemed happy and grateful when Jane Louise did it for him. He had been brought up by a rigorously unfussy woman who *did* feed herself out of cans. Eleanor hated to cook, hated most housework. She was, as Edie often said, a being without much interest in traditional gender roles: the perfect mother for a boy, since she taught Teddy what she knew about—gardening, bicycle riding, and bird identification. She had set him up to be charmed by a person who smelled wonderful, who was not at all frilly, but who gave him a taste of the domestic life he had been deprived of.

"Let's go to the country this weekend," Jane Louise said. "It'll be nice to sleep in that bed again, since that's where it all happened."

CHAPTER 4

Jane Louise had met Teddy in Marshallsville, where Edie's parents had a house. Teddy's mother lived down the road. She was not keen on the Steinhauses, since they were the sort of weekenders and summer people who walk around misidentifying wildflowers with great authority and complaining that the dump is not kept open for their convenience. Furthermore, they imported their social life instead of taking an interest in the town. Marguerite Steinhaus routinely hauled Teddy's reluctant mother to a cocktail party or two, since Eleanor was the sort of country person the Steinhauses understood: an avid gardener from a very good family whose house was full of real period furniture. Marguerite could never keep black spot off her roses, whereas Eleanor's roses were magnificent, and her house was on the local garden tour.

In their later years the Steinhauses had begun to travel extensively, often on behalf of charitable organizations, and the house was Edie's whenever she wanted, provided her brothers didn't want it first. She and Jane Louise often spent weekends in the country when neither had anything to do. In all the years she had been coming up, Jane Louise had never met Teddy. And even though she had passed his mother's house a million times, and had even been introduced to Eleanor, he had only been pointed out innumerable times on the road.

When she was off at college, he was off at graduate school. When she was at art school, he was studying chemistry in England. By the time he came back and was working as a chemist, and Jane Louise was beginning her career as a book designer, she was old enough to find being around Edie's parents so awful that she felt it was morally incorrect to take advantage of their hospitality, and she stopped going up to Marshallsville altogether, although Edie nagged her about it constantly.

The summer she met Teddy was hot and wet. The Steinhauses went off on one of their fact-finding, do-good vacations. Edie's brothers had rented adjoining houses at the seashore, and the Marshallsville house stood empty. One torrid week Edie prevailed. She gave Jane Louise the keys to the house and the key to the car and told her to get out of town.

"There are no damp remains of my parents or brothers," Edie said. "It *is* my house, too, even if I only get sloppy seconds. *There's no one there.* I want you to go up and have a nice time."

Jane Louise had been working hard. The weather had worn her down. She was too tired to say no. Besides, deep in her heart she loved Marshallsville in the way you might love a married man: She loved everything about it and felt there was no way she would ever be connected to it. Her feeling for it often felt specious to her, since she didn't live in it and hadn't grown up in it. It was something like the landscape of her childhood, and she loved it in her bones.

It was late summer. A few big storms had cleared the air, which was now hot and dry. The golden light was heavy with pollen.

Everyone who had hay was getting it in, and the air was pungent with the scent of fresh grass.

Jane Louise and Teddy met by chance late one afternoon on the path to the lake. He had spent the day haying with Peter Peering. He was brown and sweaty and he had hay in his hair. He smiled at her. She smiled back, and then stopped.

"I'm Edie Steinhaus's friend," she said. "Jane Louise Meyers."

"Oh, yes," Teddy said. "I ran into Edie last week in the city, and she told me you were coming up. I'm going for a swim. Are you?"

Jane Louise was in fact returning home from swimming, but she followed him down to the lake.

They dropped their towels and their jeans on a bench. Jane Louise was suddenly covered with embarrassment. She had never spoken to this person before, and she was about to enter a body of water with him, half naked. She was wearing a two-piece bathing suit, and her thick, straight hair was tied back with a ribbon.

Teddy walked the length of the dock. He was lean and rangy, with a long back and muscled shoulders. In an instant he dived into the water, surfaced, and yelled for Jane Louise to jump in.

She dived modestly—actually she was afraid the top of her bathing suit would fall off—and swam to catch up with him. Then they raced back to the dock. Jane Louise, who had been swimming since she was a toddler, was very snobbish about other people's swimming styles. Teddy, she noted, swam a long, elegant stroke. They rested on the dock. Teddy scanned the sky.

"I think there's one more day of good weather left," he said. "It can't last. Are you going back to the city on Sunday?"

"I have Edie's car," Jane Louise said. "I can give you a lift."

Teddy shook the water out of his hair and smiled at her. "That would be nice," he said. "I came by bus and my old friend Peter Peering—he's the organic farmer on Rexhill Road—picked me up."

They walked slowly from the lake to his mother's house, and he invited her in. She went, but something told her not to stay too long. Upstairs in the guest bedroom was a big bed with a carved headboard: a basket of fruit and flowers and two fat little cherubs.

"What a beautiful bed!" Jane Louise said and shut her eyes against a vision of her and Teddy in it.

"It belonged to my grandmother," said Teddy.

"I'll call you Sunday morning," said Jane Louise.

But the next day some profound restlessness overtook her. Her heart was racing. The air was suddenly thick. The sun turned silvery and menacing. She could not contain herself. She walked right over to Teddy's house. She knew that Teddy's mother was in England, and she did not care if Teddy misinterpreted her. She felt propelled. He was standing at the door as if he had been waiting for her. Neither of them smiled. From their faces it might have been thought that they were embarking on some dire enterprise.

He took her hand and led her up the stairs. The window was blocked by a rose of Sharon tree that made the sunlight come in speckled. In that bed she and Teddy were as speckled as leopards. They connected with a kind of ferocious thirst and stared at each other in rapture. They could scarcely catch their breath, and they stayed in bed all afternoon as clouds moved across the sky and the sky darkened and it began to rain. They told each other everything, and Jane Louise listened carefully because she knew somehow that this was the only time she would hear these things.

Now he was her husband, and she sat next to him in his mother's car on the way up to Marshallsville. This car was a relic, an old British Rover kept immaculately by Eleanor, who was in other matters an indifferent housekeeper. Because of her lack of interest in what she called the girlish sides of things, her curtains needed cleaning and the sink was far from bright, but she rubbed her furniture with beeswax and kept her shoes in perfect condition with neat's-foot oil, which had also preserved the car's leather seats. This car had been made in the time before bucket seats, and therefore a person could sit quite close to the driver. Jane Louise slipped her hand under Teddy's thigh. Her hands were always cold, and she had gotten into the habit of using his leg as a warmer.

Her husband squinted into the twilight. The leaves had turned. Everywhere Jane Louise looked the road was carpeted in gold and red, and the wind shook the leaves against the windshield. Eleanor was never profligate with heat, so Jane Louise had packed a winter nightgown, and since there was never much in the way of food, she had provisioned herself and Teddy a large basket, which included coffee for her and decent tea for Teddy.

Since it was a posthoneymoon weekend, she had splurged and bought French butter, goat cheese, and a very expensive steak because Teddy had invited Peter and his wife, Beth, for dinner.

Peter and Beth were everything Jane Louise and Teddy were not, at least in Jane Louise's opinion. Peter had grown up in Marshallsville, gone away to college, and then gone to Africa to study sustainable agriculture. When he came home his father gave him a hundred acres, and he had started his organic farm. He had met Beth in Africa, where she was doing fieldwork, and they had married and produced three daughters in a row: Laura, Harriet (known as Birdie), and Geneva. Beth baked cakes and made jam. She was on the board of the child development center and was the head of the Parent Teacher Association. She took her girls to the farmers' fair, where they regularly won the prize for the best pumpkin or the nicest calf.

When Jane Louise looked at Beth and Peter, she saw stability, fidelity, people to whom lewd or unseemly or seditious thoughts were unknown. She did not imagine that Beth had had time to have much of a checkered past before she married Peter—after all, she had been only twenty-four—whereas Jane Louise had been in love quite unsuccessfully a number of times and had done any number of stupid things in the name of romance. She often wondered if Teddy would have been happier with a less blemished person, and she often asked him. His look told her that her question was totally moronic to him, and also that he was puzzled. Why would you marry someone if you didn't mean to?

For a relatively cheerful person, Jane Louise's need for reassurance was quite intense. For a man who seemed on amiable terms with life itself, Teddy seemed quite unwilling to give it, as if it were something fluffy and unnecessary, like a flounce on a skirt or painted decorations on a car.

In Jane Louise's experience life was a series of scrambles—to make friends in a new school, to get comfortable in a new town, to scrape together the money to take a trip. She had the deep optimism of a scrapper, but she felt she needed to be told quite often that the roof was not going to cave in.

Whereas Teddy, who seemed so able to get through the things of life without scrapping, could not be turned to for reassurance that everything was going to be all right because, in his experience, it often hadn't been.

CHAPTER 5

It was cold when they got there. On the hall table was a long note in Eleanor's precise, prep-school hand to remind them to spray for whitefly in the glasshouse with the organic compound in the old mayonnaise jar and to cut back the last of the mums.

The house was chilly and damp and exuded a smell of must, beeswax polish, and lavender wax that Jane Louise found irresistible: It almost brought her to her knees.

It was Eleanor's intention that when she got too old to cope with stairs, she was going to build herself a trim little one-person cabin and turn her house over to Teddy and Jane Louise. She had bought four acres on Cabbage Hill Road overlooking the swamp where, every summer, a great blue heron came to nest.

Jane Louise could not remember living in a dwelling owned by her and her family. They were renters. When she was a baby, her parents had rented a summer house and had then stayed on, year-round, for years. When they moved to Boston, they had lived in a rented apartment, and when they made their last move to a suburb of New York, they had rented a large garden apartment. The idea that Eleanor's house would someday be hers filled her with a mire of emotions. She did not want to inherit this house because she longed for something that could truly be her own. On the other hand, she loved Eleanor's house, every single board of it.

It was a white clapboard house set by John Crampton's apple orchard. It had a large, sunny kitchen with a big harvest table and a wood stove that was used only when Teddy and Jane Louise visited. Eleanor was as indifferent to food as she was to the cold, and in her pantry were dozens of dusty, unidentifiable jars of this or that, the castoffs of her occasional attempts to produce something interesting for a dinner party. At Eleanor's table Jane Louise had encountered a kind of food she had never seen in her life. Lilly, her own mother, was lavish. Even when money was tight and the car was barely functioning, she produced standing ribs, smoked salmon, and filet mignon. Eleanor offered starker fare: roasts of a kind Jane Louise was unfamiliar with, which were tough and required intensive chewing. Frozen vegetables, watery potatoes.

Her living room was plain and comfortable. The tapestry on the wing chair was frayed, and the old Persian rugs were worn. The mullioned windows looked down a grassy slope to a stone wall. On the other side were the apple trees. If you woke up early enough in the morning, you might see deer grazing on the windfalls.

Teddy and Jane Louise slept in the ornamental bed in the guest room. His boyhood room had been turned into Eleanor's study. On a shelf above her desk she kept the things he had brought home to her from Vietnam—he had been drafted and served for eighteen months—a little bamboo cricket cage, a brass Montagnard bracelet, a bolt of woven fabric, a basket. Her own bedroom had nothing in it of a personal nature except for garden catalogs, but the bedroom window overlooked her one great extravagance:

a greenhouse, which she called a glasshouse. It had been put together by Teddy, Eleanor, and Peter Peering from a kit. On Sunday mornings Eleanor liked to read her newspaper and listen to music in it. On the coldest day, it was warm. In this space she set her cold frames, her orchids, her miniature roses.

When Jane Louise went upstairs she saw that Teddy had brought up the bags and also that he had turned down the bedcovers. Teddy was not generally expressive, and when he was, Jane Louise felt like a person in a fairy tale whose heart had been pierced by a rose thorn.

In this house her husband assumed a posture she did not normally see. This was his house, his history. The intimacy of the occasion struck Jane Louise. She did not know this house, did not know where to find the extra string or the clothesline. It was not second nature to her. Teddy was the rightful inhabitant: She was still the guest, no matter how many wonderful meals she had prepared in its kitchen.

Downstairs Teddy was putting things to rights. He had turned up the thermostat to heat the living room and had lit a fire in the wood stove. When she got to the kitchen, he was filling the kettle.

"Let's go for a walk," Teddy said. "Then we can come back and have tea." This was also his custom. He liked to get out into the air and take possession of the landscape. Jane Louise also believed that in some way he needed distance from the house in order to get back to it.

They pulled on their sweaters and walked out.

The sun was just going down, and the light was beginning to turn a faint lavender. Small yellow leaves blew off the trees and scattered at their feet. Brilliant red maple leaves as large as demitasse saucers floated down onto the road. It was suddenly cold: You could see your breath. Jane Louise huddled next to Teddy. They walked arm in arm, and their long strides matched.

By the time they had walked halfway down the road, it was almost dark. They could hear the purring of screech owls, who let you get very near and then vanished.

Coming toward them they could see Eleanor's neighbor, Dr. Harting, who was elderly and walked with a stick.

"Hello!" he called out. "Mr. and Mrs. Parker!" He said this with genuine delight, and when he got near he took Jane Louise's hand in his.

"How very nice!" he said. "Eleanor told us all about your lovely wedding. Mrs. Harting sent me down to you with this." He held out a jar with a gingham-wrapped top. "It's her own special paradise jelly," he said. "Apple, quince, and cranberry. You can have it on your toast for breakfast." He coughed slightly as if the idea of Teddy and Jane Louise waking up together and having breakfast embarrassed him.

"How is your arthritis?" asked Teddy.

"Oh, it hobbles me," Dr. Harting said. "There's some young doctor up in Threadford who uses bee stings and says it works, and some other fellow over at that Vision of the Immortal— what's the name of that place over in Bryanston, Teddy?"

"I never get it right," Teddy said. "Do you remember, Janey? We passed it last summer."

"Fellowship of Possibility," said Jane Louise.

"She's my memory," said Teddy fondly.

"Well, there's a fellow there who cures it with acupuncture, and I'm going to give it a try. Mrs. Harting and I were in China three years ago and were very impressed by the acupuncture clinic. Well, I'm off. Got to do my two-mile constitutional."

"Please thank Mrs. Harting for the jelly," said Jane Louise.

How like a foreign language these conversations were, she thought. Proper and formal, and all sentences well constructed and in the right place. In thirty years would Teddy refer to her as "Mrs. Parker" instead of "my wife"?

They walked home in the dark. The air was cold enough to cut through Jane Louise's sweater. The lights from the house looked warm and yellow, a beacon for a lonely traveler. She clung to Teddy under an old maple tree that year after year was deformed by lightning strikes but year after year put out leaves. These leaves drifted down now, grazing their heads. She wanted everything to be all right, to make everything all right, to be Teddy's happy memory.

He was her husband now, for better and worse. Better was his level, lighthearted side—Teddy was a fixer. He could fix the jammed lock on your hall door, or a sticking window. He could get underneath your car and do minor repairs. He could put together a greenhouse from a kit and help if you could not follow the directions that came with the answering machine. He could read the stars in the sky or tell you what bird you were hearing. As a boy he could have walked out into the woods and then told you what the weather would be for the next three days.

He knew how to camp out, to travel with a knapsack, to talk to foreigners who needed help in a city. If you took his hand you felt secure in a forest or a bad neighborhood. He did not really want to know, but because he had been in a war he knew about weapons. In Vietnam he had had a civet cat for a pet before his Montagnard guides had eaten it. He could take wonderful photographs. Beth Peering often said that if it were not for Teddy, she would have no decent photos of her girls. One of Jane Louise's treasured possessions was a picture he had taken of herself and Birdie at the lake, both wearing hats and black T-shirts, looking up from their sketchbooks and smiling. It was that photo that made Jane Louise know how much Teddy loved her and how deep into his life she had gotten.

For, despite his equitable spirits, his belief that things in the world could be fixed, his ability to deal with life as if life were some sort of trainable dog, there was a seam of despair in him that was thin but deep. Jane Louise abided with this, and when he fell into its crack, he was remote as stone, friendly but distant. He even turned his public face to her, which broke her heart when it happened. It had taken her months to realize that he was not approachable in this condition. It covered him like fog, and he gritted his teeth until it went away. Jane Louise could pet him and stroke him. He kissed her abstractly in a way that told her that she was no help. He had gone through these moments since he was a child, when they had been much, much worse.

Jane Louise had first seen him fall silent after a conversation on the telephone with his father, who had wanted him to do something or other for Martine's brother. She had tried to find out what had transpired. It was made clear to her that she was not going to find out. Teddy's desolation had on it a keen edge of anger, flashy as a newly sharpened blade. She had felt her heart shrink in fear—fear of the person she loved best in the world.

Now as they walked home in the dark she knew she would never know what he was thinking. They had met too late in life to be each other's perfect other, but she felt toward him a kind of teen passion as well as a kind of grown-up gratitude. It didn't matter if she would never quite know what was on his mind: He was hers.

She felt she had stepped into his life, something new and alien, like a modern chair brought into a room full of family furniture. The fact that she loved him, that he had chosen her, did not bridge this river of differences. Why had he not married some nice girl from nearby? Or an upright girl like Beth Peering who had been brought up in a small New England town, with a father who was a professor of agriculture and a mother who raised children and made pickles? Teddy had married a Jewess, a nomad, a woman with a checkered romantic history. She gave a shiver.

"Are you all right?" Teddy said.

"I always think you should have married someone from *here*," Jane Louise said.

"I didn't want to marry someone from here," Teddy said. "I wanted to marry *you*."

"I'm freezing," Jane Louise said as they opened the door. Teddy stoked up the wood stove.

"I meant my heart was freezing," Jane Louise said. Teddy gave her a look of puzzlement and pain, a look that said: What do women want? He took her in his arms.

"Do you think I married you for some funny reason?" he said.

"I think you married me for complicated reasons."

"Everyone marries someone else for complicated reasons," Teddy said.

"Not Beth and Peter," Jane Louise said into his shirtfront.

"Beth and Peter just look uncomplicated," Teddy said. "They don't think in complicated terms."

"They have perfect lives."

"Birdie has a learning disorder," Teddy said. "She isn't reading. They're very worried about her."

Teddy was Birdie's godfather. He singled her out and for years had taken her to the county fair while the other two girls went with their parents. He was sensitive to her being the underdog and the middle child. Her sisters were traditional child beauties, with blond hair and blue eyes, whereas Birdie was brown eyed and brown haired, serious and undervalued: a problem.

Jane Louise loved Birdie, too. She took her off alone whenever she could. Birdie gave her hope, connection. When she took Birdie to the beach, the feel of that skinny hand in hers made her heart expand.

One afternoon last summer, Edie and Jane Louise had taught Birdie how to make sugar roses—they were decorating a cake for Mokie's birthday.

"Did I do it right?" Birdie had asked Jane Louise. She had produced a slightly lopsided but very nice-looking rose.

Jane Louise had said: "It's perfect. Oh, Birdie, someday I would like to have a little girl just like you."

"Like me?" said Birdie in total disbelief.

"Just exactly like you," Jane Louise said.

When she and Teddy took Birdie to the county fair, the summer before they got married, Birdie took both their hands and skipped between them. It was clear that Teddy was longing for a child of his own. They both knew it: It was only a question of time.

CHAPTER 6

Because she had been brought up by her mother, that fiend of etiquette, Jane Louise was highly attuned to social nuance. So, for example, the meal she served to Peter and Beth must not be too fancy but it must not be unfancy. A meal too fancy might be something of an affront—the city person showing off—while a dowdy meal might be an affront as well, the expectation being that if you came up from the city you ought to bring a few nice things to amuse your country friends. Jane Louise grilled a steak and made a chocolate soufflé.

At dinner they talked about Peter's younger sister, Marjorie. Everyone, it turned out, was concerned about her. She had finished college and then had gone off to study something called animal body work.

"What's that?" Teddy said.

"Well," Beth said, "it started with horses. The theory is that if you massage an animal it performs better. Marjorie says it's a big thing at racetracks. Then it spread to cows. The idea is that massaged cows give more milk."

"Kobe beef," said Jane Louise.

"What's that?" said Peter.

"Japanese beef cattle," Jane Louise said. "They massage them and feed them on corn and beer. They say it's the best beef in the world, and it costs about a million dollars a pound."

"Oh, dear," Beth said. "I hope Marjorie never hears about *that*. It would break her heart. These people are *vegetarians*."

"How about cabbage massage, Pete?" Teddy said. "Don't you notice your cabbages do better with a little healing touch?"

"I sing to them," Peter said.

"I haven't told you the other part," Beth said. "Marjorie confided this to me. They do dictation."

"Dictation?" Jane Louise said.

"They feel they understand what the animals say," Beth said. "Marjorie said that they sort of commune with them and write down what they reveal."

"It's just like Dr. Dolittle," Jane Louise said. "What *do* they reveal?"

Beth cleared her throat. In the candlelight she looked serious and matronly. She wore a sweater she had knitted herself and a necklace made of shells—a piece of jewelry made by one of her daughters. "They say things like: 'The good grass' and 'How fortunate we are to live near such good grass.'"

"That's what Steve Bowser used to say when he had his little marijuana plantation over on Three Farms Road," said Teddy.

"How fortunate we are to live near such good grass," said Jane Louise dreamily. "I feel that way all the time, don't you, Teddy?"

"I think Marjorie should come and sing to your little cabbages," said Teddy.

"I think she should get married and have a baby," said Beth.

"I think I'll go and get the dessert," said Jane Louise.

———

On the town green was a stone marker with a brass plaque listing everyone in Marshallsville who had been in the war. Almost every male from three years younger to three years older than Teddy was listed: Charlie Weil; Teddy; Peter; Ralph Barrados, who ran the family lumber business; George Rozens of Marshallsville Gas and Oil; Melvyn Herman of Herman's Plumbing. These were Teddy's childhood friends, and they were still his friends. Even though he had gone to study in England, and had come back to live in New York, and had married Jane Louise, who was dark and Jewish and, as far as they knew, a city girl, he was their own.

But not one of these men, not even Teddy or Peter, who were as close as brothers, mentioned being in the war. Every now and again Jane Louise heard them speak of what they referred to as "the military" with a kind of grim cheerfulness, but never at the end of a dinner party did they ever tell a war story, or reminisce about anything that had happened to them there.

In her first days of courtship, when she and Teddy lay in the ornamental bed in his mother's guest room and told each other things, he had told her about the war, his buddies, the highlands of Vietnam where he had been stationed, about the Montagnard tribesmen.

He had given her his Montagnard bracelet—a circle of hammered brass—when he asked her to marry him. She had never taken it off. When Peter had seen it on her wrist he knew at once that they were going to get married. It was after this that he began to call her Janey, and she realized with gratitude that Teddy's old friends might accept her after all.

Now she lay in that ornamental bed. Teddy had drifted off to sleep. The dishes were done, the leftovers put away. During dinner it had begun to rain. The drops clattered on the roof, and the last leaves rattled on the trees. There was not another sound.

Teddy had put hot-water bottles at the foot of the bed, under the covers. The rest of the room was freezing: This was the coldest room in the house. Jane Louise turned toward her sleeping husband. He breathed evenly. She wondered if she made him feel safe.

Love did not always scatter the barriers of private life. Teddy's thoughts were only partially accessible to her. How eccentric people were! How unknowable and how amazingly various they were! People suffered, rejoiced, fought wars they never spoke about, and took dictation from animals. They had past love lives and personal histories. They were positively rich with living. Often this thought was a source of exultant happiness to Jane Louise. Often it left her with a pounding headache. Who had carved the bed she was sleeping in, anyway? Why did a person think a headboard ought to have pomegranates and wheat carved into it? Was it a person who felt that a bed's true purpose was as a place in which to conceive babies? Was it someone who had studied the still lifes of Rembrandt Peale? Or some itinerant cabinetmaker with an eye for odd decoration? Eleanor's mother had inherited this bed from her mother. Who else had slept in it? Who had been conceived in it? Our lives, Jane Louise thought to herself, are like tiny nail snips. If you can hardly begin to fathom your own husband, how can you know anyone?

"It is rich with possibility," she said, quoting something Sven liked to say.

Teddy stirred in his sleep. Sometimes he had what Jane Louise called his "Victor Charlie" dreams, in which he was being sniped at by the unseeable enemy. In the country he slept like an undisturbed child. The night folded over them. All over Marshallsville, citizens were asleep in their beds and animals were dry in their stalls. Even the coyotes, called coydogs in these parts, were silent, hiding in their burrows.

Jane Louise sighed. She fitted herself against her warm husband. How fortunate we are to live near such good grass, she said to herself, and fell asleep.

The next morning she let Teddy sleep: He loved to sleep. It often seemed to Jane Louise that he must have been deprived of it as a child, but the fact was that the state of suspension, the idea of not moving, of not having to relate to anyone, was heaven to him. Besides, he worked very hard, and at the moment his firm was under a great deal of pressure. There was a rumor that they would be bought by a large German natural pharmaceutical company. They were scrambling to create new products, and Teddy was their chief product designer.

He had designed furniture polish made of citrus oil as well as an extract that nullified other bad smells: This was in constant demand among cat and dog owners. He created non-petroleum-based car waxes as well as agricultural soaps for insect control.

Jane Louise was an early riser. She liked her hour of solitude. She had lived alone for a good part of her adult life, and she needed that hour to collect her thoughts. She put Teddy's old cashmere turtleneck over her nightgown, slipped on woolly socks and slippers, and went downstairs to light the stove. The sky was an intense, cloudless blue. The day blazed up before her. She put the kettle on and got the coffee she always brought up to Eleanor's out of the fridge. Eleanor made the most terrible coffee, and Jane Louise was very particular; she brought her own filters, too.

Jane Louise had brought her clothes downstairs and set them on a chair by the stove. She dressed, rummaged through Teddy's jacket for the car keys, and set out for Gartner's General Store and Butcher, where you could also get the paper. She thought she would make a large pot of bean soup and would leave the leftovers for Eleanor to have when she came home from Boston.

Out in the car she drove the long way to the store, past the garage, up Winding Road, and down Rattlesnake. Dark gray clouds appeared in the northwest, but that signified nothing in this part of the country. The clouds would roll over; in an instant the sky would be brilliantly clear again.

Jane Louise had come to know this territory, which was imprinted on her heart. At home in the city she calmed herself to sleep by wandering around the countryside. She imagined the seasons: the woods inflamed with red and yellow. The sight of an entire mountainside ablaze. The bare, naked landscape in the winter or the trees hung with snow. Her earliest memory as a child had been the forsythia bush outside her bedroom window encased in ice. She dreamed of skating on Marshallsville's pond or on Dog Pond, fringed with willows. Last year the ice had frozen five feet thick. Teddy had taken her skating on Dog Pond and had driven the car right out onto the ice. A bonfire blazed out in the middle. She had spent early mornings during mud seasons lying in bed watching the icicles melt.

Often Jane Louise, who loved living in the city, felt that leaving the country was like tearing the bandage off a wound. The feelings of her childhood overcame her. Being in the country was second nature to her, and she could hardly bear to leave it. But it was not her country: It was not the landscape of her childhood. She had borrowed it from Teddy. In the car she was overwhelmed with desire for a place that was *hers*, that she had a right to, that she could claim. The feeling washed against her like rain on a windshield. Tiny yellow willow leaves blew up against the windows. She took the turn on River Road and went to get the morning paper to bring home to Teddy.

CHAPTER 7

"She takes dictation from horses," Jane Louise said. She was in her office on the phone to Edie.

"I often feel that's what I do all day," said Edie. "Marjorie was always a little dim. The Teagardens are after me again."

"The wilted flowers?"

"They didn't wilt," Edie said. "These people dog their food. They hauled the child off to church and did whatever they do. They dunk the kid's head or pour water on it or something."

"They cast out Satan and all his works," Jane Louise said.

"And how do you know that?" asked Edie.

"Mrs. Samuelovich told me," Jane Louise said. "She was brought up in rigorous Episcopalianism."

"How is Dita?" said Edie.

"The usual."

It was pretty clear that Dita had dumped Jane Louise. Dita had shut up like a fan, although in person she behaved as if nothing had happened. She called Jane Louise by all the old endearments. This drove Jane Louise crazy. Furthermore, Dita was always in motion, and it was impossible to sit down and try to find out what was wrong. Apparently Dita felt nothing was wrong, but Jane Louise noticed that often her door was closed, or if Jane Louise happened to be on the editorial floor and looked into Dita's office, Dita just happened to be on the telephone and waved in a way that said, cheerfully, Don't come in here.

"Strangely enough," Edie said, "Mokie had to straighten them out on a number of points. You can imagine how well that went over. The Teagardens being counseled in the niceties of christening etiquette by a nig-nog."

"How did they take it?" Jane Louise asked.

"Mokie said they looked at him as if he were a talking dog."

"They took dictation from him," said Jane Louise.

"Actually, I took dictation from them. The little woman called to ask me what my partner's background was. She said: 'He seems so very well versed in these things.' I said it had nothing to do with his father being an Anglican priest and his brother Paul a doctor of theology. That sort of shut her up, and then she was back on me again. She wanted something called 'sculpted plates' for the cake. Apparently you make marzipan roses and daisies and strew them across the plates—you should have seen the plates, darling."

"Oh, yes?" said Jane Louise.

"Flora Danica. Four hundred bucks a throw. Or more."

"Isn't life wonderful?" Jane Louise said. "How my mother would die for those."

"Wouldn't she just," said Edie. "I guess I'll talk to you six or seven more times."

"And I you," said Jane Louise. That was their traditional sign-off.

Jane Louise was in the middle of designing a jacket for one of Dita's books, *Fractured Selves: Psychoanalytic Images of Women*, for which she had taken a postcard of the Mona Lisa and another of Whistler's mother, cut them into strips, and was pasting them next to one another. When she was working on a design Jane Louise felt as focused as a high-intensity lamp. She did not hear Sven come into her office, and she didn't notice him until he was so close she could feel his breath on her neck.

"Go away," she said.

He picked up her wrist and felt her pulse. "Nice work," he said, looking at her composite.

"How about getting your hands off me?" Jane Louise said.

"I'm trying to determine if you're pregnant yet," Sven said.

"You'll be the first to know," said Jane Louise.

Sven dropped her wrist. "I think Mrs. Samuelovich will very much admire this jacket sketch," he said. "When she comes back."

"Back from where?"

"Mr. Nick, world-famous photographer and White Russian, took her to Alaska for some last-minute salmon fishing."

"Dita went salmon fishing?"

"Oh, yes," Sven said. "She stuffed her little Mark Cross suitcase full of the works of Henry James, put on her cashmere sweaters, and off she went. He fishes, she reads. They stay at a lodge run by some other Russians where the food is terrific and a person can lie in front of the fire and read elevating books whilst one's husband goes out with an expensive Inuit guide. I see that this is news to you. Don't you two girls confide anymore?"

Jane Louise was silent.

"I warned you that she was a dangerous friend," Sven said. "She's the kind of person who has three best friends from childhood and the rest are just crazes. Expendable, if you see what I mean. I bet you thought she adored you, right?"

"Would you mind terribly if I went back to work?"

"I wouldn't," Sven said. "I just fell by to feel your pulse and to tell you that there's a meeting in the conference room in an hour—you, me, and Erna."

"What does *she* want?"

"Big Arctic book," Sven said. "Demanding author. Heavy design values. Be there at eleven."

Erna Hendershott was a tall, commanding woman and the editor in chief. Wife of political adviser Alfred Hendershott and mother of four. She was an almost perfect person. She belonged to the Royal Guild of Needleworkers, and her embroidery could be seen on her pillowcases (she had cross-stitched every pillowcase in her house with pine trees and initials) as well as her handkerchiefs and bed linen. If you went to a staff dinner at her house, you might find the fresh pasta she had just rolled and cut hanging over the handlebars of her son's bicycle to dry. She made towering cakes for the bake sales at her children's school and sat on the boards of a couple of worthy charities. In her closet hung a number of stately and official-looking gowns for the elaborate parties she said she hated but which, out of duty to her husband, she not only attended but got herself photographed for in the society columns. She had straight, lank hair, pale blue eyes, and the piercing gaze of a hawk.

Jane Louise watched her with fascination and despair. Erna, she felt, was like a preadolescent, at the mercy of drives she did not understand. Jane Louise thought she had a major crush on Sven. She was constantly batting at him, or cuffing his hand, treating him as if he were one of her children. Sven did his part by driving her crazy. He became languid. He stared into her slightly rattled eyes and smiled what Adele called his "big sex smile." He treated her as if she were a large, underused horse. This made her blush and stammer and become furious. Their battles, which Sven took in stride and Erna slammed doors over, were legendary.

But nothing would ever happen. Erna was as safe as a Georgian house on the main street of a prosperous country town. How could a person run the editorial department of a publishing company *and* cross-stitch pine trees on all the sheets? Jane Louise had seen her at editorial meetings with her embroidery frame, stitching away as others spoke. Erna had attempted this at a design meeting, but Sven had removed it as a mother might take something dirty away from a child, and Erna had never embroidered in his presence again. For the Christmas party Erna produced a large, English Christmas cake with shiny white frosting. If she gave a party at home, her charmingly dressed children passed the hors d'oeuvres.

She counted among her friends a score of single or divorced people: lawyers, hatters, poets, bankers, and lieder singers who either had families far away, or families they did not speak to, or no families at all. She gathered them to her table at holidays, making them aware, Jane Louise felt, that they were floating specks in space, while the Hendershotts had achieved the stability of an old piece of fine mahogany furniture.

Sven lounged at the conference table in a blue-and-white-striped shirt and banana-colored trousers. His socks were rose colored. He was quite a vision.

It was a freakishly hot day, although it was November. Jane Louise had pulled her hair off her neck in a ponytail and tied it with a piece of silver ribbon she had found lying around in the art department. She wore a shapeless white turtleneck and a plain gray skirt. Erna, whose dresses were made for her by a Swiss woman in her neighborhood, wore a flowered print, with pearls.

Jane Louise set her pad down on the table, catching sight of Erna's wedding ring. Erna wore a tiny band of white gold—a ring that announced that she was so married and for so long that the trappings hardly mattered.

"Well, congratulations and welcome to the club!" Erna said to her cheerily. "I do think marriage is heaven."

There was little Jane Louise could say to this.

"Of course I was almost a baby when Alfred and I got married," Erna said. "In my parents' garden. Half an hour before the ceremony it began to pour, and then by a miracle it stopped! There was a rainbow, too. Totally, soppily sentimental. I think everyone should be married."

"Even nuns?" asked Sven. "Even wife beaters?"

"I mean *nice* people," Erna said.

"Nuns are often extremely nice people," Sven said.

"How do you know *that?*" Jane Louise said.

Sven gave her a look.

"Now, children," Erna said. "Let's get serious. We have a very big book here, and it has to be produced just right. Hugh Oswald-Murphy has turned in his masterpiece."

"Author of *Polar Weekend*," Sven said to Jane Louise. "It was published before you got here."

"It was called *Eskimo Faces*," said Erna. "I wish you would behave, Sven."

"*Eskimo Love Nest* was the sequel," Sven said.

Erna turned to Jane Louise. "He's an anthropologist and explorer with a towering literary style. You should read *Eskimo Faces*, Jane. It's one of the *great* books."

"It had everything about Eskimo nookie," Sven said.

Erna flushed and turned to Sven. "You're like a little boy!" she said. You could tell she wanted either to slap or kiss him. "It's got to be plain but handsome, if you see what I mean."

"Like the author, no doubt," said Sven, stretching and yawning. "Any photos? Line drawings? Poems in Eskimo? Drawings in the text?"

"Nothing," Erna said. "But it has to look majestic."

"Janey, call that guy who does the gold leaf. We could probably get a list price of about six thou per copy."

"Enough, Sven," Erna said. "I would like a top stain and a full cloth cover."

"I'll get right on it," Sven said, yawning again.

"And Jane, I'd like a beautiful typeface. Devinne or maybe Bembo."

"We can't get them," said Jane Louise. "I can get you Garamond or Caslon." She doodled on her pad. Erna was a fountain of little-used or almost extinct typefaces. Jane Louise believed that Erna spent her nights browsing through old type spec books, and Jane Louise was not entirely wrong.

"Oh, these beautiful old fonts," Erna said. "What a tragedy."

"It's nothing compared to teen pregnancy and wife beating," Sven said. "I'm sure Janey can get you Bembo for display type."

A few minutes later Erna withdrew to the editorial floor, leaving Jane Louise with an enormous, untidy manuscript.

"I wonder if old Alfred slaps her around," Sven said. "Jesus, it's like having a whole stable of nervous horses in here. I wish she'd shut up about type. It just goes to show that girls *are* ruined by reading. Even her nasty children have opinions on these subjects. She told me that her oldest had a fondness for Baskerville."

"All fourteen-year-olds do," said Jane Louise.

Sven gave her a look almost of longing. "That's my girl," Sven said to her. "These women with important parents. Her father was some big judge. It makes them overheated, like your little friend Edie."

"Edie is taller than you are," Jane Louise said. "I never should have introduced you two."

"Is she married to that spade or do they just live together?"

"He's her business partner," Jane Louise said primly.

"Yes, and I am a Chinese emperor. Does she feel her distinguished father would have a stroke if he thought his white-fleshed daughter was in bed with a darkie?"

"We feel he'd have a *stork*," Jane Louise said. "Now I'm taking this untidy manuscript into my cave."

"They do it under bearskins," Sven said. "They all sleep together in their little snow houses. Then it all heats up. The walls melt a little and then turn into ice."

"Edie and Mokie?" Jane Louise said. "Actually, they have a nice loft near the river, and Edie is allergic to fur."

"Eskimos," Sven said. "They swap wives."

"Gosh," Jane Louise said. "Maybe they'll let you join."

At her desk there were four messages: two from Edie, one from Teddy, and one from her mother. Jane Louise knew what they were about. She looked out the window. The sky had gotten dark, and the temperature was dropping. In a few weeks it would be Thanksgiving.

Soon the holidays would be upon them like an oncoming train, loaded with complicated feelings. These days Jane Louise felt like one of those floating specks Erna gathered around her festive tables—those waifs and strays she cheerfully collected. Jane Louise's mother produced an elaborate Thanksgiving that included a large number of Charlie Platt's relatives and children and grandchildren. Lilly adored them all and looked almost sadly at her solitary daughter. Jane Louise's sister, Nora, rarely made an appearance with her two perfect sons and her very rich husband, Jaime Benitez-Cohen. They traveled first-class and stayed at an expensive inn. Or else they stayed in San Francisco and entertained Jaime's enormous family.

As for Teddy, these holidays made him feel like an underdressed child standing on a dark road. His childhood had been the scene of holiday battles—who got him for Thanksgiving, Christmas Eve, Christmas Day. As a very little boy he dreaded to leave his mother. As an older boy he dreaded both his mother and his father. How lovely it would have been to live in a society with no holidays whatsoever! There was not enough of him to go around. He longed to get sick before an occasion so he would not have to do a thing except lie in bed.

His father's wife—he could not bring himself to say "step-mother"—was unlike Eleanor in every way. When Martine sat you could see the lace of her slips, and in the morning she came to breakfast wearing a bright quilted robe with bows. She and Teddy's father lived clear across the state, and it had been easy enough to ferry Teddy from one place to another. But as Martine produced her three daughters, Lisbeth, Moira, and Daphne, Teddy became less necessary, although he was still picked up from Eleanor's and brought home again. But the visits diminished. "With all those children, it's too much for Martine," Eleanor said. And while Teddy had been relieved, he had also been hurt in his secret heart. How easy it must be for his father not to love him!

Jane Louise sighed. Eleanor had Thanksgiving with the Peer-ings. Edie and Mokie often catered for others, which was Edie's way of avoiding *her* family. This year Jane Louise had decided to protect herself and Teddy and do Thanksgiving on her own. After all, it was their first year of married life. She was going to ask Eleanor and the Peerings, and Edie and Mokie, and her mother and Charlie, who would say no. Teddy would ask his British col-league, and they would invite their landlady, Mrs. Berger, whose children lived in Israel.

She did not anticipate the outcry this decision would cause.

"Oh, dear," Eleanor said. "The Peerings have been planning this for months."

"Couldn't they come to us just this one year?" Jane Louise asked. "Beth could bring her pies, and Mrs. Peering could bring her sweet potatoes."

"Well, I just don't know," Eleanor said. "It would be so much easier if you came here. There are eight of us and only two of you."

It was not much better with Jane Louise's mother.

"It's totally impossible," Lilly said. "It's been planned for weeks. I have the guest cards and the menus, and Charlie's nice friends from Palm Springs are coming, and we were sure you and Teddy were coming, too. We were counting on it."

"We thought if we did it ourselves we could have both mothers-in-law at the same time."

"I've already written to Eleanor," said Lilly, who was nothing if not correct. "I know she likes to stay up in the country, but we hoped this first year of your being married she'd come to us."

"Supposing she wanted you to come to her?" Jane Louise said.

"There's only one of her," Lilly said. "I'm afraid there are tons of us. It just won't work. But I'm counting on you and Teddy."

"The problem is," Jane Louise said, "Eleanor is counting on us, too."

"Well, darling," said Lilly. "You'll have to work it out the best way you can."

CHAPTER 8

Dita appeared in the office three days before Thanksgiving with her arm in a sling fashioned out of a large, expensive silk scarf. Jane Louise found her on the editorial floor just about to try to pour herself a cup of coffee from the communal coffeepot.

"This fucking arm," Dita said.

Jane Louise poured Dita's coffee for her and carried it to her office.

"I sprained my wrist," Dita said. "Sliding down some ridiculous glacier made of pebbles. I had to be taken to the doctor by canoe. Thank you for bringing my coffee in."

Dita's hair shone under the lamp. She was wearing a black skirt, a white silk blouse, and a pair of suede shoes. Her cigarette box was open on her desk, and next to it was a little gold lighter and a big black fountain pen.

"You better scoot," she said, as if to a child. "I've got Jacob Elitzer coming in with the copyedited manuscript of his translation. Do you know if Sven has anything back on that? It's called *End of the World: Three Latin American Poets.*"

"I'll just check it out," Jane Louise said.

"And close the door behind you," said Dita.

"Dita," said Jane Louise. "What's going on with you?"

Dita looked up. She seemed for an instant like a cornered cat. Then she smoothed out her features—Jane Louise had seen her do this a thousand times after a crying jag or rant—and assumed the posture of a harried worker.

"Darling, I'm half crippled and I just got back!" she said. "I've got a pile of stuff on this desk that would choke a horse."

"I don't mean now," Jane Louise said. "I mean—"

"Kiddo," said Dita. "Scoot out. I can't have this sort of conversation on my first day back. Nothing at all is wrong."

Jane Louise felt a great number of things were wrong. They had once had a standing Tuesday lunch date: "First my analyst, then *you*," Dita had said at the last one.

Those days were over now. Whatever had happened to Dita was not going to be shared with Jane Louise. Dita existed to prove that people were never knowable: It was a hard lesson—the hardest lesson in life.

Jane Louise counted on friendship with women. Without Edie she felt she could barely live, and she had considered Dita a very close friend. But then Dita did not have close friends, it seemed.

She was also slightly suspect at the office. For instance, Erna, who had been two years ahead of her at college, did not approve of her. Erna did not approve of divorce, or short skirts, or female editors having lunch with their male authors and then coming back at four in the afternoon looking haggard.

Erna did not approve of Dita's Nick, who had been her classmate. He was restless and easily bored. When bored he spoke in Russian or made rude noises. He was a dicey prospect at a party, since you never knew whom he might be awful to. Sven said he was Dita's front man and running dog—the pit bull she set on the others she was far too mannerly to be snooty to.

To someone like Erna, Dita was an affront. Intellectuals ought not to read fashion magazines and have exotic hair treatments at lunchtime. While it was perfectly all right for a bluestocking to wear perfume and lacy slips, it was not all right to show any amount of thigh or laugh in a dirty way. Furthermore, delicate-looking ladies ought not, when they blew their noses, to sound like foghorns. Erna believed that most women had a mandate to stay home and take care of their children—they had a mandate to reproduce, she felt—but those with a Higher Calling ought to find maternal and loving child care and take a four-day week.

Around holiday time the office was invaded by little Hender-shotts, who trooped in wearing school uniforms or pinafores: Simon, Eva, Ben, and Winnie, the baby, who, left to wander, wandered into Dita's office and came out smelling of Dita's perfume and bearing a large chocolate truffle in her hand. Dita's method with children veered from the cavalier to the seductive. She felt, she told Jane Louise, that children were fooling you. "Behind those child eyes, they know all," she said. "If Erna's baby isn't allowed chocolate she should have told me. It's clear those children are totally deprived. Why, that poor child looked as if she'd never seen a truffle before."

Jane Louise, who did not expect children to be wild, found the Hendershott children remarkably well behaved. She said as much to Sven.

"That's because they aren't *real* children," Sven said. "They're props. She got them at that theatrical rental place around the corner. Also, their father is an android. Although that little Eva is going to be quite a honey in a few years."

"For crying out loud, Sven!" said Jane Louise, who always

hoped that in Sven's case, children were exempt. She had seen him run a meandering gaze over his own beautiful daughter, Anik, but she also knew that Sven was much too interested in his sense of cool to contemplate anything as tacky as incest.

"I said 'in a few years,'" said Sven. "I'm a democrat, little Janey. I like 'em young. I like 'em old. I like 'em in between. Remember Mrs. Leigh Bracken-Rodgers?"

Jane Louise remembered very well. A small, well-made woman with white hair and beautiful cheekbones who was a curator and had done a book on miniature chairs. She was close to seventy. This had not stood in Sven's way, although whether or not he had been successful in his pursuit was not known.

Jane Louise came downstairs to her office feeling bereft. Was it the looming holiday, which, after all, had a terrible underground effect on Teddy? Or was it because it was plain and clear that she had been dumped by Dita, who had so vigorously and ardently taken her up? In public Dita was as perfect as a new white shoe, whereas Jane Louise alone knew that Dita had been unable to resist a young playwright named Joe Ching, whose play, *Harvest of the Forlorn*, she was publishing as part of the New Theater Series. This person, half Chinese, half Irish, seemed eager to run away with Dita. Dita treated him as you might treat a small dog, although she said he was as silky as a seal without his clothes on.

She had described to Jane Louise her first marriage, not a success in any way. She told the long story of being carried out of her fancy apartment one afternoon by Nick and taken to his grungy flat, where the two of them had holed up for several days, causing her second husband to divorce her and her mother to be outraged. She had been on the verge of confessing something or other about Sven. This, Jane Louise imagined, was part of the reason that Dita no longer dialed her extension, dragged her out for lunch, had girls' dinners with her when Nick was away and

Teddy worked late. And then, not to acknowledge that anything had changed! Jane Louise looked into Dita's beautiful bony face for some acknowledgment of anything and found a beautiful bony face, as closed and unrevealing as a closed door. She knew in her heart of hearts that Dita never looked back. She had left her first husband without the slightest trace of remorse or regret: It had been a mistake on both parts, and the cleaner one cut one's losses, the better. This face said: I don't want to have any idea what you are talking about.

In her own office Jane Louise closed the door and realized that she was in a rage. She wanted to throw things against the wall. She wanted to take Dita by the shoulders and shake her until she said something, anything. Instead she called Edie.

"I hate her," she said into the telephone.

"There, there," Edie said. "She's not a normal person."

"It's so unfair. It's so out-to-lunch."

"It may be that people who get married a lot aren't very steady," Edie said.

"What about people who have a lot of boyfriends?" said Jane Louise.

"That's different," Edie said.

"How?"

"Boyfriends are part of the evolutionary process," Edie said. "You and I don't trust people who marry their high school sweethearts, do we?"

"We envy but don't trust them," Jane Louise said.

"The point is you didn't marry anyone except Teddy. You think marriage is serious. People who get married a lot don't, like Sven."

"Sven is more faithful to his poker buddies. He says that Dita has three friends from childhood and the rest of us recent acquisitions don't matter."

"You poor duck," Edie said. "The problem with Dita is she's fast. I don't trust people who take other people up so quickly. As Mokie's mother used to say, 'There'll be tears.'"

"I love Mokie's mother," Jane Louise said. Mokie's mother was a black Scotswoman, a native of Glasgow who was quite a curiosity in South Carolina.

"I'm very angry," Jane Louise said.

"Well, go *say* something to her," Edie said.

"What am I supposed to say? 'You dropped me! You did a kind of friendship seduction on me and then split!'? I know her. She'll give me that look and make me think I'm crazy."

"Tell her to go fuck herself," Edie said.

"I'll never be given the opportunity," Jane Louise said.

CHAPTER 9

It turned out that no one went anywhere for Thanksgiving. Eleanor stayed home and had dinner with the Peerings. Lilly stayed home and had dinner with Charlie and their innumerable friends. Teddy and Jane Louise stayed home and had Thanksgiving with Edie and Mokie and Mrs. Berger from downstairs. Mrs. Berger owned the building and lived on the first floor. Teddy and Jane Louise lived on the parlor floor. Above them were the young Calzones (the older Calzones lived down the street) and on top, Frank and Ross, a team of interior designers whose attic flat was done in green and white.

Jane Louise cooked a small turkey, sweet potatoes, chestnuts and onions, and a green salad. Mokie made a mince pie, and Edie baked a pumpkin cake in the shape of a pumpkin, glazed in orange icing with a chocolate stem and marzipan vine leaves.

Over dinner the subject of multiracial children reared its head. Mrs. Berger said that her late husband, Mr. Berger, had been very much against this sort of thing, but she, Vesna Berger, was not. She began, after dinner, on the subject of her late husband.

"You know," she said, "I went to the bookstore the other day, and there was a whole shelf of widow books. Widow this, widow that." She paused for a tiny bite of pie. "Now, my late husband, Mr. Berger, was a very charming man and very well organized. He bought this house so cheap! On the other hand, he was so very annoying. I looked in these widow books and there was not one word about a husband's being annoying. For example, I could never buy the Sunday paper on Saturday night because the sports page had to be the last possible edition. And then social life! He didn't like this one or he didn't like that one. He would never have rented to the boys in the attic because he disapproved of men living together."

"What about lesbians?" said Mokie.

"It would have given him a heart attack," said Mrs. Berger. "He came from another world, where those things are not supposed to exist. For instance, black people. Do you know, for all the years he lived on this block, and you know he had a factory—women's gloves, he made—no black person ever sat down at the table with him? I'm sorry to say this to you, Mokie, but there are such people. Such a shame! Not to be able to sit down with someone who makes such a nice mince pie."

"I put up the mince myself," Mokie said.

"I hope you don't take what I said the wrong way," said Mrs. Berger.

"Well, *you're* sitting here, aren't you, honey?" Mokie said.

"I'm very happy," Mrs. Berger said. "My alternative was to go to my sister in New Jersey, and I'm sorry, but every day I listen to her problems. On the holiday I like to have a little fun. I always ask myself why it seems to be so hard to have a good time with one's family."

This was a question everyone at the table had asked many, many times.

"You know," Mrs. Berger said, "my daughter lives in Tel Aviv, and my son is in Haifa. They want me to come and live with them. They say how lonely I must be. But I tell you, I mean I can be perfectly honest, I am extremely happy to be alone. I was a very nice wife and mother, and now I get a little chance to be myself. I could be sitting in New Jersey listening to my sister fight with her daughter, and instead I am here. Now, Edie. May I have another little tiny piece of that lovely cake?"

She took a nibble of frosting and sat back in her chair.

"I'm so happy," she said. "Now you nice children tell me about where you were supposed to be."

"Well," Edie said. "I was supposed to be in the country with my parents and my brothers and my brothers' wives and my perfect little nephews, and my Uncle George and his wife. I was probably supposed to help with the cooking and chase the boys around and set the table and serve and do the cleaning up while they sat around the fire and drank their coffee because I am a girl and there is no reason to think I shouldn't be a drudge since I am a lowly pastry chef instead of a prosecutor or a judge."

"That's nice," said Mrs. Berger. "Next?"

"I am missing out on a huge family party in Charleston," Mokie said. "Six thousand aunts and uncles. Fourteen cousins I can't stand. Too much food. Lots of religion. Of course, if I walked in with Edie they would all drop dead. My parents love her, but our relatives are kind of separatist."

"It's too bad," Jane Louise said. "What a heavenly wedding you'd have. Your huge, horrible family on one side, and Edie's huge, horrible family on the other. After dinner, mixed partners for dancing, like a checkerboard. You could have one of those cakes that comes out in little chocolate and vanilla squares."

"Eventually we'll get pregnant and go down to City Hall," Mokie said.

Jane Louise gazed at him. "Remember, Edie," she said, "we're going to coordinate this."

"Don't do anything without us," Teddy added.

"We wouldn't dream of it," said Edie.

A baby! Late in the evening Jane Louise was putting away the dishes while Teddy swatted the sofa pillows back into shape. A baby rounded everything out. Two more places at the table: her baby's and Edie's. A Thanksgiving with babies crawling on the floor or playing with blocks while the grown-ups ate. She saw herself floating through the living room, a pregnant woman, full of purpose, just like Erna, who had often reminded her of the woodcut of Dorothie, *Great with Manie Children.*

And what, she wondered, was Erna Hendershott doing right this minute? Putting away her dishes—the family Wedgwood—or poking the fire while her happy guests—happy to be in her warm and happy orbit—finished their coffee. Her children would have been sent sleepily off to bed, the youngest with some adorable and worn bed toy, the older with an appropriately elevating and obscure English children's book. The remains of her turkey would be neatly tied up in cheesecloth and waxed paper. Erna made a point of cheesecloth and waxed paper. In fact, the insides of her fridge reminded Jane Louise—who had once been dispatched to the kitchen during a party to get another bottle of cold champagne—of a foreign country: the eggs in a French wire basket, juice in a Swedish pitcher, butter in an English butter box. The Indian lime pickle, the ricotta draining in a tub. When Jane Louise described this to Teddy, he said: "It isn't a fridge. It's the UN."

Erna made her feel like a worm. Oh, the safety and surety of that huge dining room table, those pink-cheeked children, that wedding band, thin as a wire, that didn't ever need to call attention to itself.

Jane Louise found Teddy lying on the couch reading the morning paper.

"Did you have any fun?" she asked. He moved over and tried to make room for her, but there wasn't room so she wedged herself beside him with one foot on the floor.

"I had lots of fun," Teddy said.

"But didn't you miss being in the country?"

"About as much as you missed being with your mother and Charlie," Teddy said. "I think holidays should be abolished."

"Maybe it's us," Jane Louise said. "I mean me. Maybe I just can't stand to be around anyone I'm related to for any period of time."

"Edie can't either," Teddy pointed out.

"Yes, but her brothers are all over each other constantly," Jane Louise said. "They play handball together. They meet for lunch. They live in the same neighborhood. Their children go to nursery school together."

"No one else can stand them," Teddy said. "As you know, they haven't any friends, and their wives look exactly alike."

"I guess if you like your family you don't need friends," Jane Louise said. "Maybe friends are a modern invention. Maybe they're just fluff that fills up some empty space where your extended family used to be."

"Let's have a baby," Teddy said.

"You mean, right now?" Jane Louise said.

"Let's practice," Teddy said. "Get in shape for it."

Jane Louise inwardly swooned. What an odd thing it was to have a husband. This person who was almost like a household object—a pillow or a lamp—who transformed you from a single entity into a unit, whose breathing at night was as reassuring as a clock, to whom you could, of an evening, pay almost no attention at all, and who in one minute, with one look, could turn into what a husband in actuality was: a sexual being.

Jane Louise's heart contracted. There was in this arrangement some frightening aspect, some scary way in which this connection went beyond connection and spilled into the larger world.

Teddy peered at her from his couch pillow. His hair was mussed. His glasses were fogged. She could feel his smooth hard chest under his shirt. She put her arms around him and kissed his sweet mouth.

"Okay," she whispered. "Let's."

CHAPTER 10

In the office Sven turned the force of his intense regard on Jane Louise. She felt picked over, ransacked, probed. He seemed to sniff her, like a mother cat. Now that she was married, she felt he saw right through her. She felt that the nights of her married life were as open to him as a book.

"What's the scene with *him?*" she asked Adele, who was herself the X-ray technician of Sven. "He's all over me."

"I think one of his girls quit on him," Adele said.

Jane Louise went blank.

"His lunchtime sweetie," Adele said.

Jane Louise was dimly aware that Sven's lunches, when not with printers and graphic artists, were spent in the company of compliant women of any age. She had once expressed the belief that he went several days a week for psychoanalysis. Adele had set her straight.

"He meets girls," Adele said. "You know what I mean."

"Do I know what you mean?" Jane Louise had said.

"He likes it with two girls," whispered Adele, and Jane Louise found this information compelling but scarcely believable.

Adele now deduced that one of the girls had taken a powder.

"You mean this twosome is a routine thing?" Jane Louise said.

"It's been going on a while," Adele said. "It started when he told this girl to bring a friend."

"Maybe he meant for a friend of his," Jane Louise said.

"He doesn't have any friends," Adele said. "Haven't you noticed?"

"What about his poker game with Al and Dave?" Jane Louise said.

"Colleagues," Adele said. "Sven only has wives, colleagues, and people he goes to bed with."

"He had to have a mother," Jane Louise said. "Isn't she alive?"

"Barely, and she calls him 'Svenny,'" Adele said. "Isn't that adorable?"

"Svenny," said Jane Louise.

"The reason he's all over you is because you got married," said Adele. "Any woman's husband is his rival—you get it? It's some primitive force."

Jane Louise looked at Adele with pure admiration.

It was hard to figure out what marriage meant to Sven. On the one hand, he had been married three times. On the other hand, three times was a lot of times. Adele always said that Sven liked to get married because it made him feel more guilty. It was Jane Louise's opinion that guilt was not in Sven's emotional repertoire. If he ever felt the merest twinge of remorse, it was like a dab of cologne.

"I think adultery means a lot to him," Adele said.

On this elevating note Jane Louise went back to her office. Her interior life was trisected: She was now a married woman, and with her husband, Theodore Cornelius Parker, she was creating an entity known as "Their Marriage." It was like a museum stuffed with breakfast conversations, fights about where the extra key had been put, dinners eaten, movies viewed, showers taken together, plans made. In sickness and in health, and in confusion. Decisions were made: to try to conceive a baby in the early summer—a communal decision. Eventually a baby would emerge, and Jane Louise would have another mental section, a quarter section to deal with known as "Their Child." They would then have an entity to inhabit called "Their Family."

Also there was the office, as thick with associations and memories as any home. Her office itself was not as richly furnished as, say, Erna's, which had family photos, children's artworks, large fossils from Dorset, a wing chair, a scarlet sofa, and a dozen needlepointed pillows.

Jane Louise had a photo of Teddy on her desk. She had taken it herself, of him standing by the lake wearing a striped shirt, the wind ruffling his hair. She had a poster of one of Edie's cakes on the wall. The cake, which cost hundreds of dollars, was called "The Meadow" and had made Edie famous. It was a three-layer cake with shiny, pale green icing. Heaped and scattered everywhere, as if a child had flung a bouquet of wildflowers, were hundreds of spun-sugar-and-buttercream pansies, violets, bladderwort, primroses, buttercups, and rose rugosa. It was a work of art.

On her desk was a clay bowl that she had made in art school. It contained paper clips. Her paperweight was a painted bronze elephant on a green base, a gift from Teddy.

Whatever was left over between office and home was some tiny slice called "Private Life." Here she absentmindedly filed Sven and his lunchtime trysts. She tried not to think about it, but he had some weird hold on her.

Weren't there, in this world, those who were immune to all this? Like Erna, who behaved like a grown-up, created a family, and never looked back, or sideways, and who did not live with the occasional fear that a swine like Sven might lean over again and kiss her neck, making her feel that an electric current had been run through her. Sven, she knew, was lying in wait. He would lie in wait for a long time, because she had not been conquered. She remembered her first months at the office—a youngish woman between attachments. Sven liked to take her out to lunch and make her drink a sip or two of his gin and tonic. He liked to say things like: "I wonder what it will be like when we wake up together."

His caressing voice seemed to curl up in her ear. A little voice inside her said, "How corny," and another voice, a more physical voice, so to speak, realized how effective he was. The hair on the back of her neck prickled.

Jane Louise had known exactly what to retort. She had said: "You mean, when we fall asleep in the van coming back from sales conference?"

By that time in her life, lots of lyrical, ridiculous, and persuasive things had been said to her by men. She was neither in the bloom of youth nor the exhaustion of age. She did not feel she was the classic lust-inducing type, but rather a more specific attraction. But Sven would wear her down, like water over rock, until she finally gave in. If she ever slept with him, he would behave the next day as if nothing had happened and she had somehow made the whole thing up.

Although Jane Louise had never thought of herself as boy crazy, she was certainly someone who had had her share of romance. She had experienced every possible kind: the kind in which you love them better than they love you; in which they love you better than you love them; in which you are madly in love and can't stand to be in the same room with them; in which they adore you but can't seem to organize themselves to be with you. Then she met Teddy, the light at the end of the tunnel.

Although he was frequently silent, prone to a kind of alienating depression, and it was sometimes very hard to have a conversation with him, in many ways Teddy was heaven. He was unencumbered by certain doubts. He and Jane Louise had fallen in love, and therefore it made sense to him that they should live together and plan to get married without any particular distress in the way. Although his parents' marriage had been a disaster, Teddy did not want to see that sort of gloom in his future. He pointed himself in the direction of a union. Jane Louise, who had always been marriage-shy, slipped right in with him. In some ways Teddy was not like a modern person. He did not have spiritual difficulties. He tended to see a thing clearly, and life in some ways was very clear to him. He had the vision of a sensible grown-up. He certainly did not have impure thoughts about decadent types he worked with, but then plant chemists are not usually surrounded by louche types.

A husband was someone you could hide behind. You could cover your head with a marriage the way Arab women covered themselves with a veil. You could stamp out unnecessary or wayward emotions. You could dispel untoward thoughts. You could pretend that all of your life was all of a piece and it was wonderful, wonderful, wonderful. You didn't have to admit to a thing. Like Dita.

Dita was amazing to watch in this way. It was known to Jane Louise that Dita had had that brief, quite intense sex wrangle with that silky, seal-like Joe Ching. In fact, Jane Louise was the only person in the whole world who knew about this fling. Dita did not tell her oldest and best friend from boarding school, Peachy Hopkins, because Peachy did not approve of philandering and had two nice children whom she walked to school each day. Eventually, when things got out of hand—when one of Dita's marriages broke up and a new one began—Peachy was told all.

This encounter with Joe Ching had eaten up a great deal of Dita's hot, intense energy. If Joe Ching called late, or was late for an assignation, or did not appear to be in desperate love, Dita went to pieces. Jane Louise had spent a couple of evenings trying to calm her down as she shouted and sobbed and insisted her life was worthless.

And then Dita turned up at a concert with her lawful wedded husband, the reportage photographer Nick Samuelovich, who had a noble head of white blond hair, clear-framed glasses for his stark blue eyes, and a long black scarf wrapped several times around his neck. He towered over Dita, who was small-boned. She brushed imaginary lint off his camel's hair coat, and smoothed his shoulders, and, after the concert, took Jane Louise and Teddy, who was still new in her life, off to a tiny Russian café where Dita called her husband Nikosh and Nikita and laughed at his jokes. You would never know a thing. Teddy thought she was pure hell.

The Arctic manuscript sat on Jane Louise's table, almost glowing with a lurid light, like a phosphorescent mushroom. I ought to take that home and read it, she said to herself, and think up some plain but handsome design.

Her mind was not on this project. Was it the result of marriage that your attention wandered and you felt that your own consciousness was like a new puppy on a leash?

She heard a voice and looked up. Sven was standing in the doorway, appraising her. How long had he been there?

"Get to work," he said, ambling in.

"I can't get to work with you in my office," Jane Louise said. "And what's your story? You don't seem to be very work oriented these days."

"It's the unsettling effect of your marriage," Sven said. "Puts ideas in a person's head."

"It's supposed to take ideas *out* of a person's head," Jane Louise said.

"Oh, yes?" Sven said. "Is that why you got married?"

"Peace and harmony," Jane Louise said. "A stitch in the ever-expanding tapestry of human affairs."

Sven looked at her. "Men and women are adversaries," he said. "Like cats and birds."

"Really?" Jane Louise said. "Don't you and Edwina get along?"

"I get along with all my wives," Sven said. "It isn't about 'getting along.' It's about what's really underneath."

"Underneath what?"

"Rapine," Sven said. "Hunting and gathering. We are primitive people."

"How interesting," Jane Louise said. "You mean when a boy and girl go out, it's really about how he kills an animal, she finds some berries, and then he jumps her?"

"You know what I mean," Sven said.

"I don't," said Jane Louise.

"Passion," Sven said, "is the sweater of pillage pulled inside out." He looked enormously pleased with himself.

Jane Louise looked at him, saying nothing.

"You probably think it's all about oneness and unity."

There was nothing Jane Louise could say to this. She did think it was all about oneness and unity.

"It's because women are receptacles that they feel that way," Sven said.

"Seen in that light, you guys are simply garbage men," Jane Louise said. "Get out of here, okay?"

This conversation rattled and upset Jane Louise. She felt her flesh creep in ways not entirely unpleasant. She also felt slightly sweaty, as if her clothes had suddenly grown too tight.

She pushed some papers around on her desk. She fiddled with some type and answered a memo. She put the enormous manuscript in her canvas bag to take home. She called her husband, but he was in a meeting.

Teddy's office, unlike Jane Louise's, was large and uncluttered. The laboratories were painted a greenish white. The light was intense and focused. The halls of his workplace were quiet, unlike the offices of a publishing company, in which people could be heard yelling at one another, or barking over the telephone, or laughing in front of the coffee maker. Here radiators and windowsills were stacked with manuscript boxes, dozens of yellowing memos, and jacket sketches, and C-prints were pinned to bulletin boards. Teddy's office seemed like a monastery in which there were no extraneous words or things, although Teddy told Jane Louise that there was enough camaraderie to keep a friendly person happy. There were football pools and, during racing season, Derby pools.

Jane Louise imagined meetings at which sober, clean-looking scientists produced and analyzed data. This was, in fact, pretty much what Teddy described. Meetings of the editorial and design department were not like that at all.

Every now and again when some book presented design problems, Jane Louise was hauled upstairs to the editorial meeting. There Erna presided over a squadron of eccentrics: Delphine Kolodny, a nasty piece of work known to Dita as "the Flatworm." Dita had the sweetest lunches with Delphine and then reported that Delphine took notes on everything she said. She felt that, given the chance, Delphine would sneak into her office and copy names off her Rolodex. Delphine had confided to Dita at one of their sweet little lunches that she wanted to be a "really top editor." Dita recounted this story with considerable relish.

Dita's left side was always commandeered by Jeff Pottker, whom Dita had once French-kissed in a darkened office during the annual Christmas party. She revealed to Jane Louise that his wife was preoccupied with such paraphernalia of infancy as baby shit and breast-feeding, which seemed to have put a crimp in his libido. There was Omar Majors, editor emeritus, a fine-looking old man with the head of a Roman general, whose brother had once courted Dita's mother. And Willa Gathers, who did the cookbooks, and venerable Thomas Moss, who for years and years and years—he had never had another job—had edited poetry, art books, and history. Jim Phillipi came in three days a week and worked on an unending series of war memoirs. It was rumored that he had been on the Long March with Mao, as a journalist. Jane Louise surveyed this mostly underdressed (except for Dita) crowd, many of whom felt that designers were like cleaning personnel, while they, the editorial staff, were towering intellects.

If she looked around the table, what an amazing amount of information she had about these people, some of whom she barely knew: Bob Lodge, senior editor (known to Dita as Blodge), was having a lunchtime affair with a dopey young woman who looked like his ex-wife when young. Little Jeannie Sprout had a terrible crush on Mike Church, head of the sales department, and so on.

At meetings and on crowded buses, Jane Louise always had the same thought: Each of these people was born with a personality and a family history and a set of unique feelings that they were truly entitled, for better or worse, to express whenever they felt like it.

CHAPTER 11

At dinner Teddy said: "What if we went away at Christmastime?"

Jane Louise thought that meant to stay with Eleanor in the country.

"I mean *away*," Teddy said. "To some nice place where it's hot."

"What about your mother?" Jane Louise said. "We already didn't go there for Thanksgiving. Shouldn't we go to either mine or yours?"

"Eleanor's tough," Teddy said. "She's feeling very liberated. All those years of struggling through Christmas. Now she's a free woman. She jumped the gun on us and she's going to England to stay with her old college friend Audra Llynch. She was afraid to tell us because she thought we'd be unhappy."

"Ain't that something," Jane Louise said. "Well, *my* mother can be heartbroken."

"Your mother can say she's heartbroken, but she and Charlie can go away to someplace hot and expensive," Teddy said. "She can have a lovely vacation and torture you at the same time."

"Maybe they'll all be heartbroken," Jane Louise said.

"Listen," said Teddy fiercely. "We're all heartbroken. I'm heart-broken. Until I met you I never had a holiday I enjoyed."

Jane Louise gaped at him. She had never expected to hear such a naked declaration from her husband. He was eating his dinner as if he had not just said a momentous thing, but his face was grim. She stood up, took his fork away from him, and threw her arms around his neck.

"For God's sake, Janey," he said.

"I don't care," Jane Louise said. She sat in his lap and pressed her lips against his neck and breathed him in. She could feel his neck pulse against her cheek. Her tears slid onto his collar. She knew he hated storms of emotion, but she needed to feel him close to her. She wanted to make up for everything: for the conflicts and loneliness of his childhood, for the year and a half he had spent, an only son, in Vietnam, racked with a free-floating guilt that his mother would be left alone. She wanted to wash away his awful feelings about his father and his half-sisters. How was she going to do this?

As she sat, with her husband in her arms and his warm breath on her neck, she felt fragile and exhausted. How am I going to keep him cheered? she wondered. How could she, a person whose life had been far from settled, make him some nice, safe place in which to rest comfortably?

A holiday away! Jane Louise imagined herself and Teddy alone in a hotel room, lying next to each other on a hotel bed, holding hands but not speaking. She imagined herself turning to her husband and watching the cloud of sadness she so dreaded rolling over him. She imagined them skating at an ice rink. Teddy on ice was as easy and secure as a bird. It was a natural element for him. She imagined them skating arm in arm—she was a pretty good skater, too—trying to skate away from the sense that they were alone and isolated at a time when people clung together with their loved ones.

Jane Louise expressed this vision to her husband. He raised an eyebrow.

"Do we know people who are happy to be in the bosom of their family?"

"Peter and Beth," Jane Louise said.

"Well, let's decode Peter and Beth," Teddy said. "Beth's family stopped speaking to her when she married Peter because he isn't Catholic. They only got back together when the kids were born. She hates them, actually."

"Why does she bother?"

"It's a hunger," Teddy said. "She wants the kids to have grand-parents."

"They have Peter senior and Laura."

"Those are *Peter's* parents," said Teddy. "Now let's take Peter senior and Laura. On the one hand, it's all very cozy, and they all live together in a small town, and Peter got such a great piece of land from his father, but Marjorie didn't inherit a piece of land from *her* father, so now she takes dictation from horses. Peter's glad he has the land, but he also has his father breathing down his neck. It's nice in a small place. It's also hell. It's not like here. Here you don't have to be careful every minute of offending someone or hurting his feelings and having the whole thing snowball. There it's different. When Peter started farming with-out chemicals, Howard Vincent and Arnold Kingshot and Jack White took it as a slap in their face since *they* farm with chemi-cals."

They were sitting on the striped couch. Teddy sat upright. Jane Louise slumped next to him. She wanted to crawl under his sweater.

"Do you think we'll ever be happy?" she said.

Teddy looked down at her. "Aren't you happy?" he said.

"I mean in the cosmic sense," she said.

"No one is ever going to be happy in the cosmic sense," Teddy said.

"I mean," said Jane Louise, "what will our life be like?"

"Listen, Janey," Teddy said, "our parents never had to think about what life would be like for them, and look what happened. And hundreds of holidays rolled around and we survived."

"I want something better," Jane Louise said. "I want to have a child who doesn't dread those occasions."

"I know what you want," Teddy said. "Safe house, warm hearth. Communion with nature. Happy cooperation. Good vibes."

Jane Louise hung her head. "Don't make fun of me."

"I'm not," Teddy said. "Those are the right things. Most people don't even believe they're possible anymore."

"I want them," Jane Louise said. She was amazed at how passionate she sounded.

"Then you'll have them," Teddy said, drawing her close. "Or some variant form of them."

"I don't suppose you could help me out, could you, Janey?" Edie said. Jane Louise was in bed with the phone tucked under her chin. "Mokie's sick as a dog, and I have another Teagarden event at the end of the week."

"Do I get a view of the Teagarden landscape?" Jane Louise said.

"*Complète*," Edie said. "You can see the child's room with the alphabet stenciled around the wall, and the heirloom quilt they got on Madison Avenue, and the nanny's room right next door, and their huge Park Avenue stately-home kitchen, and the paneling in the library from a Norman church, and the Old Masters in the hallways."

"And do they have a live ancestor sitting in the drawing room wearing a mobcap?"

"The old parents are always sequestered," Edie said. "Mrs. Teagarden hasn't renovated them yet. They're said to be in Palm Beach."

"Yum-yum," Jane Louise said. "What's the occasion this time?"

"They celebrate things I've never heard of," Edie said. "But this is just a simple winter party. The house decorated in pine branches. Big beeswax candles, all the silver candlesticks out. Tiny lights. Baby orchids. Like that."

"The piano rubbed with beeswax," Jane Louise said.

"Naturally they use only natural household products. The servant does the windows with vinegar," Edie said. "Mrs. T. has planned a simple but elegant dinner of simple but elegant caviar on roast potatoes, followed by a lovely but modest pile of lobsters, followed by a large, tasteful platter of white Belgian asparagus, and for dessert she wants something she calls a Sugarplum Fairy Cake."

"A live ballerina pops out of it," Jane Louise suggested.

"White icing, lots of spun stuff, silver dragées, and tiny white sugar rosebuds."

"What about the fairy? Is it one of those plastic jobs?" Jane Louise said. "I guess you want me to come over and spin the sugar for you."

"I'm very much afraid," Edie said, "that this will have to be done in Mrs. Teagarden's state-of-the-art kitchen. She prefers things done 'on-site,' as she says."

Teddy said, "Who pops out of what?" when Jane Louise had hung up. He was half asleep on his side of the bed.

"The people with the christening want Edie to do another

party," Jane Louise said. "Mokie has the flu, so I have to help. They invented something called a Sugarplum Fairy Cake with spun sugar, and Edie and I have to produce it. I said I'd help."

Teddy yawned and turned on his other side. "Do you really know how to spin sugar?" he said.

"Oh, sure," Jane Louise said. "All girls can. Edie taught me. You do it with this wooden thing that looks like a giant comb."

"I want to come and watch," Teddy said. "I didn't know I had married a woman who knew how to spin sugar."

"You never asked," Jane Louise said.

"These people have a lot of parties," Teddy said sleepily.

"These people have a lot of money," Jane Louise said. "Maybe we should give a lot of parties. It feels just like family life, but everyone goes home afterwards."

"Are you all right?" Teddy said.

Jane Louise thought for a moment. "I want a great big family that has been in the same place for centuries and has never moved. I want dozens of cousins and millions of relatives."

"Really?" said Teddy.

"Not really," Jane Louise said. "I can hardly stand the ones I have. I often feel horrible that I love Edie better than I love my sister."

"Edie is a hundred times nicer," said Teddy.

The next evening Jane Louise stood in Edie's kitchen listening to Mokie sneezing in the bedroom. Mokie and Edie lived in a loft that was almost totally utilitarian, except for a wall on which was hung Edie's collection of hats (which Jane Louise thought looked very much like Edie's cakes) and a large shelf for Mokie's collection of salt and pepper shakers, all in the shape of black cooks, some smiling, some frowning, and some with mottoes written in fake gold paint, such as, GIT IN THE KITCHEN, BOY! YAS! YAS!

Everything else had its proper storage bin, drawer, or closet.

"But what about the fairy?" Jane Louise said. "I thought about it all day."

Edie said, "Mrs. Teagarden wonders if we can find a small, bisque doll. Money is no object. She is, however, open to suggestions."

"I'll make one," Jane Louise said. "I'll make one out of cardboard, doilies, and those reproduction Victorian cupids."

"Do you think that would work?" Edie said. "I think she wants this to cost a lot."

"Tell her it will cost two thousand dollars, and give the money to me and Janey," said Mokie, ambling into the kitchen. He was wearing wrinkled blue pajamas and his horn-rimmed glasses.

Mokie was beautiful, with a beautifully round head. Together he and Edie looked like a negative and positive of the same person. Their elegant, bony wrists shot out of anything they wore—everything was too short on them. Mokie was languid. Edie was jumpy. She was wearing a blue shirt and slacks, and a pair of dark red shoes, highly polished. Her feet were long and skinny.

Jane Louise never tired of watching them. They were like a pair of giraffes, graceful and ungainly at the same time. Edie's voice was low and calm, while Mokie, who was not as easily flapped, squeaked when he was rattled.

"Is this more Teagarden horse manure?" he said. "Oh, these people. I've had Mrs. Teagarden on my case all morning. She wants something called Sandpine for her greens. I told her it grows only in Florida, and she said, 'Don't you have people there?' I thought she meant darkie relatives, but I guess she meant a branch office."

"Maybe we should do institutional catering in a prison," Edie said. "These people are beginning to get to me."

"Don't worry," Mokie said. "We've got a book full of charities to make you feel better. Next week, indigent families, then unadoptable orphans, then rare heart disease, and after the New Year we have all sorts of good stuff: tennis for disadvantaged youth, the penniless or soon-to-be-penniless film archive, and poor struggling writers and poets."

"Great," Edie said. "We can give them that dinner of rice water and gruel we've been working on." She ran her hand through her hair. "I'm sick of working for rich people," she said.

"We all are," said Mokie. "But they're the only ones who have any money."

They sat around the table drinking tea and eating chocolate biscuits and watching used tissues pile up next to Mokie. His eyes teared, and he looked forlorn. His sneeze was amazingly loud.

"The thing about men is, who told them they were allowed to sneeze like that?" Jane Louise said.

"My mother loved my sneezing," Mokie said, sniffing.

"Women are taught to repress sneezing," Edie said.

"It's symbolic," Jane Louise said.

"I thought we were talking about rich people," Mokie said.

"They aren't our only clients," Edie said. "We do for nice people, too."

"Not nice enough," Mokie said. "Nice people don't have caterers. I'm going to go to divinity school and become a preacher like my old man."

Edie looked at him, her brow furrowed. There were times when it must have occurred to her how unalike she and Mokie were. And yet he was the son of a distinguished preacher who had been influential in the civil rights movement. In his family, like Edie's, achievement was everything. Just as Edie had been groomed to take her place in society, so had Mokie, and they had both met as renegades in Paris, making candy roses and spun sugar and learning restaurant management, the last thing either the Fraziers or the Steinhauses had in mind for their offspring. Their essential life was a secret: their relationship, their line of work. When they finally broke down and got married, would they hide their little mulatto offspring, too?

"Teddy wants to go away for Christmas," Jane Louise said. "All of us."

Edie had been doodling on her notepad. Her head shot up. "Won't we feel horrible that we weren't *en famille?*" she said.

"We're old enough to have our own holidays," Mokie said. "I like them better that way. But don't we have some parties to cater?"

"We only have the ghastly Teagardens. They're paying us a fortune. We have a few wedding cakes, and then nothing till after the first. After all, we deserve some time off, too."

"Where are we going?" Mokie said. "Are we going?"

"I don't know," Jane Louise said. "The whole thing is sort of depressing."

"Depressing!" Edie said. "It sounds like heaven in a teacup."

"I guess we'll be each other's families again," said Jane Louise.

"We might even have some fun," said Mokie.

"Fun," said Jane Louise. "What a weird thing to think about at holiday time."

CHAPTER 12

In the end they bundled into Edie and Mokie's old car and drove to Vermont, four very tall adults in a not terribly large space. Mokie and Teddy sat in the front, and since the seats were pushed back to accommodate their legs, Edie and Jane Louise squashed into the corners of the car and stretched their legs out crossways. Jane Louise passed around a thermos of coffee. In the trunk were four pairs of ice skates, and tied to the top of the car were Teddy's cross-country skis.

They stayed at an inn kept by an old Swiss couple. The four of them were the only guests. The hostess had kept fires going in their rooms and put hot-water bottles into their beds. It was freezing cold.

After they gulped down a few excellent sandwiches, they crawled into bed. Jane Louise woke in the night to see that it was snowing. The fire in the room had died down. At dawn she woke up again to find herself inside a greeting card from another century. Outside the snow fell straight down in large, flat flakes. The room was wallpapered with a print of cabbage roses. The Persian rug was faded. One of the inn cats was asleep on a blue chair. It was Christmas Eve day, and she was far away from her family.

Teddy was fast asleep. Down the hall was her closest friend in the world, the person who knew her longest, understood her best, and knew her past as well as her own. The idea of a holiday with her mother and her stepfather suddenly seemed impossibly appealing, although in her mother's new house and with her mother's new husband she felt tense and uncomfortable. Teddy's breathing was a solace to her. But were they not as strangers, all alone?

Since the beginning of mankind, men and women had gone off together to form a unit, a couple, an entity with a history behind it and a destiny in front. Was it easier when you did this in the context of an enormous family, or worse?

Jane Louise shifted around. Her husband had broken down and put on his pajamas in deference to the cold. She covered his shoulder and watched him sleep: He was as relaxed as a child. The tension of the day had left his face. He smelled sweetly of sleep. How easy it would be to do wrong to a sleeping man!

Such availability, such access! Jane Louise shivered, and she huddled next to him. He turned and put his arms around her. His embrace was so familiar, and so remote, it caused her almost to shudder. They were now related to each other by marriage and were protected by law from any number of incursions into their privacy. They were a legal and economic unit. To undo their relationship would take the intervention of a court of law. And yet they were in this bed because they loved each other, and were meant to love each other in spite of everything, for ever more. It was their mandate to create a family, and fill their lives with photos and memories and trials, and odd bits of family lore and family occasions, and their children would go out into the world and say: "In our family, we always . . . " and, "We feel . . . " She and

Teddy, these two unprepared tall humans, whose backgrounds included rancorous divorce and financial uncertainty, were supposed to create some unswerving, stable, and dependable structure. How were they supposed to do that?

As Teddy was shaving, a tap came at the door, and there stood Edie in a dark green robe and striped slippers.

"Oh," she said. "Yours woke up. Mine says it's too cold and went back to sleep. I think he expects breakfast in bed."

"As you may remember," said Teddy, squinting into the mirror, "I suggested someplace *hot*."

"It was too expensive to go someplace hot," Jane Louise said.

"Think of the wonderful amounts of money we'll pay in doctor bills for bronchitis from freezing our asses off up here."

"It is pretty cold," Edie said. "The radiator's tepid."

"It's because of these quaint, old-fashioned fireplaces," Jane Louise said.

There was another tap on the door, and in walked Mrs. Schuldes, the owner's wife, bringing a large basket of what looked like shale.

"Cannel coal," she said. "Burns very hot. It was five below this morning, but it's supposed to warm up to ten above. Come down to breakfast. The dining room is quite overheated."

They went to breakfast; Mokie came, too. They wore silk underwear, leggings, T-shirts, turtlenecks, heavy sweaters, and three pairs of socks. They ate dozens of muffins, piles of toast, and cups and cups of coffee with hot milk.

After breakfast they ambled into the sitting room, sat in front of the fire, and read the papers.

"Gosh, this is romantic," Mokie said.

Then it was time for lunch, and then they went up to their freezing rooms and took naps under their down quilts and blankets. If the Schuldes family was celebrating Christmas, there was little sign of it, although the sitting room was full of pine branches in enormous glass jars, and there were wreaths on every door. In the late afternoon the smell of mulled cider wafted up the stairs.

Jane Louise realized that she was exhausted. They were all exhausted. The idea of lying around napping took them by surprise, like a fall on the ice, and they surrendered to it. When they came down for dinner—Edie and Jane Louise in long skirts and long underwear—they were surprised to find a cheerful group of people they had never seen before. Mrs. Schuldes explained that these were friends and relatives who always came for Christmas supper and evening skating. Guests of the inn traditionally were included.

They stood in the living room, drinking hot cider, until the doors to the dining room were pulled back to reveal the kind of table Edie said Mrs. Teagarden would have paid several hundred thousand dollars to have someone fix up for her. On the large sideboard were three roast ducks, a glazed ham, an enormous glass dish containing a mountain of beet and herring salad, greens, roast potatoes, and a gigantic Christmas cake.

"This is the most beautiful thing I've ever seen," Edie said.

Jane Louise looked around her. It made her feel almost panicky to be sitting at a Christmas table surrounded by people she had never seen before.

As they began their dinner the front door crashed open, and in walked the three big Schuldes boys and their dogs. They had just come from cleaning off the pond and setting out the flambeaux: huge torches on poles. They sat down and began eating quantities of food Jane Louise found mind-boggling. "Did you and Mokie eat that way when you were teenagers?" she asked Teddy.

"Honey, I *still* eat that way," said Mokie. "This is heaven."

He looked around the table, used to being the only person of color. This group was polite and not very talkative, so Mokie started in.

"My wife and I are caterers," he said. "Actually, Edie is a cake decorator and pastry chef. She has raised cake decoration to a fine art. And I am a caterer, but I have *never* seen such beautiful food." He lifted his glass toward Mrs. Schuldes.

"My husband does all the cooking," she said. "It must be very interesting to cook professionally."

"You do," Mokie pointed out.

"We only do breakfasts, except for Christmas Eve," Mrs. Schuldes said. "Do you have many interesting clients?"

Mokie, Edie, and Jane Louise sighed audibly.

"Tell them about the fairy cake," Teddy said.

"The sugarplum fairy," Mokie began. "We have a client who is what you might call extremely demanding. Every little thing, every big thing, every middle-sized thing. She likes to get it all right. This year our client had a winter party, and she had a vision of something called a Sugarplum Fairy Cake."

"Is that one of those hollow cakes with a lady popping out of it?" Mrs. Schuldes said. "You hear of these things at stag parties."

"She was unclear what it was," Mokie said. "But my genius wife decoded this to mean a cake with a doll ornament. We made her prototypes in cardboard, we found Victorian Christmas cards, we found little dolls of the fifties. Finally Jane Louise found an old bisque doll and dressed it up, but by that time our client had forgotten all about it and was onto something else."

"*Forgotten!*" Mrs. Schuldes said. "After all that work?"

Mokie smiled a beautiful smile. "These people aren't afraid of hard work, ma'am," he said.

Jane Louise looked over at him. The name of this smile was "the Nigger Funereal Smile." She and Mokie had in common that they never felt they were where they ought to be, and when they were where they thought they ought to be, they longed to be somewhere else. Mokie's manners were flawless, a kind of self-parody. He had the very best kind of Sunday church manners. He called women over a certain age "ma'am"; he almost bent double to shake the hands of shorter people. It often drifted into Jane Louise's mind to wonder what he was like in bed. She wondered this about a great many people: In this regard she was a variant form of Sven. As she ate her dinner, she reflected on this question.

Sven the Lover she saw as a kind of mechanic, a man with a workbench in his basement, slowly taking the parts apart and slowly putting them back together, with tremendous concentration but no real personal interest. Mokie she imagined as hot and languid, the sort of person who sighs and props himself on one elbow to take a sip from a bedside glass of water. Teddy was ardent and straightforward, like a boy. Unlike Sven, who doubtless went in for accoutrements, or Mokie, who might be able to take a telephone call in the middle and then peacefully continue the enterprise, Teddy did not much go in for frills. Rather, he himself was thrilling. His feelings were the main thing. It amazed Jane Louise, who felt her emotions were pretty obvious, that a person so restrained in daily life could be so carried away. He was a hungry man.

Here they were, the four of them, at this big table in the middle of nowhere on a major holiday, surrounded by people they had never seen before. Jane Louise was eating her duck and thinking about sex. What was anyone else thinking about?

After dinner they piled on their coats and scarves, gloves and boots, and went down to the pond for an evening skate. The Schuldes boys had lit the flambeaux. Near the benches, where you could sit and put your skates on, they had lit a bonfire. The pale quarter moon hung in the cloudy sky, and the stars peeked in and out of the fleeting darkness.

They put on their skates and tested the ice. It had frozen several feet and was as black as obsidian.

Teddy was a wonderful skater. It was like dancing to him. Recently he had taken their skates to be sharpened, and he circled the pond, his scarf flying behind him, his hands locked behind his back. He skated over to Jane Louise and led her onto the ice.

Jane Louise, who had usually been the person with the least amount of money in the fairly fancy places her parents moved to, had spent her teen years hanging around the skating club that she could not afford to join. All her friends belonged, and kept their skates there. Members had a little red number tag laced into their skates. How Jane Louise had longed for that! She had never, since money was always tight, asked for lessons, and she had learned by watching. Skating with Teddy was nicer than any skating she had ever done.

Over on the other side Mokie and Edie were being silly. They looked like a pair of storks. Atop their curly hair they wore stupid-looking hats with pom-poms, and they were attempting to execute an ice tango: They looked like the photo of the scientist dancing with the sandhill crane. At pastry class in Paris they had eyed each other solemnly, and when Edie had come to class with her skates over her shoulder, Mokie made his move. They spent their two years in Paris in bed, in class, on the ice, or in cafés perfecting their French. Now they were waltzing and twirling, and Edie was laughing.

Mr. Schuldes skated while smoking a large curved pipe and wearing a Tyrolean outfit and feathered hat. Mrs. Schuldes wore an old mink coat. One of the guests, who had been a professional skater in her youth, took off her coat to reveal a pink skating costume and heavy pink tights. She glided out into the middle and executed a series of twirls and leaps.

As they skated past the torches, their faces were momentarily lit up. The warm light cast a glowing shadow. Then they skated into darkness. The three Schuldes boys pushed a round wooden table onto the ice and covered it with a cloth. Mrs. Schuldes skated out with a tray of hot chocolate and cookies.

"I have died and gone to heaven," Edie said to Jane Louise. "This isn't really real, is it?"

Jane Louise thought it was like a fairy tale out of the Old World, like a Victorian postcard or the *Nutcracker* ballet.

"God, wouldn't old Mrs. Teagarden die for this?" Mokie said.

Teddy drank his chocolate and kissed his wife. He seemed able, every once in a while, to enjoy his life without any anguish or static. It was dark. It was Christmas. He was on ice skates with his wife in the freezing cold, drinking hot chocolate and eating the kind of powdery nut cookies that melt in your mouth. For an instant life was frozen. There was no past—no days in an under-heated house or overheated apartment while adults fought or complained. This was heaven.

In the flickering light Jane Louise looked up at Teddy. His face, like his face in sleep, was free of worry. He looked completely happy.

It had begun to snow fine, needlelike flakes that buzzed and stung. Jane Louise felt her heart open. Maybe everything would be all right after all, and if you worked almost till you dropped, roasting ducks and sharpening your ice skates and planning to move a table out onto a frozen pond, and if you kept your fires burning and picked your friends with care—maybe if you made sure that every single thing was just so, life would not spin out of control and make you sick with anxiety and concern.

Teddy took her arm. She was suddenly sleepy, and she leaned

against him, yawning. Little by little the ice was clearing. The torches sputtered. The chocolate had all been consumed. The platter of cookies was empty except for crumbs.

"Someday," Jane Louise said, as she and Teddy took one last, slow skate around the pond. "Someday we'll get a house with a pond and have a party just like this, except we'll all do it together and have all our family and friends."

Teddy held her tighter. He knew perfectly well that in this world few events pop off so well, and few families and friends gather so peacefully. He did not want to say that this evening had been lovely because Mokie and Edie were their family by choice.

But of course he did not have to say it. As they walked arm in arm back to their rooms, he knew perfectly well that Jane Louise realized exactly the same thing.

PART II

CHAPTER 13

On a sleety February day Sven ambled into Jane Louise's office and sat down.

"When do you think you will be announcing your maternity leave?"

"And what makes you think I'll be asking for a maternity leave?" Jane Louise said.

"You got married," Sven said, lighting a cigarette. "You're not a kid. It's bound to be in the works."

"I'll let you know first thing, Sven."

"I find this whole idea of conception very touching," Sven said. "It's my opinion you can feel a direct hit. All my wives say that."

"I'm sure all your wives say a great many things," said Jane Louise.

"I'm sure they do," Sven said. "Now tell the truth, Janey. Are you secretly pregnant, right this minute?"

"Guess what?" Jane Louise said. "It's none of your beeswax."

"Don't be touchy," Sven said. "This subject interests me. Half of Edwina's pals have been to one high-tech fertility doctor or another. There's little I don't know."

"My mommy told me to make sure I had a nice spring baby," said Jane Louise. "And that's what I shall have, or we'll adopt one."

"Get on it," Sven said. "You're probably losing ovarian viability with each passing minute."

"Thank you for your concern," Jane Louise said. "Did you come in here to talk about my ovaries?"

"There's a lot of rumors all over town that this place is up on the block."

"You mean they're going to sell it?" Jane Louise said. She felt instantly white with dread.

"That's what 'on the block' usually means."

"But why?"

"No heir, for one thing," Sven said. "Expansion, for another."

"Expansion into what?"

"Oh, bigger things," said Sven. "Books that make more money, more commercial fiction, a new paperback line. You know."

"I don't know," Jane Louise said. "I hate change. It's usually for the worse."

"It's on the street that movie people or Europeans want to buy us. Everyone says it's totally false, which means some part of it is true."

The press was owned by a not entirely benevolent millionaire by the name of Hamish Levey, who had inherited it from his father.

Hamish ran his company for fun and profit. He had been heard to say that he had hired his staff in order to replicate the sort of cultivated and amusing people you might find on an ocean liner. He liked his female employees to be beautiful, brainy, with impeccable pedigrees and manners, and his male workers to have gone to Yale, to play tennis, and have a sharp eye for art and commerce. He liked a winner. When Jane Louise looked around the company, she was always amazed at how many people had independent incomes.

His wife was named Emerald, a former Broadway actress with an immense head of red hair. She knew the name of every employee and sent booties when you had a baby and flowers when you lost a relative. Their office parties were ravishing.

Hamish felt, since salaries were so laughable, that it was morale boosting to throw a big office bash once a year at his house. Everyone was invited, from the newest editorial assistant to the boys in the mail room to the board of directors. Towers of luscious food were produced, and famous people often played the piano. The older staff drank too much, while the younger ones could be found in the garden, trying to pretend they were not smoking dope. And since authors were also invited, those sweet-looking, peachy editorial assistants often revealed the next day that Pulitzer Prize–winning authors had tried to feel them up. Later there was dancing, coffee, and wonderful cakes.

Jane Louise herself had been hit on by a number of famous and not so famous people at these parties. She had once been invited by Hamish to a small dinner given for an author over whose book she had slaved. At this party liveried servants hovered in the dining room, and Emerald, in black satin and Victorian jewelry, fussed over everyone regally. Upstairs you could hear the barking and snuffling of their brace of pug dogs. Their children, almost grown, were either at drama school in London or banking school in Switzerland.

Just as Jane Louise had had a few unsuitable paramours, so had she endured a number of lousy jobs. Just out of art school, she had worked for a slave-driving, maniacal designer who threw tantrums, threw objects, and expected Jane Louise to vacuum her rug.

By the time she had been through a few of these places, the press appeared to her a beacon of reason and calm. Day after day a nice lady named Lillian answered the telephone as she had done for forty years. A number of people had been hired by Hamish's old father, and their loyalty to the firm was prodigious. Year after year the press produced the kinds of books a person might like to take home and read or send to friends.

"What will become of us?" Jane Louise asked.

"One day," said Sven in his caressing voice, "we'll be working all alone in a small office together. It will be a Saturday, and no one else will be in the building. Your husband will be off in the country helping his mother rototill, and Edwina will be somewhere with Piers. There will be a huge, scary thunderstorm, and only the two of us in here on a rain-soaked afternoon."

Jane Louise gave him a long, bland look. "I've heard this somewhere before. What's next? I know: 'His hot hands ripped at the frail fabric of her blouse, and he pressed her to his throbbing need.'"

Sven gave *her* a bland look. "Cute," he said. "Where'd you get it from?"

"I used to read romance magazines as a kid." She put her head down. "If we get bought, will that be the end?"

"You look as if you were going to cry, Janey."

"These things scare me."

"Don't be silly," Sven said. "Roll with the punch. You buy a company because you like what it does and the people who do it."

This did not console Jane Louise. Teddy had once worked for a company that had been sold to a group of investors who then decided they had no interest in plant chemistry. They had sold it to a group of Germans who offered everyone severance or jobs in

Düsseldorf. Teddy had been briefly out of a job, but these things didn't bother him overmuch; he knew he would always work. In fact, he had turned down jobs for lots of money at places he didn't want to work and for work he didn't want to do.

He was interested in creating an environment free of poisons, and Jane Louise often felt that this was an appropriate urge in someone who felt that his childhood had been polluted by two well-meaning people perpetually at war. He liked a nice, clean space. Jane Louise did, too.

"When Teddy's company was sold, they put his division out of business," Jane Louise said.

"You never know." Sven shrugged. "This place makes some money, but Hamish doesn't need capital. Whoever buys it will turn it into a real business."

Jane Louise sighed. She knew what that meant: early retirement for the faithful retainers. No more laid paper for the poets. No more poets. No more parties, no more biographies of obscure literary figures. No four-color jackets except on potential bestsellers. No beautiful typefaces that were hard to find. No illustrations in the text. . . .

"What does Erna think about this?" Jane Louise asked.

"Oh, Erna," Sven said. "She's waiting to see which is the winning team before she joins it. She's the sort of person who is already learning the new national anthem as the invading army approaches." He stared at Jane Louise. "You poor kid," he said. "We know you wouldn't learn the national anthem of the invading army, would you? We know you'd join the underground, or quit, or get fired. Right?"

"How about getting out of here?" she said.

Sven looked hurt, but he left, and Jane Louise closed the door behind him.

She put her head down on her desk, as tired as if she had just had a three-hour crying jag. A great many things she did not want to think about flapped across her brain.

I should never have married Teddy, she said to herself gloomily. He should have married some cheerful Christian who would give him a great big family and a pack of dogs. Someone who likes rabbits, and dreams of little Brownies and Cub Scouts running all over the place. Someone who belongs to the Congregational Church and does good works. I am anxious, Jewish, over the hill. What if my ovaries have withered? What if I do have a child and I'm a grouchy mother?

What if there were to be no baby?

Jane Louise felt ardently that Teddy deserved to have a baby of his very own, one who looked just like him and could grow up to dispel some of the things that had haunted him.

Furthermore, she was sure she would soon be out of a job. Hamish would sell the company to people who would install time clocks and go in for genre fiction instead of belles lettres. Her beautiful designs would be ruined, her artful jackets wrecked.

She did not notice how dark it was in her office until Sven had opened the door and put his head in.

"Hi," he said. "I was just checking up."

Jane Louise looked at him with a kind of loving hatred. "Fuck you," she said.

"No bad language and no weeping," Sven said. "I told you it was a *rumor.*"

"Please go away, Sven," Jane Louise said.

"Okay," he said. "No more brooding. Keep your pecker up."

CHAPTER 14

The enormous manuscript of *In the Polar Regions*, by Hugh Oswald-Murphy, had been placed on Jane Louise's desk three times and taken back three times by Erna Hendershott. Then, just as Jane Louise felt she had a grip on what this thing should look like, Erna would appear in a tearing rush and inform her that the author had added to it or taken something away, or that most likely it had been pushed off the spring list or that he had decided that some Eskimo artist would do little line cuts to be scattered throughout and, furthermore, that his photographs—still to come—would have to be keyed in.

Jane Louise finally made Erna sit down in her office. This had never happened before: Erna did not sit down in the offices of others. She stood and watched over the peons, who sat. She was a magisterial woman, the sort of person who might be in training to be an empress or to be the person in the world most like Theodore Roosevelt. She had a clear voice, a firm stance, and long, strong legs with dancer's calves. Her clothes bordered on the matronly, but she had not changed her style since college.

Erna wore the kind of suit one's mother wore—cherry red wool, or soft, heathery tweed—with silk blouses and pearls. She was a clubwoman to the tips of her Italian pumps, except that her club was made up of important journalists, distinguished writers, renegade lawyers, or political figures with literary notions. She was a man's girl. Jane Louise watched her with the utmost fascination, as if she were a giant bug. She would have liked to take Erna home in a jar and study her.

These flying visits from Erna drove her crazy and often made her angry. Erna did not much like it when the peons acted like regular folks with civil rights and work of their own. Therefore, when Erna crashed into her office breathless, as if her secretary were running after her with a cordless telephone, Jane Louise decided she would stare her down and get her to behave.

"You'll have to sit down, Erna," Jane Louise said. "I have preliminary specs on that book, unless you're here to tell me we're killing it."

"Killing it! *Polar Regions?*" Erna shrieked. "Dear girl! This is the sort of book you stop press for."

Jane Louise had heard this song before. Erna's books were often the sort of book you stop press for.

"Well, there's a little problem with the book as it stands," Jane Louise said. "It's extremely long. With no illustrations or photos, it's going to be unbelievably expensive. With photos—out of sight."

"We have to cut, but Hugh isn't ready for the editorial process," Erna said.

"Then I can rip up these specs, right?"

"Well, can't you get me at least a sample page so he can see the type?"

"Show him the Jacobsohn book on Scottish domestic architecture," Jane Louise said. She knew exactly where the Oswald-Murphy file was but was having a lovely time making Erna wait. "It's exactly what you want."

"Not a bit of it!" said Erna. "I want something plainer and grander."

"It is plain and grand," Jane Louise said. "You said so yourself. I did exactly what you asked, and I think it came out perfect."

"I'll look into it," Erna said. "I think we'll have an absolutely finished manuscript in a month, and I want you to have a clear desk for it. Okay?"

Jane Louise glared at her with what was now bleak hatred.

"Sho' nuff, massa," she said, but Erna had already left.

Jane Louise, who was diligent and organized, had already taken the huge, untidy manuscript home and read every word. It had had a curious effect on her. She found the prose an impediment—vast reaches of stately, important sentences. She said as much to Teddy: "This guy leaves no musk-ox unturned."

Yet Jane Louise, who was almost relentlessly domestic, whose idea of a nice time was to stay home, found herself enthralled, creeped out by, and totally taken over by the idea that actual people lived at the top end of the world, people who had no access to wood except what drifted to shore, or metal except what fell out of the sky in the form of meteors; who made their clothes, food, implements, and houses out of animal parts, bones, and hides, and tusks. The idea of endless snow, of ice floes, of a place where there was nothing but silence, seemed to call out to her.

One night Teddy came home from playing squash with Mokie to find her stretched on the couch reading Admiral Peary. He came over and kissed her on the nose.

"'Civilization began to lose its zest for me,'" Jane Louise intoned. "'I began to long for the great white desolation, the battles with the ice and the gales, the long arctic night, the long arctic day, the handful of odd but faithful Eskimos who had been my friends for years, the silence and the vastness of the great, white, lonely North.'"

"They don't write like that anymore," Teddy said.

"I could live without the handful of old but faithful Eskimos," said Jane Louise.

"It's the imperialist, white-supremacist Zeitgeist," Teddy said.

Jane Louise raised her eyebrows. "What have *you* been reading all day?"

"Long-winded German letters about distillates," Teddy said. He flung himself on top of her. "Let's have a baby," he said.

"It isn't spring yet," Jane Louise said.

"It was the equinox weeks ago," Teddy said. "Besides, we might not get it right the first time. Come on, we're getting older every day."

"You're crushing my book," Jane Louise said. She could barely look at Teddy. He seemed in this instant a perfect stranger for whom she was nothing more than a vehicle for his heirs. She was a faceless, personless thing that by a trick of biological nature could produce a little infant. Her heart pounded.

"You don't want me," she said. "You want a baby."

When Teddy was not defensive, he was very persuasive.

"In order to get the baby, I have to have you," he said. "Unless you don't want me."

"What happens if I can't have a baby?" Jane Louise said.

"We'll buy one," Teddy said. "Or we'll rent one on a long lease."

Jane Louise was suddenly struck by the apersonality of it all. She was an egg; Teddy, a box of seeds. They could be anybody. They could be a couple of overheated teenagers in the back of a pickup truck. They could be two people who met five minutes ago on a blind date. They could be Eskimos or impoverished South America Indians. The whole machinery of baby production had to do with luck and timing, both mysterious and beyond anyone's control. The whole enterprise involved karma and destiny.

And out of just such machinations had come Jane Louise herself and Teddy, who were about to start the whole thing all over again. It was not just your own personal baby you were creating, but a piece of the future, a citizen, a person who would one day have little to do with you but might run things, or go to jail, or change the face of North American art or commerce, perhaps be the first person to do something or other.

To embark on such a project seemed heroic, impossible. And furthermore, you passed your own inheritance, genetic and otherwise, on to these fragile new people who did not ask to be born. Here was Teddy, who seemed to walk between the dark and the light, trying always to be even-handed and steady, and who revealed his sadness only when it was unbearable. Or Jane Louise, whose passion for spareness, order, and a plain, stripped-down style of decor was simply a cry for peace and order against chaos—a way of quelling anxiety. Would this baby be long and skinny and anxious, a good swimmer with a head for math? Prone to fits of depression? A plant chemist or book designer with an almost adequate salary?

The whole enterprise was fraught with risk and peril. Jane Louise seemed unable to move. If you were about to try to conceive a child, oughtn't it be done with great solemnity—wasn't that the spirit of the thing?—in a proper bed, perhaps with candles or torches? She said as much to Teddy, who was much more lighthearted about these things than she was.

"Shut up," he suggested, kissing her.

It seemed a good idea for the time being. Jane Louise relaxed.

Perhaps they would have a baby, perhaps not. She was a leaf, a twig, a crumpled bus transfer floating on a breeze, or a feather rushing on top of white water. She was as effortless as a salmon or a porpoise. She was as concentrated as a waterfall. As she moved toward Teddy, her heart gave an inward lurch, and her destiny, unknown to her, unfolded before her.

CHAPTER 15

For a while everything stood still. It did not seem to Jane Louise that she was pregnant, and it did not seem that the press was going to be sold any minute. Jane Louise felt that her life was a time bomb. One day she would wake up, feel queer, and have a baby. One day she would walk into her office and be told that it had changed utterly and that she was out of a job. Or one day she would discover that she could not have a baby and she could slink off into the darkness, leaving Teddy to find some fertile, uncomplicated woman who would never give him a moment's pause and present him with a big, fine family.

It rattled Teddy to see her so worried: She tried to mitigate her feelings. It was her job, she felt, to be breezy, efficient, to get the job done cheerily, even if she felt she had a stone for a heart, one that was radiating terrible waves of panic.

Suddenly it was spring. In Mrs. Berger's little front yard, crocuses began to bloom. Teddy came home one night with a flat of primroses and a pot of paper white narcissus. In the mornings the sunlight woke Jane Louise up. Nothing woke Teddy; he was an ardent and unflappable sleeper.

On the weekends Jane Louise let Teddy sleep. She closed the bedroom door and had coffee in the living room by herself. On Saturdays she and Teddy knocked around. Often they knocked around separately and met for lunch. As the weeks went by, Jane Louise began to wonder why she felt so bereft. She and Teddy seemed, to her, as happy as possible in the modern world. They liked where they lived. They had jobs they liked. And yet, as they wandered around holding hands, Jane Louise felt an empty space that got emptier and emptier.

On the morning she woke up feeling terrible, she realized that what was missing was a child. She prayed she felt terrible because she was pregnant.

It was Sunday, cloudy and gray and not entirely warm. Teddy was fast asleep—he had had a week of conferences and presentations. For a country boy, he was a late riser. Jane Louise had her coffee, quietly got dressed, and kissed him on the head. She felt queasy. He stirred in his sleep, opened one eye and said, "Where are you going?"

Jane Louise said, "It's very early. I'm going to the flea market, and I'll wake you when I get back."

Jane Louise was not an acquirer like Edie, who collected everything: old rolling pins, straw hats, old lace tablecloths, white clothes from the turn of the century, rayon dresses of the forties, homespun linen, floral tablecloths.

She herself was after plain white ironstone and table silver, and on Sunday mornings she went to the flea market in a parking lot to hunt. Even at the crack of dawn it was crowded with dealers, with traders, with hunters like herself who were similarly addicted.

She knew the real estate agent with the pink glasses and the fancy jackets who looked for picture frames. Or the tall man in black who wore a top hat and collected old teddy bears. And the tourists, and the antique linen and button collectors. It seemed to Jane Louise that there was a dealer for anything a person might have a passion for.

Jane Louise had, from her earliest recollections, gone for the very plain, the unadorned. She hated anything with gold on it.

The idea that objects had rich personal histories, totally unknown to her, filled her with a kind of grief. At a tag sale in the country Teddy had bought for Jane Louise a potlike vase, made by a child whose name, Scott, had been scratched on the bottom. It had an unintentionally elegant shape and had been glazed a fierce robin's egg blue. Made by a child, and someone had sold it! Had it been left behind when a house was sold? Had Scott broken irreparably with his parents? Had he grown old and died, or sold that object himself—a grown-up, with no more connection to the child that had been?

Jane Louise wandered aimlessly through the aisles of the market. She passed the couple who sold clocks and china from the thirties, and the woman from Belize who came up twice a year for a month and sold piano shawls and white nightgowns. She wandered past the upscale dealers who kept their stock under glass and sold fancy silver, Sèvres, and little bronzes.

At the top of the center aisle was a clutch of tables on which a young dealer named Albert threw the contents of his house sales: large piles of household linens smelling of naphtha; dishes, glasses, and plates; a rack of fur coats; piles of books. Jane Louise ambled by. There, on the corner table, were the immaculate contents of some person's library: the works of Sigmund Freud, the *Grove's Dictionary of Music,* the poetry of Heinrich Heine, the plays of Bertolt Brecht, *The Story of Opera*. Jane Louise opened a copy of *The Life of Schiller*. On the flyleaf was a bookplate, a line cut showing Cupid resting under a laurel tree eating a cluster of grapes and reading a book. It said: EX LIBRIS DR. FRANCES ROSEN-WASSER.

Instantly Jane Louise felt she knew exactly who this person was: a psychoanalyst who fled Vienna or Frankfurt in the late thirties, when you could not take your money but could take your things. The set of Rosenthal china on the next table was doubtless hers, as well as the napkins and damask cloths. Jane Louise picked up a copy of *The Hebrew Melodies in English und auf Deutsch*. On the table among the china she found a set of napkins, heavily embroidered with poppies and wheat, and a tea cloth to go with them. She found a little green vase in the shape of a monkey and bought it for Teddy. The whole lot cost eight dollars. Then she walked slowly home.

She felt awful. Was it the weather, or was she pregnant? She clutched her purchases to her and imagined Dr. Frances Rosenwasser's apartment—a long dark hallway, a window ledge full of snake plants, a dining room with limp chiffon curtains and etchings framed in gilt. People got born, grew up, acquired things, and then, in a flash, it was all over: sold in a heap, dispersed, given away. Why did Dr. Frances Rosenwasser's children, if she had children, or her friends, not want her *Grove's Dictionary of Music*? Why had someone not claimed those beautifully embroidered napkins?

She walked home slowly, immersed in these melancholy thoughts. If Teddy was awake, she would not tell him how queasy she felt. Suppose she merely had the flu? Jane Louise's impulse not to disappoint Teddy was ferocious. She owed him this, she felt; life owed him this. The glitches in hers had been cosmetic:

moving around, never having enough money, feeling like a perpetual outsider. But the fracture in Teddy's life was deep as a fault. She wanted life to prove to him that things could be made whole.

He was up, showered, his hair wet and slicked down, wearing a pair of blue jeans and an old T-shirt. He looked about sixteen years old, reading the paper at the table.

She put her package down. Teddy offered his forehead for a wifely kiss.

"I feel rotten," Jane Louise said.

"How rotten?" said Teddy.

"I don't know. Queasy."

Teddy looked over the top of his paper. He peered at her inquiringly.

"It's probably flu," said Jane Louise. "It's going around the office."

"Maybe you're pregnant," Teddy said. "Is that going around the office?"

"It sort of went around the office six years ago. Erna had Winnie, Sven had Piers, and Gwen, who used to be Erna's secretary, had twins."

"Maybe it's a slow-acting pregnancy virus," Teddy said.

"I don't want to think about it," Jane Louise said. "I don't want to be disappointed."

"I'll put you to bed," Teddy said. "Would you like some tea?"

Instead Jane Louise crawled into his arms. She made a clumsy fit, all legs and elbows. She did not want to say, "I want this to be a baby! I want to be some child's mother. It's taken me over! I want it! I want it!"

She said nothing.

Teddy said, "If it's a baby, we'll have a baby. If it's not, you'll have the flu, and we'll have the baby later."

"And will it be all right?" asked Jane Louise. "I mean, do you think anything will be all right?"

"I do," Teddy said. "I really do."

CHAPTER 16

It was the first of June. The office was suddenly quiet. No-one could stand to stay in at lunchtime except on rainy days, when people ordered piles of sandwiches from the local delicatessen and made gallons of coffee in the coffee maker near the ladies' room. Otherwise the noon hour was calm as a nursery at nap time.

Jane Louise sat at her drawing board with a calendar in front of her, idly doodling. She had just come back from the gynecologist, whom she now had to call her obstetrician since she had just learned that she was going to have a baby. She had conveyed this news by telephone to Teddy, who had said, "Oh, my gosh! Oh, my gosh!" a number of times and then had hung up in order to call his mother. Eleanor was stoical by nature, but she was longing for a grandchild, since Teddy was her only shot at having one.

The idea that there was to be a baby was about as remote as Saturn. Jane Louise was entirely unchanged. She was as skinny as ever. In fact, she was rather skinnier since she was definitely off food. She did not look five minutes pregnant, although she was actually six weeks gone. Her doctor had shown her a photo of what looked like a translucent little salamander. This was what had taken up residence inside her. She had heard herself giggle—she who was not prone to giggle—but the whole thing was so outlandish and odd.

She and Teddy had decided to tell a few close friends and then keep the news to themselves. Soon they would go on vacation. By the end of the summer she would be showing, and that was time enough. Furthermore, in the first three months anything could happen, although Jane Louise did not want to think about that. A wave of the most intense, almost furious protectiveness had come over her. Her hands balled into fists. This little creature was *her* creature. She was the container for some future citizen. This seemed to her the most serious thing in the world. Strangely, when she had looked around her on the bus back to the office, it was teeming with large pregnant women, and no one seemed to give it a second thought. Even at the doctor's, women who looked about to deliver sat waiting for their appointments, reading *Business Week* or using their briefcases as desks.

Jane Louise closed her door and dialed Edie.

"Guess what?" she said.

"*Okay!*" said Edie. "I'll have to get right on this. I mean, if we want to go comparison shopping for layettes and stuff. Mokie's out looking over a client's apartment. I'll jump on him when he comes home. Though I have to say, I've been feeling sort of awful myself. So maybe it won't be necessary."

"It's very serious," Jane Louise said.

"Oh," Edie said. "Did I get it wrong, and you're sick and not pregnant?"

"No, you got it right. It just feels so . . . serious. I mean, this is about future *people,* whose early history is in our hands. I mean, characters to mold and personalities to form."

"God, it makes a person talk *funny,*" Edie said.

"Well, for Chrissake," Jane Louise said. "It *is* serious."

"I know it's serious, but aren't you glad?"

"Oh, I'm so incredibly glad," said Jane Louise, her voice quavering. "I'll call you later," and she splashed tears all over the receiver.

This tiny thing, this spark of life, was going to change everything. Jane Louise contemplated the five million things she would soon have to think about: maternity leave, baby clothes, choosing a pediatrician, appropriate gear for carrying a baby around or putting it in a car, baby backpacks, proper baby toys, schools, to say nothing of labor and delivery.

Being pregnant and not telling anyone was like a state of suspended animation. In the ladies' room, where Jane Louise went to wash any tear streaks off her face, she realized she was wearing a strange grin—a sort of involuntary smile.

The person to avoid, she knew, was Sven. He would be able to intuit her state. There was no doubt, Jane Louise was not immune to his fearsome charm. He seemed to be only about sex. You did not think of Sven in connection with nice meals, or having children (despite his four), or walks in the park. You only imagined him in the act of, and there was no doubt that he would be very good at it since it was all he ever thought about, except running the art department, which was, in his opinion, much less complicated.

Sven made a person think of sheets and sweat, of hotel rooms and assignations, of deep kissing on empty side streets, and things like that. Was that because of Sven? Or because of her?

A person who was pregnant ought not to have impure thoughts about other people. Why couldn't a person seal her life up, as a book is packed in shrink wrapping? Safe, immune, immured, like Erna Hendershott and her fortresslike marriage, her fortified castle of children, her homemade pasta and needlework. Her bake sales for the children's schools, her dinner parties, her security and safety against things that didn't fit. You wouldn't catch her thinking about Sven in connection with rumpled sheets, at least not whilst in the elevated condition of pregnancy.

Meanwhile there was business to do. The enormous Arctic manuscript by Hugh Oswald-Murphy had been pulled back yet again by Erna, who claimed that the author was recasting it and that all work on it must stop.

"Who is this guy, anyway?" Jane Louise complained to Sven when he promptly appeared in her office. She felt she must only talk business.

"Erna thinks he's a genius," Sven said. "Did you read it?"

"I thought it was kind of soppy," Jane Louise said. "He uses the word *vast* a lot."

"I guess it's kind of vast up there," Sven said. "Now listen, here's another of Erna's geniuses. Martin Barlow."

Jane Louise groaned. "Carole Santangelo literally threw that manuscript at Erna the day she quit."

"Carole had many other reasons to throw things at Erna," Sven said. "Now, Janey, you're our good girl. Take this home tonight and get on it. He's coming in next week."

"May I ask when he delivered this thing?" Jane Louise looked at this manuscript, which was large and untidy.

"It isn't when he delivered," Sven said. "It's when Erna scheduled it. She wants to crash it for the fall."

"Why?"

"Here's why," Sven said. "The first deal Hamish had lined up to sell us fell through. There's Germans or Swiss wandering around upstairs. No sane person would authorize the kind of money Erna's planning to pump into this book. She claims she wants it out for the Christmas season, but really she wants it out before we get sold."

"What's it got?"

"His wife did the woodcuts, let's put it that way," Sven sniffed. "It's not so bad. It's just huge."

"*The Literature of Nature*," Jane Louise read. "*The Magnificent Language of Outdoors*. What a lousy subtitle. It sounds like one of those ever-popular anthologies to me."

"Uh-huh," said Sven, no longer very interested. "The author needs restraining. He refuses to cut a line of it unless someone shows him that the design won't be affected."

"Oh, I see," said Jane Louise. "I'm supposed to be the mouthpiece for Erna's cuts, right?"

"Beautifully put," Sven said. "See you around. If you baby-sit him nice, I'll take you out to lunch after. You'll need a drink, doubtless, unless by that time you'll be worrying about fetal alcohol syndrome. Any news on that score?"

"Sven, don't you ever give up?" Jane Louise asked.

"It's just that I can't wait," he said. "You can't know how I look forward to it. You, pregnant. There's something about pregnancy in a tall, skinny girl that has a kind of magic to it."

"When I get there, I'll let you feel for me for a dollar and a half," Jane Louise said. "Please go away."

Sven looked at her musingly. "Cheap at twice the price," he said.

On her way home from work it occurred to Jane Louise that she might bring home some flowers for Teddy. He had called a number of times during the day, which was most unlike him. He told her how happy his mother was and how delighted Peter and Beth Peering were, and how Birdie hoped that she could sit for the baby when it came.

"Did you tell your father?" Jane Louise said.

"I'll write him," Teddy said, and shut up like a clam. His dread of his father, his stepmother Martine, and his three half-sisters was considerable. He felt they breathed a different-colored air and lived in a familiar yet entirely alien atmosphere. The fact that he was connected to these three big, silly blond girls, by blood, amazed and alarmed him. They had nothing in common whatsoever. His half-sisters were shoppers and consumers, devotees of beauty parlors and nail salons. They read fake historical novels whose heroes were named Brad and whose heroines were called Topaz.

Even grown up, they still adored stuffed animals. They were strongly and tightly bound to one another, and they found Teddy useless and superfluous. As for Jane Louise, she barely registered as female for them. She was too thin, too plain, too uninterested in jewelry, and her clothes were too odd. And she worked for a publisher and didn't show any interest in children.

In the old days, under the old order, a wife might feel it her job to bring a family together, but in the face of modern exigencies this was impossible. How could you get Teddy's parents ever to be in the same room harmoniously?

Surely in the face of all this uncertainty in the world, there might be a way to celebrate the news of an impending birth. Did the couple go out for dinner? Did the wife make dinner? Did she rush home and set the table with the good silver and the wedding china? Of course, Teddy and Jane Louise did not have wedding china. They had the large number of ironstone plates Jane Louise had collected, and they had half a set of Eleanor's mother's silver, filled in with things Jane Louise had picked up here and there. For their wedding they had gotten odd things like art pottery and a tea set in the shape of oranges and lemons. Teddy's half-sisters could be seen at the wedding thinking, Weird friends, weird presents, and they're weird, too.

Jane Louise stopped to buy flowers, then bought a large bunch of grapes and a pomegranate. Seeds seemed appropriate. If you hadn't any rituals, you might as well roll your own, Jane Louise thought.

Would roast chicken be a nice dinner to celebrate a baby? And a bottle of champagne, although she supposed she shouldn't drink any. Perhaps a nice bottle of nonalcoholic champagne, if such a thing existed. Green beans, rice, and something from the bakery. As she gazed into the bakery window, she saw Teddy at the counter waiting for a package. He had a bunch of flowers under his arm.

Suddenly Jane Louise felt washed over with shyness. Her own husband. Their own baby. Now what was she supposed to say, or do, or be? She was standing at the bakery door when Teddy came out.

"Hi, Dad," said Jane Louise.

"I just got us a little chocolate cake," Teddy said meekly. "To celebrate."

"Isn't that funny," Jane Louise said. "I got a chicken."

They stared at each other almost uneasily.

"Maybe I ought to carry you home," Teddy said, "in your fragile condition."

"Maybe we both ought to start working out in a gym and build up our stamina," Jane Louise said. "What else did your mother say?"

"You know her," Teddy said. They walked down the street in the early evening light.

"Wouldn't it be nice," said Jane Louise, "if we could just be ecstatic about this without having to think about all this other stuff?"

"Like what?" Teddy said.

"Well, like your father, and my sister. She got there first, kidwise. I'm telling you, in some way she'll hate me for this. And then there's my mother and her countless notions. I don't know.

I guess it makes me sad that I have to tell her husband rather than my father."

"It'll all be fine," Teddy said. "Who cares, anyway? You *are* happy, aren't you?"

"I worry about being an unfit mother," Jane Louise said. "I worry that something will happen and I'll lose the baby." She was very near tears.

Teddy grabbed her by the shoulders. He looked at her fiercely. He never, ever, made public displays of anything. He looked her in the eyes.

"Nothing is going to happen to this baby. You're a very healthy person. Dr. Pivnik told you that, didn't you say? We're going to have this baby, and you will be a wonderful mother, and I will be a wonderful father."

Jane Louise looked into his hazel eyes. Teddy's features were round and mild. To see him in a passionate state disarmed Jane Louise completely.

"Did you marry me just so I could be the vehicle for your baby?"

Instead of getting angry, Teddy enfolded her. He said, "I married you so I could sleep with you all the time. Now you're knocked, and I feel like a million bucks. I'd like to call everyone I know."

Jane Louise walked along next to him in silence.

"You should have married some nice girl in her twenties so you can have dozens of babies," Jane Louise said. "Instead of the president of the Withered Crone Society."

"Shut up, Jane Louise," Teddy said. "I'm the depressive in this family, not you. So, march nicely, and let's have a little fun."

CHAPTER 17

Martin Barlow's colossal anthology was divided by landscape categories: fen, heath, moor, meadow, field, bog, swamp, dale, and so forth. Since the integrity of the book was of great importance to him, he would not give an inch.

"Do we need *all* these pages on marl?" Jane Louise asked. She felt sweaty even though it was cool. There were strange twinges and flutters in her lower region—signs of the presence of her little tadpole. At the moment she did not much care how many pages the pink-cheeked and sweet-looking Martin Barlow had on the subject of marl.

"Do you know how little has been written about marl?" Martin said. "It took me *months* to track it. Listen, I'll combine it with moraine, but that's as far as I'll go. There isn't very much on either of them."

Jane Louise sighed. Martin was to be treated with kid gloves, she knew. He had been signed up for three novels about country life of the rather steamy, existential sort: *A Big Storm Knocked It Over, Marauding Dogs Will Eat It,* and *Snow Makes Everything*

White. He was considered a literary hot ticket, and his first book was ready to be published. Jane Louise had skimmed through it. On the first page a girl says to a boy: "I'd like to bite into you like a grape."

Jane Louise regarded Martin, who had round, innocent brown eyes and an adorable lock of brown hair that fell into his eyes. He looked about twelve years old. Jane Louise didn't so much want to bite into him like a grape as to nip him fiercely, like a terrier. Why wouldn't he listen?

"Well," she said. "Can we cut a little of the desert? That's a *really* long section."

Martin looked as if she were about to shred his clothes. "Why, no," he said. "I mean it. This isn't just your ordinary T. E. Lawrence stuff. This is *art.* I don't want to disturb the balance."

I'd like to disturb your balance, you petulant little jerk, Jane Louise thought. Why do I have to be nice to this self-congratulatory twit? And why does Erna land me with this stuff?

Jane Louise said, "Can we cut a little of Hugh Oswald-Murphy? There's so much on ice. Besides, Erna's doing his big Arctic book any minute."

It seemed to her that Martin gasped. "Cut Hugh Oswald-Murphy?" he said.

Jane Louise looked at him hard. "I didn't mean him personally."

"No," said Martin Barlow.

He was wearing a faded work shirt. His pink, ripe neck and a triangle of hairless chest were revealed. Jane Louise wanted to smack him.

"Lookit, Martin," she said. "If you want anyone to *buy* this book, it has to be cut. Didn't Erna tell you that? You said you'd cut in accordance with the design. I'm telling you, if you don't cut this by *one hundred pages,* no one will be able to afford it.

This book, which will have only tiny woodcuts, will cost *more than fifty dollars,* and we will have to scrimp on important items, such as binding and the jacket."

She thought Martin would cry. Then he gazed back, and she had the eerie feeling that he was trying to look down her shirt.

"Martin," Jane Louise said. "Erna and I—we went over this manuscript very carefully. All the proposed cuts are carefully marked. I want you to go into the conference room and meditate on these cuts, and then I want you to accept them."

"I'll look at them," Martin said, "and see what I think."

When he left, Jane Louise slumped over her desk, drinking the remains of the lemonade she had brought with her that morning. It seemed to settle her stomach.

"How'd it go?" asked Sven. He was standing in the doorway, wearing what appeared to be her jacket.

"He's a mule," she said.

"Your shirt is unbuttoned," he said. "Maybe that'll encourage him to give in. Cute underwear, though. Coral—nice color. By the way, is this your jacket or the hub's?"

He disentangled himself from the jacket and hung it over her chair. Jane Louise realized what a mistake it had been to tell Sven that she and Teddy sometimes shared clothes, because Sven had promptly discovered that he and Jane Louise also shared the same size.

"I borrowed it to go to a meeting," he said.

"It's mine," Jane Louise said.

"How sweet," said Sven. "Sort of like wearing *you.*"

He also liked to drink out of her coffee cup, which he said was the poor man's substitute for other forms of contact.

"Where's *your* jacket?" Jane Louise said.

"Probably being worn by someone else," Sven said. "Paula Pierce-Williams."

Jane Louise felt an unwelcome stab of jealousy. Paula Pierce-Williams was a part-time designer, a trim, straight-haired woman with a generous mouth, a headband, and thick brown hair. She had two small children, a stockbroker husband, and a house in the country. She had a slight air of being overheated; Sven treated her with a kind of deference.

"Paula Pierce-Williams is the best person who has ever lived," Jane Louise said sulkily.

"Oh, for sure," said Sven. "I knew her older sister Mollie during a difficult period. She was at the tail end of a dead marriage."

"Oh, yes?" Jane Louise said. "And were you helpful?"

"Always," said Sven.

"And did you hire Paula hoping some similarly difficult period would evolve?"

"Hamish hired her. Paula's husband is one of his squash partners. That's the way the world works, honey doll, except for you. You were hired on *merit*."

He spun on his heel and was gone, just as Adele was coming in.

"Hi! You look awful," Adele said. "Is Sven being mean to you?"

"I think he's going to put the make on Paula Pierce-Williams," Jane Louise said.

"She could use it," Adele said. "What a bitch. She treats me as if I were her personal body servant. Also I can't believe that anyone who dresses that way could possibly do any kind of artistic work." Adele believed that creative people should dress accordingly.

Paula wore what squads of women of her class wore: plain skirts, blazers, little black patent leather shoes, a Chanel scarf, and a handbag.

"She's very neat," Jane Louise said. "And she's good with type."

"Who cares?" Adele said. "Sven likes her around the way cats like to play with mice. They don't eat them. They just tease them until they give up."

"She'll never give up," Jane Louise said. "She's not interested."

"Well, speaking of interested," Adele said, "here's some news. Dita quit, but you knew that already, didn't you?"

Jane Louise did not know; Dita rarely spoke to her now. She seemed insignificant to Dita. Jane Louise had become some mere girl in the art department.

"She quit?" Jane Louise said.

"Yes, and she left that huge book on the gardens of France on Sven's desk with a little note."

"A little note," said Jane Louise.

"You know, those notes that you could decipher and no one else. Sven seems to think that something is going on between Dita and that guy who has the gardens, or who took the photos, or wrote it."

"He wrote it," Jane Louise said. "Philippe de la Vernard. His garden is in there."

"Gee," Adele said. "She certainly is glamorous."

"Well, I have some news," Jane Louise said. "Close the door and sit down. I'm going to have a baby."

Adele sprang from her chair and grabbed Jane Louise's arm. "Oh, how wonderful!" she said.

Jane Louise gazed at the rows of books on her shelves, recalling which of them she had designed for Dita. So Dita had quit and was going to run off with Philippe de la Vernard! She tried imagining telling Dita the news that she was pregnant, but it was not a scene she could picture. Dita was not interested in children. The friends she had who had children had grown-up children. One felt they had always been grown up. But it hardly mattered. Dita was quitting without a word to her. Jane Louise was almost embarrassed by how much this hurt her feelings.

"Oh, I'm so happy for you, Janey!" Adele was saying. "And wait till Sven finds out. He'll swoon, or maybe you haven't heard him on the subject of pregnant women."

Jane Louise began to feel as if she were in a falling elevator.

"What *are* his feelings about pregnant women?" she said. "He hasn't shared them with me."

"Oh, he *respects* you," Adele said. "Around us he says any old thing. The other day I heard him tell Dave, 'It is my fantasy to enter a room full of women, all of whom are pregnant with my child.'"

"That's pretty humanitarian of him," Jane Louise said. "But you know I'm not his type."

"You're one of his types," Adele said. "Barbara, from contracts, saw him on the street with some girl, and she was tall and dark, like you."

Jane Louise felt an inward flutter, not the sort connected to the early stages of pregnancy. Sven got to her, it could not be denied. Married three times, and it seemed to have no effect on him whatever! A daughter in college, a set of teen twins, and a kindergartner, and it all seemed his due. A roomful of women, each pregnant with his child! Jane Louise yawned. Perhaps it was the presence of all those sperm that made men like Sven rove, whereas an egg was like an anchor. The key to Sven was that, if you thought about sex all day long, it drew sex vibrations to you. Sooner or later, the most upright of people would wonder what it would be like to be in bed with you, except of course for Adele, who never thought any such thing. She was about marriage and family in the least sexual of ways.

What a thing! Jane Louise thought. Just found out I'm pregnant and instead of flowers and sweetness, I have a recalcitrant author and a boss who wants to feel me up.

"Why is life like this?" she said to Adele.

"Like what?" Adele said. "Listen. That must be Martin Barlow knocking at your door."

The door opened and Martin came in as Adele slipped out. "I've been through the manuscript," he said.

"That's impossible," Jane Louise said. "You haven't been in there long enough."

"I know this manuscript front to back," Martin said.

He set it down and came around to stand next to her. She could feel his warm breath near her face. He leaned very close. He radiated heat. His cheeks were flushed.

"Martin," said Jane Louise. "You're *breathing* on me."

"I'm terribly sorry," he said, sitting closer. "Now look, I've accepted this cut on page three twenty-five." He leaned his arm across her, brushing her ever so slightly.

"You accepted one cut, and I'm supposed to be glad?" Jane Louise said. "How about the other fifty?"

Martin looked at her. His round glasses and round eyes made him look like a little spotted owl.

"Okay," he said petulantly. "All right. But it isn't my book any-more."

"Oh, shut up, Martin," said Jane Louise. "This is an *anthology,* not a novel. Erna claims she never lays a glove on your golden prose. I'm asking you to knock out a little Hugh Oswald-Murphy and Gilbert White. One's in Greenland, and the other's dead, so what's it to you?"

"You also cut Hal Borland," Martin said.

Jane Louise shrieked, "I did not cut Hal Borland. I took out two very similar passages about summer, for crying out loud. And he's dead, too!"

"It's about integrity," Martin said.

Jane Louise felt like baring her teeth. "Okay," she said. "I'm going to put this manuscript in as is. I'll ask Erna to take money out of your ad budget so you can make cuts in galleys. I give up."

"I think you're doing the right thing," Martin said. "This *is* the right thing. You'll see. I'm starving. You wouldn't like to come out and have lunch with me? My treat, of course."

He beamed at her with a kind of expressionless radiance that Jane Louise identified as the deep warmth of self-love. How happy Martin Barlow must be.

"Are you all right?" Martin asked. "You seem to be yawning a lot."

"You're a very tiring guy," said Jane Louise.

"Well, maybe I'll just go back on the train. I'm pretty tired, too. We have a little baby named Lucy, and she gets up very early."

"Oh, a baby," Jane Louise said. "How nice! How old?"

"Ten months," Martin said, "I think. I never quite get it right."

"It's really easy," Jane Louise said. "You try to remember her birthdate and then count forward from there."

He gave her an unfocused look, as if this hadn't occurred to him.

"Good-bye, Martin," said Jane Louise, who passionately wanted to see him leave. "*Think small.*"

He gave her a crushed look and slunk out.

CHAPTER 18

According to her birth book, with each day Jane Louise's salamander was becoming more and more a human creature. The fact that this process was happening inside her was often so startling to Jane Louise that it caused her to lose her breath. Why? Even Sven's wives had had babies, and Sven was a father.

Jane Louise and Sven both took their vacations in August. Sven and Edwina went to Martha's Vineyard with little Piers and his half-siblings: Anik, who now studied at the Sorbonne, and Allard and Desdemona from San Francisco.

Anik was gorgeous, with white blond hair and very dark eyes. Her mother was also a great beauty. She lived with a French Marxist aristocrat.

"Her stepfather's a count and her father's a Jew prole," Sven said of Anik.

Jane Louise said she did not think there was anything particularly Jewish or proletarian about Sven.

Anik was a very sensible girl who treated her father as if he were totally beside the point. Jane Louise enjoyed watching Sven get cut down to the size of a normal, boring parent.

Sven always brought Anik to the office. This was like the switch that threw many things into motion: the summer desk clean-up, the last wrap-up meeting, the pre-vacation lunch.

In August Jane Louise and Teddy would house-sit for Teddy's mother while she toured the gardens of Britain with her old college friend. Teddy's father had hated driving and touring. Although a Brit himself, he was firmly expatriate and never wanted to go back. He hated gardening, and as soon as he and Teddy's mother had gotten divorced, he had moved to a suburban housing complex where he met his second wife, Martine. Eleanor had brought Teddy up in *her* mother's summer house. There Eleanor gardened freely and joined the garden club and the Cottage Garden Society. She was perfectly happy to raise her child in the tranquillity of the country, where she was known to everyone and knew everyone. She only wished that Teddy's father might have died so she would not have to bear the stigma of divorce.

Jane Louise and Sven always had lunch together before they went away. They would discuss the upcoming fall list, like good colleagues. Jane Louise never thought of these lunches without a kind of compelling dread. It would be bad news if Sven ever decided to focus on her.

On the day of the meal she went to find Adele for moral support, but Adele had already gone out to lunch, leaving behind on her desk a magazine called *Consumer Bride*.

Sven sauntered out of his office wearing a biscuit-colored linen jacket. He poked at the magazine as if it were a dead mouse. The fact that Adele was getting married was nothing to him.

They went to Sven's hangout: a highly polished, old-fashioned saloon with sawdust on the tiled floor and really good food.

"So," said Sven absently, surveying the menu. "You and Teddy—same as usual this summer?"

This caused Jane Louise to blush. This summer would not be quite the same as usual. At the end of it she would be almost five months pregnant.

"The same," Jane Louise said brightly. "We're going to visit Martin Barlow. He lives about half an hour from Teddy's mother, and I'm going to beat him into line."

"Hmmm," said Sven. "He's very pushy."

"He's really just a sweet, spoiled boy," Jane Louise said.

"You watch him," Sven said. "Those nature boys are like octopuses—or octopi, I'm sure he'd say—all hands."

"He seems pretty harmless in that way," said Jane Louise, who did not believe this for a minute.

"Mark my words," Sven said. "He probably hasn't recovered from the sight of our coral-colored underwear."

A truly integrated person, like Erna, who did not have little parts of her personality flying around, would have been immune to Sven, especially when pregnant. But Jane Louise felt overheated and therefore much more vulnerable.

"And your vacation?" she said.

"Oh, ever the cheerful dad," said Sven. "Everything as smooth as silk. Anik and Desdemona work on their tans and meet the not-too-well-behaved sons of rich, well-heeled writers and lawyers, Allard plays softball, and little Piers digs in the sand, covered with sun-block. We all watch the meteor showers with Allard, since he's the family astronomer."

"I've never seen a shooting star," said Jane Louise. "Teddy says they're very cheering."

"That's the difference between us and them," said Sven. "Gentiles are on such chummy terms with the unknown. I find shooting stars intimidating."

"I never think of you as finding anything intimidating," Jane Louise said.

"Only the void," Sven said. "Let's order."

After the waiter had departed, Sven sipped his gin and tonic and mused on summer weather.

"I like a meteor shower," he said. "I like those sultry, hot nights when the sky looks dark red instead of black. I like when it's clammy and sticky. People kind of stick together or they get all slippery."

"Uh-huh," said Jane Louise. An elaborate club sandwich was set before her. It looked somehow sinister, with nasty pieces of bacon poking out and mayonnaise dripping down its toasted sides.

"It's a good thing we're both going away," said Sven. "I've been dreaming about you. Maybe it's the change of season."

Jane Louise stared at her sandwich. A wave of something or other washed over her. How uncool it would be to be sick while at lunch with Sven.

"I dreamed about Teddy, too," Sven said. "In my dream he was . . . oh, never mind what he was. Like should never get together with like. That's why homosexuality is so impossible to a guy like me. Jews should marry gentiles, women should marry men."

"You must think my friend Edie has a match made in heaven," said Jane Louise sleepily. She really did feel sort of awful.

"That cute dark husband. It sets the mind to work," Sven said. "Basically people are *against* one another. That's what sex is. The great bridge across."

Jane Louise stared straight ahead. She was ravaged by exhaustion. After this lunch, how was she going to put one foot in front of the other and actually walk back to the office? If there was an *us* and a *them*, she wanted to be a *them* like Teddy, whom Sven felt was on such happy terms with the unknown. At least Teddy's conflicts were clean and clear and not a holy mess of sex and office politics, and marriages and children all over the place, like Sven's.

She felt Sven's warm hand on the back of her neck.

"Snap out of it," he said. "I've been talking to you for five minutes. Don't fall asleep on me, Janey. Eat your lunch."

Jane Louise looked again at her sandwich. Suddenly she was ravenous.

"Don't wolf your food," Sven said. "You know, you have all the earmarks of a person in the early stages of pregnancy."

"I've already promised that you'd be the first to know, or have you forgotten?" said Jane Louise, wiping mayonnaise off her chin.

"The first?" said Sven coyly.

"Oh, Teddy'll know the minute it happens," Jane Louise said. "These Christians have industrial-strength sperm. They know the minute it takes."

A slow, almost malevolent smile spread over Sven's lips. It was the smile of a serial killer, a snake coiling to strike.

"I see," he purred. "I can feel these things long distance, so to speak. Pregnant girls are hotter—their skin, I mean."

Jane Louise felt breathless. She picked up Sven's glass and drank the dregs of his gin and tonic. There wasn't much left, and most of it was water. At least she needn't worry about fetal alcohol syndrome.

"There's something essentially loathsome and creepy about you, Sven," she said.

"That's my girl," Sven said.

CHAPTER 19

Teddy's mother's house was so unlike anything Jane Louise had grown up with. Her mother, Lilly, was an urbanite. She liked cut flowers and vegetables that were delivered from the local green-grocers. In her house the idea was order and comfort in a formal setting.

As for Eleanor, her old garden boots were always in the hallway. She had a mud room—the sort of space Jane Louise's mother had never heard of—where she kept wooden boxes of seeds, neatly marked, trowels, unopened bags of chicken manure, garden cata-logs. A smell of earth and must rose from this room, which also contained a very old washing machine. Eleanor hung her washing on a line and only washed when the sun was out.

Teddy's mother was a traveler, not a domestic being. Her tiny library, once a pantry, was filled with travel books, which, when opened, threw out a rich aroma of mold, and her kitchen was not messy but minimal. She herself lived on tea and salad. Even in the winter the little greenhouse provided her with lettuces.

While Eleanor preferred not to cook, she had her stand-bys.

For the library bake sale she made her chocolate loaf. For the annual garden society fund-raiser she sold her bread-and-butter pickles and rhubarb-and-strawberry jam. And for entertaining she made curry as it was served in New England tearooms, with little dishes of coconut and peanuts and raisins. The note she left for Jane Louise said: "Dear Jane Louise: Use anything you like and throw out anything that looks frowzy—you know I can't bear to pitch anything away."

So Jane Louise, happily taking up Eleanor's invitation, would rummage through the cupboards throwing out musty bags of unlabeled spices that had no taste or smell.

In the mornings she let Teddy sleep, and while the water was boiling for coffee, she put on Eleanor's battered old straw garden hat and went out while the dew was still on the leaves and picked vegetables for lunch and dinner.

In back of the house behind a stone wall Eleanor grew beans on poles, and English peas. Her tomatoes ran up an arched trellis. She grew garlic, onions, chard, and celery. Along the stone wall in back of the garden was the blackberry and raspberry patch. In a sunny corner near the potting shed was the asparagus patch, now green, fuzzy, and full of ferns. Her rhubarb was forty years old.

Jane Louise went out barefoot. The coolness and softness of the lawn gave slightly beneath her feet, and from the misty earth rose up the smell of grass, air, and the deep, rich smell of soil.

She shook the bags of human hair Eleanor hung on the fence post to keep the deer away, and she scattered fresh mothballs under the lilies. The deer loved Eleanor's lilies and especially liked to nibble the young buds. She emptied the dead slugs from their saucers of beer into the compost heap and put fresh saucers out. Then, before the sun broke through the mist, she did a little hoeing and went inside to make coffee, thinking about her husband and this house.

140

What had made her so brazenly barge in on Teddy, so entirely sure that he was waiting for her? The boldest thing she had ever done in her life was to knock on Teddy's mother's door with the sole intention of getting Teddy into that big ornamental bed. When he had answered the door she could see he had been waiting for her. She remembered how restrained they had tried to be. Had Teddy asked if she would like a cup of tea? Had she said yes, and had they had a cup of tea? Or had they simply rushed into each other's arms and then proceeded to that beautiful bed where the afternoon light had speckled them?

She climbed the stairs to the guest room, remembering. Teddy was awake and lying like a child, on his back, watching the sun make patterns on the ceiling. Down the hall from this room was Eleanor's study, where she kept her garden books, her endless correspondence with the Cottage Garden Society, and her voluminous notes on the Marshallsville Garden Club, of which she had been president for years. She was on the board of the Hopkins County Botanical Organization and the secretary of the Agricultural Resource Center. She was the person you called if your next-door neighbor, whose vegetable garden bordered yours, began spraying with pesticides while you tried to garden organically. She was a master of diplomatic persuasion. When things got rough, and sprayers were intransigent, Eleanor hoisted her big guns—her presidentship of practically everything—and leaned mercilessly on the culprit until he or she gave in. She was remarkably successful in her methods and had gotten the sod farm in Hopkinson to stop using chemical fertilizer and had organized a compost center at the dump. She fit into her society like a foot into a well-made shoe.

Jane Louise put his coffee on the night table. Teddy opened his arms, and she crawled into them. Teddy took an hour or so to wake up. He was unshaven, and he looked unfocused and very young.

"You smell of digging," he said.

"I got some baby carrots and tiny little beets. The saucer was full of the most enormous slugs," said Jane Louise.

Jane Louise's heart expanded. It smelled so wonderful in the country. The curtains fluttered in a mild morning breeze, filling the room with the scent of chamomile, which grew wild on the lawn, and thyme, which grew between the cracks of the marble slabs leading to the front door, and lavender, which Eleanor grew in profusion in her two front gardens: one for cuttings, one for herbs. Jane Louise stretched back against the pillows and felt she could stay here forever.

She felt liberated not only by the country air, but by the fact that she was now free to be pregnant without worrying that Sven was going to hang around the office checking out her body. Her stomach was not as flat as it had been, and she felt herself to be almost chemically tired. She turned groggily to Teddy, who was going back to sleep. She curled up next to him and drifted off.

When they woke it was raining.

"That's funny," Jane Louise said. "When I got up this morning it was sunny. That was an hour ago."

"Berkshire weather," said Teddy. "It'll go away. What are we doing?"

It occurred to her that they had not planned to do one single thing.

"Let's go to the Hopkins diner and eat a huge breakfast," Jane Louise said. "Let's get some of those biscuits. Then we could go get some eggs from Mr. Kossuth and some corn from the Deans. Maybe by that time it'll clear up and we can go swimming."

"We should drop by and see Peter and Beth," Teddy said, yawning. "They were away visiting Beth's mother, but maybe they'll come for dinner."

"This time next year," Jane Louise said, dreamily, "we'll be here with a baby. It'll be five months old. Can you imagine?" She sank back into the pillows, imagining. She remembered the first time she had met Beth Peering, who had jumped down from her van and unloaded her three girls, who all wore white shorts and shirts and white socks. Beth had looked ruddy and freckled, her face glowing. Jane Louise remembered how dark and diminished she had felt. I am a New Yorker, mother of no one. I will never emerge from a van with three little girls. I will never have that maternal confidence. If I have a baby, it will be a treat, a good luck charm, a piece of magic, not something I expected and got in the normal course of things.

Jane Louise thought of Beth's middle child, Birdie, whom she loved with all her heart. Birdie loved her back. She had none of her mother's bounciness and all of her father's seriousness. She and Jane Louise drew together—that was Birdie's skill. In the summer Jane Louise gave Birdie art lessons—that was how Beth saw it. Jane Louise did not think of what they did as lessons. The two of them sat at a table by the lake and did watercolors together. This connection was precious to Jane Louise, who often wanted to snatch Birdie up and claim her.

"Hey!" Jane Louise said. "Is that the telephone ringing? It sounds like an insect."

Teddy sprang out of bed and ran downstairs.

He called up a moment later, "It's for you. Martin Barlow. He says we're supposed to come for lunch, and you're supposed to bring him some pages."

"Oh, Christ," said Jane Louise. "Tell him to hang on." She went downstairs, still not quite awake.

"Hello, Martin," she said.

"Welcome to the country," Martin said. "I hope you haven't

forgotten that we're supposed to see each other today. We'd like you to come here for lunch, and then we can go over the pages together while the others go for a walk."

"The others," said Jane Louise.

"I mean my wife, my child, and your husband," said Martin.

"You're very well organized," Jane Louise said.

"We're vegetarians," said Martin. "Does that bother you? Nicolette is an amazing vegetarian cook. We'll expect you at about twelve-thirty."

"But Martin—" said Jane Louise, but the receiver was dead. Martin had hung up.

CHAPTER 20

"My life," said Jane Louise in the car. "Pregnant, on vacation, and I have to go see some paradigm of self-congratulation and hold his hand while about five words are cut from his precious anthology."

"Watch out for Route 18," Teddy said. "It's around here somewhere. We want Greenhaven. What do the directions say after Greenhaven?"

"It says three miles exactly to a fork in the road—Frozen Dog Lane, can you believe it? It's the right fork. Then two miles through the town of Candlebury and the first right at the general store. Their house is the third on the left, and it has a dead tree in front of it."

"Dead Tree Lane," said Teddy. "Did you check the map?"

"I thought you thought maps were for twinks," said Jane Louise.

"Maps are for geniuses," Teddy said. "Asking at gas stations is for twinks."

Martin and his wife, Nicolette, lived in a restored farmhouse near an historic village. The big dead tree stood in front of their salt-box, a ghostly yellow-white, full of holes.

"What happened to it?" said Jane Louise.

"It was struck by lightning," said Martin. "We keep it for the woodpeckers."

Jane Louise felt sure she had just heard the titles of his next two books.

The Barlows' baby, Lucy, spent her time in a backpack being carried around by her mother, who had long, curly hair worn Pre-Raphaelite style and wore a gauzy long skirt. Jane Louise tried not to evince too much interest in the baby—it was none of Martin Barlow's business that she was pregnant—but her attention constantly wandered to this creature, blond and curly haired, who once out of the backpack sat on the floor playing with a collection of rubber pigs.

Nicolette fed them a vegetarian lunch, and then it was arranged that Nicolette and Teddy would walk Lucy down the road to visit their neighboring farm and visit the farm wife who grew her own indigo and spun her own wool. Martin and Jane Louise would go over the final proofs of *The Literature of Nature*. By the time they came back, Martin and Jane Louise would have finished their work, and Lucy would be ready for her nap if she hadn't passed out in her back carrier.

Jane Louise watched them from Martin's study as they walked down the road. Except for the gauzy skirt and the curly hair, that was a vision of her future: Teddy and Jane Louise and an unknown baby in a yet-unpurchased conveyance walking slowly down a country road.

Martin's study at the back of the house was so flooded with light that it was almost impossible to see. Jane Louise could not figure out how he got any work done between twelve and three in the afternoon.

She was wearing a yellow sundress and green sandals. As she had put on her dress that morning, she had realized it was starting not to fit. In a few weeks it would be unwearable. She also knew that she would doubtless feel Martin Barlow's bare hands on her back.

As she squinted over the proofs, what she had known would happen happened. She was spun around. Martin Barlow pressed his hands against her back and kissed her.

"Go away, Martin," she said, as if to an annoying dog, although for the moment she felt as if she could have stood in that spot kissing him for hours. He was as hot as a high school boy—an earnest, hungry kisser. What did this mean? After all, she had spent part of the morning kissing her husband, another extremely accomplished kissing partner. "Go away," she said, giving him a little shove.

He did go away. He retreated to the one dark corner of his study like a punished child.

"I'm horribly sorry," he said. "Really I am, but I just was dying to kiss you."

"I was dying to kiss you, too," said Jane Louise before she could stop herself.

"Really?" said Martin. "You don't suppose—"

"I only said that to make you feel better," Jane Louise lied.

"Being a writer and everything," Martin said, "sometimes I feel I need more experience."

"That's why God gave people imaginations," said Jane Louise.

"Did God give them?" Martin said. "I don't know. Nature. Manhood. There's more somewhere." He looked extremely sad and ridiculously young.

"Try oceanography," Jane Louise said. "Skydiving. Hot-air ballooning."

"You're making fun of me, but you don't understand because you're not a writer or a man."

"True enough," said Jane Louise. "And you're not a designer or a woman."

"Sometimes I feel so ambitious I think my head's going to explode," Martin said. "I feel consumed with power."

"Gosh, how scary," said Jane Louise.

Martin grabbed her hand. "Listen," he whispered. "You're a great designer. I feel totally connected to your sense of design. I just feel we have a bond."

"Authors sometimes feel that way about a nice-looking book," said Jane Louise.

"Please, please," said Martin.

"Get a grip, man," said Jane Louise.

From downstairs came the sound of a slamming door.

"Martin! Martin!" called Nicolette. "Lucy can say 'sheep'!"

"I can't say what I feel," Martin whispered hoarsely. He grabbed Jane Louise's hand again and kissed it. "Thank you," he murmured.

"And thank you," said Jane Louise.

That night was the night of a meteor shower, according to the newspaper. Jane Louise was apprehensive. She was not keen to peer into the void. Sven had sent her a postcard, as was their custom: "Don't forget to contemplate the Almighty as you watch the stars fall down. Very scary. Hot up here. Good for the dream life."

Teddy was more than happy to be her guide to the heavens. The sky had cleared, and his mother's house had an upstairs deck on which you could take a sunbath, hang the towels to dry, or bird-watch. Eleanor used this deck to set out her seedlings in the early spring. It was a perfect viewing spot.

Teddy was enraptured by the thought of fatherhood. It held no terrors for him that Jane Louise could detect. Her pregnancy had unfettered his spirits. This made Jane Louise occasionally feel awful. She felt she should have gotten pregnant the instant they met, although as Edie pointed out, Teddy had delayed being a father for about as long as she had delayed being a mother, so it was obviously the right time for both.

He read birth books in which he discovered that in not too long this creature would begin to move around, and he would be able to feel it. How he longed for this day! Meanwhile, the thought of motherhood was not so clear a path for Jane Louise.

How would this child be brought up? What sort of a school would it go to? What would happen if Jane Louise was too old to run after it, if when this baby was ten she was an old wreck? At night in bed she worked a kind of mother-math in her mind: When this child is x I will be y, and when it is z perhaps I will be dead or decrepit. What sort of a mother would she be, a person who allowed Martin Barlow to put the make on her, and who tolerated a lizardlike Sven waiting under a rock to get her?

At eleven o'clock Teddy set out the chaise longue. He carefully read the bottle of insect repellent—even though it was entirely herbal—to see if it was safe for use on pregnant women before painting Jane Louise's arms with it. Jane Louise had made a pot of tea and set it on a little metal table.

Teddy wedged himself in back of Jane Louise, performing the service of a back rest, and handed her her mug of tea. He put his arms around her waist.

"Look!" he said. "Over there!" Jane Louise leaned back against his chest to see a star—or something like a star—blaze across the sky, and then another and another. At a corner of the horizon, lights flashed. There was not a sound. Above her the sky was as mute as black velvet, sprinkled with rhinestones. It covered the whole planet. It was everywhere. So this is the universe! Jane Louise thought with a shudder.

The night sky, like the God of Moses, was unending, incomprehensible, full of enormous, indecipherable messages. Who wouldn't be anxious in the face of this?

Teddy breathed happily. It was all science to him. He knew the constellations as familiars and often pointed them out to Jane Louise, who could recognize only the Big and Little Dippers. To Teddy the sky was as readable as a face. Teddy knew what he believed, and therefore the incomprehensible did not throw him into a swivet.

"These mosquitoes are treating me like French toast," Jane Louise said. "Anywhere there's no repellent, they're having a picnic."

"Look!" said Teddy. "There's more!"

Jane Louise lifted her face from his shoulder. She realized she had turned in her seat and was clinging to him. This really *was* some big deal. Above her was the amazingness of outer space, and meanwhile, she was a container for the miracle of inner space. The enormity of it made her tremble.

The sky flashed. The comets blazed.

"Martin Barlow made a pass at me in his study," Jane Louise said.

"What nerve!" Teddy said. "I hope you made him cringe like a dog."

"I did, actually," said Jane Louise. "Teddy, I think I've had enough of these Perseids. They're sort of giving me the creeps."

"Okay," said Teddy. "Let's go and give Little Catherine or Little Heathcliff a rest."

How simple it could be! The answer to the problem of being anything was *being* it. How admirable Teddy was! From the ashes of his broken childhood he had formed a decision to be a cheerful person, a do-gooding scientific type with a knowledge of English literature. That he had undercurrents of sadness as long and deep as a river was not the point. He had claimed a territory for himself and did not think too much about the complications. People settled on what they were going to be and *were* it, like Erna Hendershott, exemplary mother, wife, and editor, board member, needleworker, superperson.

Maybe being a mother, Jane Louise thought, would somehow make her immune to edges, snags, surprises, having passes made at her in sunlit studies by overzealous writers. She would have a baby and be all of a piece. The world would fall, gently as snow, into an attractive shape. She would find her place in the celestial order and no longer feel even the remotest twinge when insects like Sven crept around.

"I'm freezing," said Jane Louise.

"I'll warm you up," said Teddy. He opened the screen door, and they walked slowly into the guest bedroom, where everything had happened with such apparent simplicity so long ago.

CHAPTER 21

In the summer Edie's parents went abroad on judicial conferences, fund-raising missions, and art tours. Edie's brothers and their wives split the house during July and August unless they went to the seashore. Edie never counted on the house. She had been cut out of this deal for a number of reasons: She had been in Paris, had been unmarried and, it was their opinion, had no interest in the country, especially since she had no children. The fact was that the Steinhauses preferred to pretend that Mokie and Edie did not live together and tried as best they could not to deal with it.

"They do not want colored people leaving smears on their furniture," Mokie said. "Basically, they hope someday I'll take a magic shower and it will all wash off."

So Mokie and Edie rented a house less than a mile from Teddy's mother so that they could spend the month with Jane Louise and Teddy. The house they rented was a collapsing farmhouse owned by a pair of psychologists named Helene and Paul Schreck.

"And so aptly named!" said Mokie, who had studied German in college. The Schrecks had made it very clear that although they were friends of Edie's parents, Edie and Mokie should be very grateful to have the privilege of paying a lot of money to live in their dirty house.

The first week up Mokie took Teddy on a tour.

"These people are *eccentric*," he said. "It's weird. A house in the country and *not one single field guide*. Hey, Ted! Look, black mold in the step of the fireplace, and yesterday we realized that the back porch steps are rotting. Is this some kind of country thing or are these people strange?"

"They're considered to be sort of incompetent," Teddy said. "Naturally, my mother can't stand them. She disapproves of wood chips around flowers, and she says that Helene hires someone to put the garden in and then sort of lets it die."

"Edie says there's a large community of Japanese beetles on the roses," Mokie said.

"That's better than termites in the foundation beams," Edie said. "Why don't we have lots of money instead of them?"

"We're nicer," Mokie said. "Listen, come out and tell me if the porch is safe. It seems to be pulling away from the house."

"Why are we staying here?" Edie said.

"To have fun!" Mokie said. "It *is* fun. I love this house. It dazzles this little colored boy."

Edie gave Jane Louise a long-suffering look.

"Let's eat," she said. "Did you bring me that platter? I looked everywhere but they don't seem to have one, although they did have some rotting leaves in the teapot."

"After dinner we will have a tour of the owner's workroom," Mokie said, carving the chicken. "And now we have an announcement. Janey, don't be mad. I sat on Edie not to tell you. This is probably the only thing she hasn't told you first, but here it is. We think our baby will come just a little after yours. What do you think of that?"

"Oh, my goodness!" said Jane Louise. The news was everything she had ever wanted.

It was one of those moments in which the world seems to stand absolutely still, as if in a photo taken by surprise. There they sat at the Schrecks' ugly dining room table, lit by candlelight. They were eating roast chicken and scalloped tomatoes. Teddy wore an old blue shirt, and Mokie had on a ripped sweatshirt. Edie sat smiling in her chair, wearing one of her vintage dresses with a design of parasols on it. This is the night of a momentous announcement, Jane Louise thought. We ought never forget what we had for dinner, where we were, how we felt. And yet soon it would all be history, something from the distant past. Someday, if all went well, they would be sitting at some other dining room table with teenage children telling them about this very night so long, long ago.

As she stared into the candles, she could see back to the first time she had met Edie, a gawky girl sitting on her dormitory bed mending a pair of polka-dot socks. She remembered the nights they had sat up drinking coffee and popping Dexamyls, trying to study for exams. She remembered Edie walking around hand in hand with Percy David, the tall, emaciated exchange student from England, and her passionate affair with horrible Fred Clarins. She remembered the hours, the days, the years they had spent hanging around in Marshallsville when Edie's parents weren't around.

She could remember Edie in her little room in Paris telling Jane Louise about Mokie, and then meeting Mokie for dinner in an Algerian restaurant. They had had so, so much life together, and it seemed to Jane Louise that there was so much more in front of her. If all went well and their babies were born, they had eighteen years of parenting in front of them, four years of worrying about their children away at college. Why not marry them off right away, if one was a girl and one was a boy? The permutations and heartache, the wrong choices, the misery—the useless emotions all could be easily avoided.

And there they were: a man who had lived most of his life in this place, who still came back to the house he had grown up in. A woman who had summered in this place all her life. A black man whose family and its traditions were from far away. A woman who had lived in any number of places as a child, who never summered anywhere, whose family plans were always thrown together at the last minute.

Our children will learn to swim in this lake, and Teddy's mother will give them little garden plots as she had given Teddy. She would pay them an allowance to pick the beetles off her roses and the caterpillars off her tomatoes. They would weed and hoe and go off to Peter Peering's to help pick peas. And would that stability make them into little snoots? If they were close to their families, would they grow up crooked and strange? Everyone at this table, Jane Louise thought, had struggled: Edie to get out from under her horrible brothers, and Mokie to leave his big, encompassing family and go to Paris, and Jane Louise to find some corner of the world to be steady in, and Teddy to transcend the early fracture of his life.

We have ended up here, Jane Louise thought. It occurred to her that she was sleepy. The air was muggy and still. It was very hot. She looked across the table and saw that Edie was yawning.

"You guys clear up," Edie said. "Janey and I have to stretch out because of our delicate conditions."

They stretched out on the not-very-comfortable sofa in the Schrecks' living room.

"These people," Edie said.

"How could you have such a nice house and let it get so

awful?" Jane Louise said. "Why would you put such horrible-looking stuff in a place like this?"

"These people. . . ." said Edie sleepily. "If I just closed my eyes I could just drift off."

"Me, too," said Jane Louise.

And a few minutes later they were both asleep.

CHAPTER 22

It was suddenly sweltering. The sky was a strange gray-yellow, and the air stood still. Teddy and Mokie decided to go canoeing on the river. Edie and Jane Louise decided to drive to the library in Marshallsville Village and then have lunch.

Jane Louise felt as heavy as the weather. Some of her clothes were beginning not to fit. Otherwise, she looked exactly as she had before, but she noticed her body slowing down. A peaceful kind of weightiness settled over her. She found it restful and benign.

She and Edie walked slowly in the heat toward the library, a tidy stone building over whose portico grew an enormous wisteria. As they opened the door, a wave of delicious cool air breezed over them.

"You know Franny Chaffee, don't you?" Edie said.

"The one with the silver hair," Jane Louise said.

"She is my idea of what a librarian should be," Edie said. "A retired English teacher. She does this for fun."

"Oh, hello, Edie!" said a voice. Behind the desk stood a tall, gray-haired woman with a cupid's-bow mouth. Her voice was girlish and sweet. "And isn't that Jane Louise Parker?"

Jane Louise was suddenly overcome with shyness.

"You're married to Teddy!" said Franny Chaffee, as if this fact had slipped by Jane Louise. "We all saw the announcement in the paper. Eleanor is so happy!"

"Really?" said Jane Louise. She was afraid her voice might crack. The idea that Eleanor was happy because Teddy had married her was an unexpected gift.

Jane Louise liked to pounce on books. Edie liked to browse. Jane Louise claimed her books and went outside on the municipal lawn. There was no relief from the heat. There seemed not to be much air to breathe. Next to an ornamental bench and under a catalpa tree was the stone marker bearing a brass plaque that she had never noticed before. Jane Louise put her books on the bench and knelt to see what the marker commemorated.

THE YOUNG MEN OF MARSHALLSVILLE

WHO GALLANTLY SERVED

IN THE CONFLICT IN VIET-NAM

Jane Louise read off the names. Theodore C. Parker. Peter S. Peering, Jr. Her own husband, commemorated on a plaque! How very deep in this place he was.

"Did you know Teddy was on this plaque?" Jane Louise called to Edie as she came down the stairs.

"Isn't that funny," Edie said. "Frankly, I never noticed it. Teddy and Peter never talk about it."

"He did say if we had a boy he was going to a Quaker school and registering for conscientious-objector status before he turns two."

"I guess that's mentioning it," Edie said.

"I guess it is," said Jane Louise. "God, it's awful out. Is Warren's restaurant air-conditioned?"

"Warren's from Florida," said Edie. "It was the first thing he put in."

Jane Louise traced Teddy's name with her fingers. She imagined him in jungle fatigues. She had seen his photos of Vietnam—he said every vet had piles of them—few of which contained any pictures of him. There was a photo in her office of a person lying on a slab of driftwood on a beach taken from a long distance. It was Teddy at the South China Sea, but it could have been anyone on any beach.

She and Edie drove over to Warren's, a little lunch and teahouse in town. The sky was an unmoving greenish lavender. There at a table they found Mokie, Teddy, and Peter Peering, sweaty and drinking a large pitcher of iced tea.

"We thought you were going downriver," Edie said.

"The canoe outfitter isn't renting because there's a severe storm warning up," Teddy said. "In fact, we ought to eat lunch and go home. This looks big."

"Don't be squeamish," said Peter. "It'll blow over."

"Not this baby, it won't. I hope you guys have plenty of candles," Teddy said.

"We don't," Edie said.

"Well, go up to Phil's and get some," said Teddy.

"Oh, you city slickers," Peter said.

"One hundred on a tornado," Teddy said. He and Peter had been making bets on any old thing all their lives. They shook on it.

As they got into cars, they could hear rumbling.

"Let's get out of here," said Jane Louise. "This looks very scary."

LAURIE COLWIN

At home they checked Eleanor's emergency stash: votive candles of every size, the bottled water, a portable gas ring, the three boxes of matches, flashlights, batteries.

"Your mom," Jane Louise said.

"Mokie said those idiot Schrecks don't have a thing, which is sort of amazing since you can count on losing power up here the year round."

They spread the candles out on the table and went and sat on the porch. A strange low wind was blowing. The sky had turned a more lurid purple. Jane Louise could feel the hair on the back of her arms stand up.

"It's so suffocating," she said. "Is that pregnancy or what?"

"Or what," said Teddy. "It's whatever this storm is."

They went around the house closing windows except for a crack. They lit two tall storm candles and put one in the bathtub and one in the bedroom. The first drops, heavy and furious, began to fall. Suddenly it was black, as if the night had fallen on top of them.

The wind blew steadily, close to the ground. The rain rattled violently.

"We may as well go upstairs and watch this from the bedroom," Teddy said.

"Aren't we supposed to go into a cellar?" said Jane Louise.

"If it looks bad we'll lie on the floor," Teddy said. "Besides, there aren't any trees on this side of the house."

It was impossible to see across the road. In the house it was as black as a well. The wind roared through the trees. Heavy sheets of water pounded down with such force that the drops flew upward. Jane Louise held her breath. Jagged lightning flashed all over the sky. She felt herself clutching Teddy. She gave a kind of involuntary groan. They sat completely still. The lightning flashed

162

as white as magnesium, filling the sky with an eerie, desiccated light.

"Sit on the floor," Teddy said.

She huddled next to him on the floor. He put his arm around her and held her tight.

"Are we going to die?" Jane Louise asked.

"Not from this, darling," he said. "We're in a minitornado belt. We've had these before. It's kind of thrilling."

The storm was directly overhead. There was a terrific tearing bang, and the bathroom light went out.

"I wonder what came down," Teddy said. "The transformer's right up the road." He picked up the telephone and heard nothing but static. As he turned to the window, a streak of lightning split a huge limb off the oak tree in the pasture.

"Holy moly," he said.

Then suddenly the rain stopped. The wind died down, but the sky stayed black. The thunder rumbled, farther away.

"We're out from under it," Teddy said. "Where's the flashlight? Let's go downstairs and see what's happening."

They walked downstairs as the rain started up again. The thunder could be heard booming in the mountains. They opened the front door and looked out: They couldn't see a thing. The barn light across the street was out, and the sky was like ink.

"There's nothing for it," Teddy said. "Let's eat by candlelight."

They had their dinner and went upstairs. The storm was over. The sky had cleared. Thin ragged clouds floated across the night sky, lit by a quarter moon. Out in the pasture the fireflies were out. Their beams seemed enormous and luminescent, like halos, as if magnified by the charge in the air.

Jane Louise and Teddy lay in bed holding hands.

"I was really scared, Teddy," Jane Louise said.

"I know you were."

"Well, I've never been in a storm like that," Jane Louise said. "I wasn't in the war, like you."

She turned to him, and he looked like a boy: He looked naked and innocent. This was his house, the place from which he had gotten on a bus with Peter Peering and gone to a plane that took them to an army base. Then they had boarded a windowless transport, frightened quite beyond speech, and flown through the air to Southeast Asia. Even people you loved and lived with were barely knowable, thought Jane Louise. She wondered if Teddy had slept with anyone else in this bed.

The air was strangely quiet, like someone who had sobbed herself out and fallen asleep. It was entirely still. She could hear the tree frogs calling to one another, and the soft trilling that Teddy told her was a screech owl.

PART III

CHAPTER 23

When she returned to her office, Jane Louise was visibly more pregnant than she had been before she left. She had gone off in her first trimester and reappeared in her second. This to her was like changing time zones.

Her only objection to pregnancy was the public aspect of it: None of her old clothes fit. She got bigger and bigger. People she did not even know *noticed*. This seemed to her an invasion of privacy. She did not yet have the nice round stomach of a woman further along and was therefore not quite ready to wear maternity clothes. She felt in a suspended state of something or other that she could not define.

Her chief dread was facing Sven, who was into Eros, it seemed to Jane Louise, in a bigger way than ever. She felt this as she walked into the office, but then Sven was on record as finding pregnant women erotically interesting.

Her first day back she stared at the stack of papers and specs on her desk. It was hard to believe so much could pile up so fast. A noise in the hallway caused her to look up.

"So," said Sven. "You're back."

"So," said Jane Louise, "I am."

"And there is much more of you than before," Sven said.

His eyes slid over her body, just as described in cheap romance novels.

"Uh-huh," said Jane Louise. "Oh, look! The specs came in on the Devlin book."

"Um," said Sven, rubbing his hand over his chin. "So, did you find out what you're having?"

"A baby, it looks like," Jane Louise said.

Sven gave her a stern look. "Aren't you sufficiently long in the tooth to need to have that test?"

Jane Louise sighed. "I am, and I will. I just don't want to know what it is when I get the results."

"So you'll know if you're having a little mutant," Sven said.

"Thank you for your confidence and support," Jane Louise said. "I hope it won't be a little mutant like *you*."

Sven ambled farther into her office. He liked to stand around her desk, as opposed to sitting with one leg over a chair and showing his crotch in profile, as he did constantly to Erna. Anyone could see this drove Erna crazy in some subliminal way, but Erna's powers of denial were formidable.

"I like to think of myself as the potential father of other people's children," Sven said.

"Do you mean putative?" Jane Louise said.

"I mean I like to entertain the thought that I might have been the father of your child."

"That would be sort of difficult," Jane Louise said. "Since we've never had . . . congress, I think they call it in the books."

"It's a metaphor," Sven said.

"You're such an insect, Sven."

"Yes," Sven said. "But I'm *your* insect. I can't wait till you get really big."

Jane Louise sat back in her chair. "How about getting out of here?" she said. "I've heard your lecture about ripeness."

"Ripeness," Sven said, "is *almost* all." He rubbed his chin again, and Jane Louise had cause to notice that his skin was always slightly reddened, as if he had spent the entire day kissing.

There definitely was something about being pregnant that put one constantly in touch with one's elemental forces. A pregnancy was the dividing line, no matter how old you were when it happened, between youth and something else. The unborn got born and turned into children, and therefore your days of lying on a musty bedspread in somebody else's house and kissing all afternoon were over forever, as were the days when you could stay in bed on rainy mornings entangled with your lover. Lovers turned into husbands, who then turned into fathers, and those rainy days would begin at six o'clock in the morning with baby shrieks or child demands, and one's thoughts would revolve around such things as diapers or play dates or pediatric visits. It was definitely the end of something and the beginning of something else.

"So, you had a tornado," Sven said. "I saw it in the *Times.* Were you affected?"

Jane Louise gave an inward shudder. The landscape of the tornado spread before her. A few barn roofs had been damaged by falling trees, and no one had been hurt, but up in the wild part of Marshallsville to the east, the landscape had been ravaged. The little shady town of Marshall Plain had lost most of its trees. Entire mountainsides of white pine and hemlock had been snapped in half. Their bare, jagged trunks pointed at the empty skies. The day after the storm she and Teddy and Peter Peering had gone out in Peter's truck to see what the damage was. In the village people stood outside their houses in a daze. The sound of power saws reverberated in the long valley.

For four days Teddy and Peter and Mokie sawed and hauled, and Jane Louise and Edie stood in the firehouse making sandwiches for the National Guard. There were not even poles left to string the telephone wires on. Route 16 was closed to ordinary traffic. Long lines of telephone company trucks and flatbeds of poles crowded the lanes. Jane Louise attempted to describe this to Sven.

He looked at her closely. "I see it all," he said. "A wee little baby and a retreat to the country. You and hubs all nice and cozy in a little country house, with a four-wheel-drive vehicle, spending the winter months ordering seed catalogs and waiting for spring. A mud room. A play group. A thriving gossip mill. Embedded in small-town life. You girls. You get knocked up and you instantly retreat."

"I grew up in the country, Sven," said Jane Louise.

"Did you now?" Sven said. "I hadn't really known that about you. You strike me as entirely urbanized."

"I revert to type when I'm not here," Jane Louise said.

Sven gleamed wickedly. "I see it now. A flower garden. Membership in the garden club. Jam making. Mushroom hunting. Shut up with your little baby and a commuting husband. There's no work there, right? These tiny, preserved, useless country towns."

"Shut up!" Jane Louise cried. "You don't know anything about a small town. You only know about living in a city and fucking people you will never see again!"

Sven reeled back, as though stunned.

"My, my, my," he said. "The unstable, raging hormones of pregnancy! We're just talking about the same thing. I don't want you to move to the country because I want you around, and you're upset because you're not anonymous enough."

"Get out of here," Jane Louise said. "Get out of here before I kill you."

"My darling," Sven said mockingly. "Is this a fond hello after a long separation?"

"Out!" Jane Louise shrieked.

Sven gave no sign of leaving.

She looked at her desk, a mire of papers, and at her calendar. On Thursday she had an appointment with her obstetrician. On Friday at lunchtime she and Edie were going to have a look at cribs. One of these days she had to adjust to being back in the city which, after all, was home. She did not like to reveal to Teddy how hard it was to leave Marshallsville. She wanted her baby to grow up there; she wanted its first experience of water to be Bright's Pond. She wanted it to learn to ride a two-wheeler on Cat Hollow Road. She wanted it to know birdcalls and the names of wildflowers. She said as much to Sven, who gave her a terrible look.

"This is your natural world," Sven said. "Lunatics, weird writers, strange colleagues. You grew up here. You're a working stiff, not some nature lover like that twit Martin Barlow with his little wife. You in a small town! Surrounded by another set of lunatics, wondering where the nice Wordsworthian serenity got to. Listen, I know from small country towns. Edwina's mother lives in one. All they do is argue about pesticides at the garden club, and who gets to fish on whose land, and then one person has a fight with someone else, and the whole little cabal takes sides. Last year some guy painted his shutters a dark burnt orange, and they almost lynched him. You'd go over really swell up there."

"It's not like that," Jane Louise lied, because it sort of *was* like that. There were people who only seemed to recognize her when she was with Teddy, although she had been introduced to them a million times. She ran into friends of Eleanor's at the grocery store, and they looked at her brightly when she said hello, without a trace of recognition in their eyes.

"It *is* like that," Sven said. "You think it's all lovely walks and autumn leaves and happy, normal people. Just because your husband grew up there, don't kid yourself. You're not from anywhere, like me, and you aren't anything. You just think being from somewhere is wonderful because you haven't had what you consider stability. There *is* no stability, kid. The only difference between the city and the country is that in the country there are dead animals on the road, and you don't have to lock your car."

"Could we please not have this conversation?" said Jane Louise.

"I love this conversation," Sven said. "After all, I have a proprietary interest in you." He paused and stared at her.

"Country life," he continued, musingly. "Those long days, those longer nights. The same faces, year after year. You know where everybody is. You drive by someone's house, and someone else's car is parked outside, giving rise to all sorts of speculation. There's no privacy. It's a bad place for sex unless you walk to it, and you can't take your dog with you because if someone phones up, the other person's dog might bark."

"You seem to know quite a lot about this."

"I do," Sven said. "In one of my marriages we used to own a house in one of those charming small towns. It wasn't easy, believe me. No nice, anonymous apartment houses. It was like having a thing with a person in a doorman building all the time."

Jane Louise peered at him. There was, on his face, a look so devoid of anything one might associate with common humanity that Jane Louise gave a start.

"Sven," Jane Louise said. "I'd be really grateful if you would get the fuck out of here."

"So well put," said Sven and left.

At noon Jane Louise's telephone rang. She knew it was Edie: She always knew when it was Edie. She could tell by the ring, and she had never been wrong.

Jane Louise said: "Is this Mr. or Miss Edith Steinhaus?"

"The jig is up," Edie said.

"I beg your pardon, madame?" said Jane Louise.

"Nothing fits. I'm popping," she said. "There's no hiding now."

"It's a common side effect of pregnancy," Jane Louise said.

There was a long silence on the other end of the phone.

"Edie?" said Jane Louise.

"I don't know," said Edie in a small voice. Jane Louise knew this voice well. It was the sound Edie made when she was intimidated by her family.

"I see," said Jane Louise. "You have to break down and tell them. This is going to blow the idea that Mokie is your business partner right out of the water."

"I guess," said Edie.

"Listen to me, Edith," Jane Louise said. This was her job, and she was doing it. "Your mother is awful, your father is awful, and your brothers are too awful to mention. They have known about you and Mokie forever, and this is just the usual dodg'em game they play with you. It's none of their damn business. They don't like being confronted by a black son-in-law because their horror at the idea compromises their otherwise impeccable credentials."

"Thank you for hating my family for me," said Edie.

"It's always a pleasure," Jane Louise said. "Just think! You're giving them a grandchild."

"They have four others," Edie said sadly. "Lily-white. Go to the right schools. You know."

"Won't it be nice when we die, Edie, and we can finally be ourselves?"

"I don't want to wait that long," Edie said. "No one loves me."

"You're a dog, Edie," Jane Louise said. "I love you, Mokie loves you. Teddy loves you. Your parents don't love anyone. It's no use trying. Give it up. You're having a baby."

"Thank you for hating my family for me," Edie said again.

"Try it yourself sometime," Jane Louise said. "It's really liberating."

CHAPTER 24

On an unexpectedly hot autumn day Jane Louise and Teddy drove up the Hudson River to go to the wedding of Teddy's youngest half-sister, Daphne. Jane Louise wore a shapeless gray linen dress with no sleeves and a striped jacket. She had piled her hair on top of her head with a tortoiseshell pin.

On the highway the haze of the city began to part. They drove into a brilliant yellow glare. The trees, which had turned early, shone as bright as foil in the sunlight.

Teddy, who was in one of his less talkative modes, was driving. He was not much of a chatterer on his best days—this was certainly not one of his best days, Jane Louise knew. He wore on his face an expression Jane Louise called his "suburban visiting look," which he principally wore around his father and his father's family. It was a look of such hard-set impassiveness it always left Jane Louise a little alarmed. In order to get your face so devoid of feeling, you must be repressing everything. When Teddy got like that there was almost nothing she could do. He had entered a world he wanted no one else to enter: the world of a small child who was uncomfortable around both his parents; who felt like a betrayer if he felt the remotest twinge of love for his father or missed him while in the company of his mother; who, when he got angry at his father, felt as if at any minute his father had the right to pack him up, stick him in the car, and cart him back off to his mother. These feelings ran so deep, so still, and they were so dull from years of constant pain, that Jane Louise felt helpless before them. She wanted to take Teddy in her arms and kiss him until he cried. She wanted to hold him all night long and let him sob out whatever was in back of that relentlessly pleasant, unavailable face.

She herself was not looking forward to this wedding. She had made her accommodations with Teddy's mother, who was grateful to Jane Louise for taking such sweet care—the sort of care she had never doled out—of her son. On the other hand, Jane Louise rather dreaded Teddy's father and his wife.

Cornelius had been a skirt-chaser and a dandy. Why he and Eleanor had ever married was a mystery. It had been one of those classic, terrible mistakes. They had met in the Solomon Islands during the war—Cornelius in the British Navy and Eleanor doing some sort of decoding. She had been a linguist in college, and to an unmarried bluestocking, the intelligence part of the war looked very attractive.

After the divorce Cornelius, who was, after all, attractive and not incapacitated, got a job working for a company whose headquarters were in London but whose branch office was in suburban Connecticut. It was there he met Martine, who was large and bosomy, given to ruffles, lipstick, and flounces. She was much scorned, privately, by Teddy's mother, for her silly clothes, her interest in the royal family, her Britishisms, her awful shoes. Her three girl children had come in rapid succession: Moira, Lisbeth, and Daphne, names Teddy's mother felt were distinctly lower-middle-class.

As far as Teddy was concerned, his father's new family had made him feel as weightless as an air letter circulated between the two households. In her private heart Eleanor had been terrified that Teddy might find life in a big family congenial, that he might adore the idea of being the big brother to these girls, rather than the only child of a single woman in the country. But Teddy had seen his sisters as a blur of female babies or small girls from whom he felt completely disconnected.

Martine's girls married and reproduced young. Lisbeth and Moira already had four children between them. This, of course, made Jane Louise feel like a Martian. By the time Lisbeth and Moira were her age, their children would be in high school or getting ready for college.

Daphne was marrying her college sweetheart, Dan McGuire, whom Jane Louise had met once and could not remember. Martine had said: "You know, Jane Louise, I mean, Dan's parents, you know . . . well, not all the time but they seem every now and again to drink a little too much." She had said this on the telephone one evening in a whisper, as if revealing a terrible secret.

Jane Louise wondered if Martine meant that Dan's parents were alcoholic.

"Oh, it's nothing like that at all," Martine said. "They're very lovely people."

Nevertheless, Martine was confused about what to serve at the reception: whiskey? wine? Ought they to have beer for the younger set?

In the car, Jane Louise yawned. She was incredibly sleepy. "They're very lovely people but they drink a little too much," she said.

"What?" said Teddy, and Jane Louise realized that she had been talking to herself.

"Dan's parents," she said. "Martine says they're lovely people but they drink a little too much."

"Who's Dan?" Teddy said.

"Your future half-brother-in-law," Jane Louise said.

"Oh, him," Teddy said. "Well, Martine and Dad are acquainted with tons of lovely people who drink too much. How do you know, anyway?"

"Well, Martine likes to phone me up," Jane Louise said. "She's much too scared of you, so she hits on me because I'll talk to her. It makes her feel better."

Teddy's face tightened ever so slightly. He was definitely getting his suburban face in order. Basically, he hated Martine with a little boy's hatred. He didn't like the way she smelled, or her shiny, smeary pink lipstick. When she had had a little too much to drink she became maudlin. Tears came to her eyes, and her blue mascara ran. Teddy remembered as a little boy how this had made the world seem out of control. Teddy was capable of pushing certain things from his mind: In some ways they were too awful to think about, and there was nothing he could do about them, anyway. The birth of his half-sisters; the shut, internalized guilt of his mother; the fecklessness of his father. He turned for an instant to look at his wife.

Even in pregnancy Jane Louise did not lose her precise edges. He loved the clean cut of her hair, the long, lean lines of her arms and legs. Even her belly seemed discreet, a nice, round size. The clothes she wore, the dishes she favored, the food she cooked, all seemed to him clean and crisp and outlined, as a child outlines a picture in black. She smelled faintly sweet—of lily-of-the-valley cologne—but her natural scent was biscuity and fresh. In moments of despair, when his bad feelings crept through his defenses, he wanted to bury himself in her.

Because she was a good girl, she knew that he trusted her. He was perfectly lovely himself. She ran her fingers down his long forearm.

"Why don't you drive off the road?" she said. "We could curl up." The warmth of the sun through the windshield, the subtle kicking of her unborn child, made her feel elemental and available. This sort of thing thrilled and shocked Teddy at the same time.

"Wouldn't that be something," Teddy said.

"Teddy," said Jane Louise. "This wedding will be okay, won't it?"

"It'll be fucking hell," Teddy said. "But that's all right, since it won't last very long."

"It's so strange," Jane Louise said. "Here we are, married and having a baby and off to your half-sister's wedding."

"What's the strange part?" Teddy said.

"Sometimes I feel I crept into your life," said Jane Louise, staring out the window. This was not what she had meant to say, but she found herself saying it anyway. "I mean, I'm sort of the last person. I don't know anyone I can say I've known all my life, but you can. Our wedding was full of your childhood. But here we are, enfolded into this family no one really belongs to."

"Little Catherine or Heathcliff belongs to us. You belong to me, and I belong to you, don't we?"

"Your half-sisters are related to you by blood," Jane Louise said.

"You're too hipped on blood and connection," Teddy said. "It must be from having moved so much. You know me better than anyone in the world, including my childhood friends. You're the only person on earth who knows me."

That was all he intended to say, and Jane Louise knew that this conversation, which was at the moment so sweet, raised many not-so-sweet specters. She *was* hipped on blood and connection. Teddy, who had blood and connection to spare, was not. The idea that she was the last person he had let into his life and that he loved her better, and she knew him better, made her feel keenly the injustice of not having known him when he was little, or having been the first girl he ever kissed, or the pal he had had a secret hideout with over on Town Hill Road. Teddy found this bafflingly sentimental, but to Jane Louise, it was the expression of her wildest love.

Once during their courtship, Teddy had told Jane Louise his recurrent childhood nightmare: He was standing in a field. His mother stood in front of him, his father in back. Both had loaded guns. He had been told he had to move forward or backward, but if he moved forward, his father would shoot him, and if he moved backward, his mother would. Jane Louise had committed this to memory and had never again mentioned it.

She leaned back against the seat, and the air that filled her chest seemed golden and sweet. The idea of curling up like a cat in a warm place seemed very compelling.

She felt a bump and realized that she had fallen asleep. These tiny naps took her by storm. She rubbed her eyes, taking care not to smudge her mascara.

"Was I snoring?" she said.

"You never snore."

"I read in one of those birth books that pregnancy can bring on snoring."

"I'll let you know as soon as it happens," Teddy said.

"Teddy," said Jane Louise. "Do you still love me?"

Teddy gave her a sidelong look that was more like a wince. How he hated these conversations!

"For crying out loud, Janey," he said.

"I know it's a hard day for you," Jane Louise said. "But sometimes you seem very far away."

"I *am* far away, for Christ's sake," Teddy said. "You can't imagine how awful these things are. I really can't stand them, and if I were alone, believe me I would have booked some trip to Africa to get me out of this. Look, we turn right here."

Jane Louise smoothed her skirt. This wedding made her nervous, too. She was not very good with other people's parents and fretted again about Cornelius. There was a good deal of dead air around him. He seemed more some stock character out of central casting than a real person. When Jane Louise looked into his watery eyes, she saw a kind of staginess and weakness, a need to be taken care of by a woman. She was constantly relieved to find not one speck of it in her own husband, who was a model of self-sufficiency.

Cornelius had been the baby of his family and had never outgrown it. Now white-haired and deaf in one ear from a war injury, he was a baby still. He had married Teddy's mother for her self-reliance, her efficiency, her ability to deal with things. She looked like someone who would take care of him, and when she did not, he had turned to Martine, soft and overly made up, with the slightly battered air of someone used to constantly doing things for others.

Her half-sisters-in-law made her feel even more uncomfortable. They were younger, blonder, reproductive. Her Jewishness pressed in on her the few times she was forced to be around them. They all lived within driving distance from where they had grown up, with husbands they had known most of their lives. *Their* parents had never been divorced, nor had they been moved around. Instead, they had been rooted like trees, and they were stable, dull, feminine girls who liked to have manicures and go shopping. They talked about hair color, child care, baby-sitter problems, and their mutual friends. They sent their children to Little People's Sunday School, where they were told about tender Jesus meek and mild, and each summer they had gone to the south of England, which made little or no impression on them as far as Jane Louise could tell, to see their paternal grandparents. In the winter they had been sent to Bermuda to play tennis with their maternal grandparents, and as a result each had a formidable collection of duty-free cashmere sweaters.

Jane Louise looked imploringly at Teddy, who looked so impassive that she wanted to throw her arms around him and kiss him until some true emotion issued forth.

"Don't be so nice," she whispered.

"What?" said Teddy. He was edging along the lane as one of the ushers directed him into a parking space.

"I said, Don't be so nice," Jane Louise said. "You have that look on your face."

Teddy parked the car. He had wavy brown hair, his father's high cheekbones, and his mother's snub nose.

"Come on, Teddy," she said, taking his arm.

"What is it you want?" Teddy said angrily.

Tears sprang into Jane Louise's eyes. If she had wanted some true emotion from Teddy, this was it. He looked stricken, cornered, and truculent.

"I'm sorry," she said. "Don't be mad at me."

He took her arm. "I'm not mad at you," he said. "I just wish I didn't have such a complicated family."

CHAPTER 25

The house was of formal flagstone with a low porch. On either side of the front door were topiary trees in pots. To get inside, it was necessary to duck under a rose trellis, whose tiny yellow fall roses had climbed into the ivy. From a low hedge in the front yard wafted the pungent scent of cat pee.

Teddy's shoulders were bunched beneath his jacket. Jane Louise, who was intimate with the physical manifestations of his distress, longed to touch him, but this was never a good idea. Teddy's feelings, which he so longed to bury, were not buried, and the lightest touch when he was upset made it worse.

As they passed under the rose trellis, they turned their heads to see Martine bustling toward them. She was dressed in fawn-colored chiffon, with a large hat dyed to match. Her square feet were encased in fawn-colored shoes with cross-straps, and she was carrying what Jane Louise believed was called a reticule, a tiny ornamental bag that looked big enough to contain a mint and a child's handkerchief. She wore a bright pink lipstick and blue eye shadow. No matter how often her daughters got on her case,

Martine applied the makeup of her youth. She kissed Jane Louise and Teddy, enveloping them in her heavy perfume.

"Ted, your dad is on the lawn with the photographers," she said. "Go help him out, will you?" She turned to Jane Louise. "The girls are upstairs getting dressed, and they're longing to see you."

Jane Louise knew that there was nothing for Teddy to help his father with and that the girls were not longing to see her in the least, but she was used to Martine. Martine was like her mother. She had an idea of the way things should pleasantly be, and she edited reality heavily to conform with it. Besides, Martine probably felt that in weddings of the royal family there was a proper and appropriate place for the pregnant half-sister-in-law.

Jane Louise followed Martine into the immense foyer and up a curving flight of stairs carpeted in a Persian runner. At the top of the stairs was a large pink dressing room, and in it were Martine's daughters, getting dressed.

For a moment it was a pink-and-gold blur. The sun poured through the pink curtains, causing the pale room to glow. In the center stood Lisbeth and Moira in lacy pink full slips. They were pulling on lacy pink stockings. Their hair was every shade of blond, and their makeup was as pale and perfect as their mother's was not. The dressing table was arrayed with pins, dusting powder, makeup boxes, brushes, and cotton puffs.

"Oh, hello! It's you!" said Lisbeth. It was clear to Jane Louise that for an instant Lisbeth and Moira had no idea who she was. "Oh, gosh! Mum told us you were having a baby. It's due this winter, right?"

Although Lisbeth was younger, Jane Louise always thought of her as older since she already had a five-year-old and a three-year-old. She belonged to a world of normal suburban matrons who married young, had babies young, had family holidays and huge parties in which thousands of children ran wild in the house. They had barbecues and birthday parties and bake sales. Their husbands went to business and the wives discussed child development.

"You all look so pretty," Jane Louise said. "Where's Daphne?"

Lisbeth propelled her into another room—the formal bedroom in the center of which stood Daphne in her wedding slip, still as a waxed statue. Her elaborate bride's dress hung from the chandelier on a padded hanger. She did not move, even to smile. A little Cuban woman—the fitter—fluttered around her, smoothing and patting. On her wrist she wore a corsagelike pincushion attached to an elastic band. "Don't move, don't move!" she cried, but this was totally unnecessary, as Jane Louise had never seen anyone hold a pose for so long.

"Can I help?" Jane Louise asked.

"No, thanks," Moira said. "We have to put these net bags over our heads so we don't mess our hair, and Graciela will put our dresses on." She motioned with her shoulder to the closet door from which hung two long pink dresses, stuffed with tissue paper and looking like disembodied girls.

"Master of the female half lengths," Jane Louise said.

"Pardon?" said Moira.

"There's a Flemish painter known only as the master of the female half lengths or something like that," Jane Louise said. "Your dresses sort of remind me."

Moira gave her the sort of look you might give to a silly child. She gazed out the window. "There's lots of people out there. Daph, you ought to put your dress on. We ought to, too."

Daphne was still unmoved. The fitter draped a net scarf over Daphne's head while Moira helped slip her dress over it. She looked like an Elizabethan child being hung with cloth of gold. The fitter smoothed out Daphne's voluminous skirt.

"Look, girls," she said. "Here I put the train up like this, and this tie keeps it up. When she will walk down the aisle you let the tie go, like this. See?" She let go of the tie, and the train slipped out. "When you walk, please walk so carefully and do not step from the red carpet because the grass will stain and these never come out."

She rearranged the train and then turned to Moira, whose sleeve needed adjusting.

There was no reason for Jane Louise to be in that room, and in her gray dress and her dark hair, she felt like Cinderella.

She remembered her sister Nora's wedding to Jaime Benitez-Cohen so long ago: the white dress, the bridal attendants, one of whom had been the younger Jane Louise, dark, uncomfortable, taller than anyone else, and unhappily in love with somebody or other while her sister, radiant in the proper bridal clothes, which had set their father back quite a number of dollars, walked down the aisle to marry somebody absolutely perfect: Jewish, rich, and from a well-connected family. In her heart Jane Louise had known she would never wear a white dress, or be entitled to wear one, walk down an aisle, get married by a rabbi, or please her mother to this elaborate extent. Watching Martine she realized what sense of safety a daughter can bring to a mother. Although Lilly liked Teddy very well, he was not quite what she had had in mind, and furthermore, he was not second nature. Lilly liked money she understood *viscerally*. Flinty old WASP New England money was not something she knew by heart, only by literature.

Daphne turned her radiant face to them. She could move now, and she was very beautiful. Lisbeth and Moira had put their dresses on. Their pinkness, their blondness, their carefully streaked hair, nail polish, eyelash curlers, mascara, the heap of things that lay on the dressing table and that Jane Louise never used made her feel that they were women in a way that she was not.

"Oh, Daph!" sighed Lisbeth. "You're *so* beautiful."

Martine called from the top of the stairs. "Girls! Girls!" she said. "You must come at *once!*"

Daphne went first. She walked carefully and serenely, as if her parts were made of glass. Jane Louise gave her a smile and was greeted in return by an uplift of her lips. Her look said to Jane Louise: *This is my perfect day. What are you doing here?*

What these girls thought of their half-brother was unknown. He was some other element. He was older, a chemist, married to someone older, from a place they had never seen. What was the point of this sort of blood relation?

Daphne's wedding books, of which she had read dozens, did not say what to do with halfs or steps. They were a minor burden, something that reminded you that life is never smooth or perfect.

Downstairs they were met by a young man from the florist's who presented Daphne with her enormous bouquet, a mass of white roses, lily of the valley, and freesia, with long garlands of white-rimmed ivy. Moira and Lisbeth carried sweetheart roses, and Martine was given a long swaglike corsage to pin to her shoulder. Martine stood patiently while it was pinned and then turned and began to rummage through the florist's box. There was a pink rose for Cornelius's buttonhole, and an extra pink rose that she gave to Jane Louise.

"I'm afraid we haven't a pin," she said.

Jane Louise said it was perfectly all right and twisted it into her hair, although it was clear that this was not the orthodox thing to do. As the girls floated down the lawn, Jane Louise went off to find Teddy.

He was standing on the lawn with his father. Cornelius looked splendid in his morning clothes, which, he explained to Jane Louise, had belonged to *his* father. His top hat was collapsible and could be made to go flat. His hair was brilliant white, and his mustache gleamed in the sun.

"Let's go for a walk," Jane Louise said to Teddy.

"*Family* portrait, old boy," Cornelius said. "We'll be wanting you for one or two snaps."

They followed him and stood obediently in the back row for two family portraits. Then they were released.

They walked into the rose garden, where they sat on a concrete bench and watched the goldfish swimming lazily in their pool.

"Did you secretly want all this?" Jane Louise said.

"You mean a big house with a goldfish pond?" Teddy said.

"I mean a big wedding with ushers and bridesmaids," Jane Louise said.

"I didn't," Teddy said. "Did you?"

"I always feel bad that you had to marry a Jewess by a Puerto Rican judge."

"Oh, for Christ's sake, Jane," Teddy said. "I *wanted* to marry a Jewess by a Puerto Rican judge. I can never figure out your free-floating anxiety about this. Nobody has to get married. At least, I didn't. I married you because I wanted to marry you. Is there something wrong with me that you never seem to believe it?"

"No," said Jane Louise in a small voice.

"Then maybe what I'm hearing is that *you* wanted all this, just like your sister Nora. Maybe you wanted me to be Jaime Benitez-Cohen with a big family and lots of money and a board membership in the synagogue."

"Is that really what you think?" Jane Louise said.

"I'm beginning to wonder," Teddy said. "Usually I just assume that you married me because you wanted to, but I might be wrong."

He gave her a grieved look, a look that said, Don't hassle me when I'm suffering. But it was this remote suffering Jane Louise wanted to cut through. She would rather have had him angry than distanced. The fact that he had snapped at her in some way made her feel better. How could you tell your husband, who thought you were a normal person, that you had never felt normal for a single minute in your life?

Teddy looked at her. He picked her chin up and saw that there were tears in her eyes. For an instant he scowled, and then his face softened.

"I married the best person in the world," he said. "Is this real upset or just being pregnant?"

"I don't know," said Jane Louise.

CHAPTER 26

Jane Louise and Edie sat on the bus on a rainy day. They were on their way to buy baby supplies and they were talking about weddings. It seemed to them that although everyone cried at them, no one had anything very nice to say about them.

Jane Louise said: "When Daphne walked down the lawn, my throat closed up. I said to myself, 'This thing is costing a fortune that would have been money better off in Daphne's bank account,' and then I realized I was just plain jealous because I could never even have contemplated any such thing being done for me. Or even wanting it."

"Tut," Edie said. "After all I did for you. My most beautiful cake."

"You know what I mean," Jane Louise said. "I mean, look at you and Mokie! City Hall, no rice, no flowers."

"There were flowers," Edie said. "You brought me that bouquet."

"I did," Jane Louise said. "I guess I kind of blur over where these things are concerned."

"And you pointed out how elegant I looked compared to all the other pregnant brides," Edie said.

"I don't know why weddings make people feel this way," Jane Louise said. "To Sven it's just legal fucking, eventual obligations, and court fees."

"He's an old war-horse at these things," Edie said.

"Well, it comes from a very deep place," Jane Louise said. "Even though Dan looks kind of a twerp and Daphne has about a molecule of brain, they looked so pretty and they pressed all those buttons: hope, promise, new starts, and young love, and all that stuff."

"We're too old for that stuff," Edie said.

"It's true," Jane Louise said. "We're about struggle, dislocation, and marrying aliens, right?"

"Well, we're having babies," Edie said. "We're still young enough for that stuff."

"Barely," said Jane Louise. "This whole thing was hardest on Teddy. He really suffered. I think it was really terrible for him when his father married Martine."

Teddy's father had sent him a suit for that occasion. It had needed to be tailored, so he had been driven into town by his mother, who had dropped him off at the local tailoring shop while she went to browse in a bookshop. It was perfectly clear to Teddy, at age eight, that his mother could not bear to witness her son's being fitted for this wedding suit. Teddy had stood, sweating with heat and embarrassment, as the tailor fussed and pinned.

His mother's awful feeling about this event—even though she had no use for Cornelius whatsoever—had burned into Teddy like acid on an etching plate. She had not wanted to burden him with these feelings, and as a result, he was almost sick with anger and dread.

Teddy had not liked Martine. The sight of his father kissing this person upset him very much. He did not like her accent or the pitch of her voice, and he had not known what to say to her when she spoke to him. His boyish feelings had been in total chaos, and yet he had found himself at his father's wedding standing beside him in a church he had never seen before. He had sat next to his father and Martine at the wedding lunch, and then had been driven home by his Uncle Charlie, his father's brother. He was sick by the side of the road halfway home.

He had been handed, pale and shaky, over to his mother, who put him straight to bed. The smell of his own house, the sight of his own room, his mother's neutral, rather astringent scent, made his eyes swim.

This was put down to too much excitement, cake, and champagne. He remembered dozing off in his bed. From his room he could hear his mother and uncle chatting pleasantly. This had soothed him and made him feel that something was almost right.

Edie had heard this story before. It was a variant form of a story Mokie told of being invited to a wedding and being taken for a parking attendant.

Daphne and Dan would have a big, leather-bound book of wedding photos. Jane Louise kept her small batch in a pine box, and Mokie and Edie had a few very nice pictures Teddy had taken the day of their wedding—the two of them holding hands, Edie in a blue smock, visibly pregnant, her fuzzy hair in a halo around her head, carrying the bouquet Jane Louise had given her. Jane Louise remembered the details of Daphne's wedding: the pink and white jordan almonds in little pink baskets, the five-tiered cake on top of which stood a tiny plastic bride and groom. Weddings were definitely about destiny, for better or worse.

Jane Louise fished a list out of her handbag.

"We should get serious," she said to Edie. "This layette business."

"It would be nice to know why it's called that," Edie said. "I think all babies should be dressed in black to show them off."

"Or white, if you have a darky," Jane Louise said.

"It is weird wondering how dark your offspring will be," Edie said. "Of course, you don't have this problem. But I may end up with a little chocolate baby."

"Or spotted," Jane Louise said. "Wouldn't that be a hoot?"

"It would make it easier on Mommy and Daddy. They could tell everyone it has a disease," Edie said.

Jane Louise always wondered that Edie still called her parents Mommy and Daddy. These frightful people, who did not, in Jane Louise's opinion, deserve to have such a nice daughter, had not taken the news of Edie's pregnancy very well. It caught them off guard. They had spent so long denying that Mokie was anything more than Edie's business partner that they had never given much thought to their strategy should he have proved to be anything more. Since they had not wanted to imagine such a circumstance, they had no presentation ready for it. On the bus Jane Louise and Edie tried to make one up.

"They could say that Mokie raped you and then decided to be a man about it," Jane Louise said.

"They could say that this is the consequence of anthropological research," Edie said.

"Or that you are part of a widespread do-good movement that believes passionately in miscegenation as the answer to world peace," Jane Louise said.

"Oh, that's very good," Edie said. "They'd love that."

"Sven refers to your impending as 'the project in black and white,'" Jane Louise said.

"How stylish!" Edie said. "Mokie feels we should have a black-and-white party when it's born—you know, date-and-nut bread with cream cheese, marble cake, black-and-white sundaes, Irish coffee."

"Yik," said Jane Louise.

"Or little plates of mashed potatoes with black caviar. Or truffles and egg whites."

"What *do* they say, do you think?"

"They lower their voices and say what a wonderful person Mokie is and that they pray life won't be awful for us as an interracial couple, and how they back us one hundred percent. And we *will* look nice at all those racial harmony events they go to. I mean, it'll show how brave they are that their daughter went the distance."

Jane Louise eyed her friend. She had never heard Edie, who was so careful and muted about her family, speak this way. Edie's wide hazel eyes were awash.

"Come along, Miss Edith," Jane Louise said. "It'll be okay."

Tears slid down Edie's cheeks. "Oh, Janey. They're so horrid. Mokie suffers this stuff so silently. He's so cheerful and stoical, but he's sort of like Teddy. Being down is pretty far down for him. It doesn't happen often, but it's pretty awful when it does. It's very depressing to see your parents not love your loved one."

"Charlie and my mother weren't so thrilled with Teddy, as you recall," Jane Louise said. "At Daphne's wedding I had a long think about Nora's wedding years ago. I was her bridesmaid only because I was her sister and she had to have me, but she didn't really want to, and for about ten years afterward my father complained that he was still paying off the debt. It was the year before you and I met at college. You should have seen it—all this stuff dragged out to impress the Benitez-Cohens, and they probably never thought much about us anyway because we didn't have any money. But Jaime! He has tons of money, he makes tons of money, they have that enormous house in San Francisco, and tons of famous people to be friends with and genius children, and Jaime gets his name in the paper all the time, and Nora gives parties that get reviewed! What are we compared with that?"

"Dust," Edie said. "Sand. Cobwebs."

"Yes," Jane Louise said sadly. "Why are people's families so horrible? And here we are, just about to start our own. Do you suppose these fetuses will someday not be able to stand us?"

"Oh, doubtless," Edie said. "But they'll have each other."

"Sven's children adore him," Jane Louise said. "Maybe our children will adore us because we'll be good, and if even a totally inadequate parent like Sven, who'd probably put the arm on his daughter if it were legal, can get love, maybe we will, too."

"Yes, Sven is a beacon of hope," Edie said. "Such a swine and such devoted children, although perhaps little Piers will turn out to be a serial killer with thighbones hidden under the floorboards. Here's our stop."

They entered a place called Bubby's Baby World. It was like entering a museum full of the cultural artifacts of another culture: rockers, strollers, things to hang a baby in, buntings, stretchies, tiny garments of every description, plus dozens of varieties of bottles, hotplates, warmers for baby food, tiny forks and spoons, some with oddly shaped handles, nightlights in the shape of ducks, lambs, cats, and moons. Rattles filled with plastic stars or beans. Objects that could be grasped by a tiny fist and made to whirl in different colors. Baby strollers, some with hoods, some with little umbrellas suspended from springs. Side carriers, Snuglis, crib blankets and sheets. One side of the store was devoted to cribs, in colonial, art deco, and rustic style. Cribs that looked as if handmade by Shaker craftspeople. Cribs with flowers handpainted on them. White, pink, and blue cribs, and cribs in natural and stained wood. The sight of this made Jane Louise's and Edie's heads spin.

In back of the clothing counter was a small old man.

"Hello, girls!" he called out cheerfully. "What can I do for you?"

"Layettes," said Jane Louise.

"Congratulations," the little man said. "Now, what would you like?"

"Well, cotton baby clothes," Edie said.

The man peered up at her. "This we don't sell," he said.

"Really?" said Jane Louise.

"Listen," the little man said. "Here we have only flame-retardant materials. You know, if you would take a piece of cotton and hold it up to a seventy-five-watt bulb, in one hour that piece of cloth would be on fire."

"I promise you," Jane Louise said, "I have no intention of holding my baby up to a seventy-five-watt light bulb for even half an hour. It never entered my mind."

"You'd be surprised," the man said.

"I would be stunned," Jane Louise said. "But you have cotton undershirts or whatever you call them, don't you?"

"These we have." He gave the girls a long look to assess their ages. "Boys or girls?" he asked.

"We don't know," Edie said.

"Most of my ladies know," the man said. "It saves so much time and worry. It takes the guesswork out."

"We didn't ask," Jane Louise said. "So we thought we'd just try to get black or brown or gray infant clothes."

The man looked at her as if she were insane.

"Those they don't make," he said kindly. "And you mustn't ever dye anything for a baby, because the baby could chew on something, and dyed fabric is poison."

"We hadn't thought of that," said Jane Louise.

"You'd be surprised," the man said. "What about white or yellow?"

"That sounds right for any gender," Edie said.

"Somehow," the man said, "I don't feel you girls are taking this very seriously."

"We are," Jane Louise said. "After all, we're pregnant."

"Besides yellow, white, pink, and blue, don't you have any colors?" Edie asked.

"Babies just need to be warm, they don't need colors," the man said. "Have a baby shower, and your friends will give you fancy. Here we have basic. Do you have a list?"

Jane Louise and Edie looked at each other. Neither had a list nor any idea what they were supposed to have besides undershirts, which, they had been told, were the most important item of baby wear.

"We don't know," Jane Louise said. "What do they need? High socks? Kilts? Earmuffs?"

"Ach! You girls are teasing me," the man said. "All young ladies are born with this knowledge."

"We're not young," Jane Louise said. "We might have been born with it, but we outgrew it."

"We'll just put ourselves in your hands," Edie said.

On the way home it began to sleet. Jane Louise and Edie hunched together on the bus surrounded by large shopping bags.

"Didn't it sort of creep you out when he said, 'Now all you need is the baby'?" Jane Louise said.

"The whole thing is so totally weird," Edie said. "Won't it just be a hoot and a half when we take the boys this weekend to pick out cribs? I liked that Shaker-looking one."

"I did, too, but it costs a fortune," Jane Louise said.

"Did it?" Edie said. "I didn't even look."

"We both better start looking at prices, Miss Edith. We're going to be moms, and neither of us has a bean. Did I tell you about that lady and her shoes?"

"Tell," Edie said.

"I was browsing around in the bookstore the other day at lunchtime. This woman came in wearing a heather maternity smock and a violet cape," Jane Louise said. "She looked as if she was about to deliver on the counter. She was wearing the most gorgeous shoes I have ever seen. Kind of that lawbook dark tan calf, very plain, low heel. I asked her where she got them, and she said they came from Andrew Paulsen. That place is extremely pricey. I've never been in it, but I said to myself, 'I'm pregnant, and I want those shoes.' So I nosed over and there they were. I looked at the price tag and realized that my days of buying shoes like that were over, what with school tuition and like that."

"School tuition for the unborn," Edie said. "Well, it's like chatting with Mrs. Teagarden. When she was pregnant, she had everything made for her and got this cabinetmaker in Maine to make the crib, and imported the nanny from Ireland, and had the room stenciled, and got one of those machines that sounds like the mother's heartbeat."

"A machine that sounds like the mother's heartbeat," Jane Louise said musingly. "I thought that was called the mother."

"She didn't intend to be around all that much," Edie said. "What with entertaining and all. She asked me if I intended to nurse and told me that she had actually managed to locate a wet nurse, but it didn't work out at the last minute."

"And did she find a dairymaid and an alchemist, too?"

"She finds them. Now she's planning a Christmas party. She said to me: 'I don't know what I want for Christmas. I *have* everything.' I said, 'What about a large cashmere shawl?' and she said, 'Oh, I have drawers full of *them*.'"

"She can send one over to me," Jane Louise said. "I wonder what *her* wedding was like."

"She told me," Edie said. "Winter fantasy. Small children dressed as cherubs."

"And a cake in the shape of a large pile of thousand-dollar bills," Jane Louise said. "I have nothing."

"Well, the thing about the Teagardens is they have to be themselves, whereas we get to be us."

"How swell," Jane Louise said. "And when we're dead we will be reconciled to it."

CHAPTER 27

As the winter began, Jane Louise became amazed at the form her body was taking. She and Edie discussed it endlessly. They felt they looked slightly ridiculous, like cranes carrying bowling balls. Every other part of them remained skinny while they bulged, spherelike, in front. Teddy and Mokie seemed to be transfixed. Their lank, fleet wives, who were so precise in matters relating to style, were suddenly slightly fuzzy and off balance.

Around Teddy, Jane Louise realized that she was paying a kind of deference to what she felt was his solemn awe at her condition. How much the idea of fatherhood meant to him humbled her, and her anxiety, which floated freely at the best of times now, took a definite bent: Supposing the baby she produced was not right in some way? Supposing she was incapable of producing a nice, straight child with all its faculties intact?

Sven, as ever, was helpful in this matter. Glancing at her round belly he said: "I don't think any baby produced by *you* would be particularly straight."

"Thank you, Sven," said Jane Louise. "Now be a good person and bugger off."

"How charming you'll look with a little wriggling baby in your arms," Sven said. "They go with everything, you know, like a string of pearls."

"Thank you, Sven," said Jane Louise. "Now be a good person and buzz off."

"Birth," said Sven. "What a thrill."

"For you but not for me," Jane Louise said.

"Oh, you'll love it, Jancy," Sven said. "I know your sort. You're in this life for the highs."

"I'm not too keen on pain," Jane Louise said, wondering how Sven knew this about her.

"Oh, pain," Sven said dismissively. "It's one of the big deals."

"And the others?"

"Sex, death, birth. Who could ask for anything more?" Sven said.

"I could," Jane Louise said. "Glamour, economic security, home ownership, freedom from anxiety, a lizard belt. Shall I go on?"

"Niceties," Sven said. "Just wait."

Jane Louise had always wondered if Sven was the sort of man to want to witness what she and Edie called "the birth event." It turned out he was and had. It seemed to her that he would very much like to witness *her* birth event, although, she pointed out to Sven, this would be a little hard to explain. It seemed to her that he saw aspects of the birth event that had not previously occurred to her, and he attempted to point these out whenever he had a spare minute.

"Everything is not related to pure eroticism," she said.

"Everything *I'm* interested in is related to pure eroticism," Sven said.

"Listen," said Jane Louise. "I'm a busy woman. I've got Hugh

Oswald-Murphy and Erna coming in in half an hour to talk about design. Can you believe it? This book gets delayed every ten minutes, I get put on hold every time I design a page, and this guy wants to come in and talk about type. I ask you."

"He's a lush."

"How nice for me," Jane Louise said.

"He's a blowhard," Sven said. "He's one of those Brit types who has been so enchanted by the sound of his own voice for so long that he goes around bleating like a sheep and expecting everyone to fall to their knees at his every utterance."

"Wonderful," said Jane Louise. "Just my type."

"Erna schlepps him around like a battered suitcase," Sven said. "He looks like he's coming to pieces. He has one of those wrecked-boy faces those alcoholic Brits have. All yearning and wide-eyed and full of despair."

"Yum," said Jane Louise.

"He's actually very charming," Sven said. "I got drunk with him once when we published the Eskimo nookie book."

"He sounds perfectly delightful," Jane Louise said. "Does he have fancy luggage stickers from famous hotels plastered all over him or just tags from old Cunard boats?"

"Both," Sven said.

"Thank you for your input," said Jane Louise.

"Don't let him lean on you," Sven said. "He has that sort of 'Help me, I'm a helpless genius' appeal."

"Erna goes in for that sort of thing," Jane Louise said, although she was not entirely sure she was herself immune.

"She likes a large, slightly ruined object with a kind of raffish, masculine charm," Sven said.

Jane Louise gave Sven a long, thoughtful look.

"You ought to write for women's magazines, Sven," Jane Louise said. "You have a lot to impart to us gals."

"Women's magazines should write about *me*," Sven said. "See you round the campus."

Suddenly Erna, looking flushed and wearing a perfectly tailored old plaid suit, appeared with Hugh Oswald-Murphy in tow.

He was a large, florid, handsome, ruined man with a graying boy's haircut and eyes full of scrutiny and appeal. He walked right up to Jane Louise's desk and extended his great big paw.

"How d'you do, my dear?" he said. "You've been so frightfully nice about all these delays, Erna says. Oh, my!" he said, as Jane Louise stood up. "With child!"

"I guess you mean knocked up," said Jane Louise, giving him a dumb look. She figured that Hugh Oswald-Murphy was one of those men who respond well to a really dumb-appearing woman.

"Children," he said. His voice was loud and low, like a bear growl. "How angelic. Such darling creatures. Have hundreds!" he said. "I do."

"Gee," Jane Louise said. "Really? Hundreds?"

"Eight," he said.

"How many mothers?" Jane Louise said.

"Now, Jane," Erna said.

"A fair question, Erna," Hugh said. "Five."

"Gosh," Jane Louise said. "Five. It makes me feel quite humble."

Hugh Oswald-Murphy gave her a look of reappraisal.

"This young woman is having me on, Erna," he said.

"She's not as dumb as she looks," Erna said.

Jane Louise felt that some day it would be enjoyable to kill Erna, right on the street, in some morbid, painful, and very humiliating way.

"She doesn't look dumb a bit," Hugh Oswald-Murphy said.

Jane Louise had been called many things in her life, but never dumb. She gazed with hatred at Erna, who was almost panting. It was sad to see someone in such obvious throes of sex longing, although Hugh Oswald-Murphy did not appear to Jane Louise as much of a worthy sex object. He was too visibly self-concerned, self-referential, and self-absorbed. Even Sven, who was nothing more than an arrow waiting to be shot, was probably capable of some state of thrill or thrall, although love and transformation were doubtless not in his emotional vocabulary.

One of the things Jane Louise most loved about going to bed with her husband was the total change in his aspect. Gone from his features was what she called "the Marshallsville Face," that pleasant visage he turned to the world to protect himself and make himself invisible. In her arms he was rapt, impassioned, ardent, hungry, and given over to feeling. He longed for her and made it clear. It melted her to see him in this condition: She was addicted to it. That she could work this change on him and make him happy gave her more than hope. It thrilled her and made her wonder if people really did have some deep center and if the soul of another did not necessarily, as Chekhov says, lie in darkness. She hoped that deep might actually call to deep in this internal way. It lightened her darkness. She had never felt this with another soul. She did not feel that if you went to bed with someone like Hugh Oswald-Murphy you would find anything more than the person now sitting in a chair across from her.

"I was thinking," said Hugh Oswald-Murphy, "that this charming young woman and I might have a chat about the type and the photos, Erna, and then we might all go out and have a bite."

"Yes," said Jane Louise dreamily. "A bite."

Hugh Oswald-Murphy gave her a curious stare, as if she might actually be thinking of biting him. Jane Louise flushed. These days a drowsy languor overtook her, as if the physical processes of her pregnant body had thrown a kind of warm scarf over her. She longed constantly for her bed—not to be in it, but on it, surrounded by clean pillows and wrapped in her down comforter.

"I can't have lunch," Erna said. "There's a board meeting."

"I would have thought that would be quite unnecessary," Hugh said. "Now that Hamish has finally caved in and off-loaded this lovely place to those loathsome toad compatriots of mine."

The words *loathsome toad compatriots of mine* floated past Jane Louise's brain.

"Oh," she said, "did Hamish sell?"

"Oh, Hugh. You shithead," Erna said.

"I'm frightfully sorry," Hugh said. "I had no idea this was still hush-hush. Pretend you never heard a thing."

"I heard a thing," Jane Louise said. "What gives?"

"I'm not at liberty to say," said Erna, with a preening expression.

Jane Louise felt a red curtain of rage flap over her eyes.

"This affects my livelihood," she said to Erna. "I'm pregnant, and my husband is not a political adviser. He's a plant chemist in a tiny firm. You tell me right now, Erna, or I'll hurt you."

"Good gracious," said Hugh.

"Calm down, Jane," Erna said.

"I won't," said Jane Louise. Her voice was definitely menacing, a tone she had never heard before. She suddenly felt a wave of protectiveness. This was the tiger aspect of impending motherhood.

"It's all very well for you to have inside dope," Jane Louise said. "Nothing's going to happen to *you*."

At that moment, Sven ambled in. "Well, well, a family huddle," he said. "Hello, Hugh."

"Michaelson," said Hugh. "Very good to see you."

"Sven," Jane Louise said. "Have you been keeping from me that Hamish has sold?"

"I just heard this morning that it's final," Sven said. "At least they're publishing people and not in kitchen appliances. But Erna knows all, don't you, Erna?"

"She's not telling," Jane Louise said. "You'll have to beat it out of her."

A speculative look came over Sven's features. What a pane of glass he was! You could tell he was thinking what it might be like to smack Erna around.

"Get out the electrodes, Janey. Let's torture her."

Erna sat down. She had the manner of a teacher telling serious news to a class of preschoolers.

"It's the Primrose Group," she said. "They own publishing companies in Britain."

"Some of which they've *ruined*," Hugh put in cheerfully.

"Do shut up, Hugh," Erna said. "They own publishers in Britain, Canada, and Australia, and a lot of magazines, and they want to be a presence here. Hamish will have a ten-year contract. We'll all be safe. They like us as we are."

"They like us as we are," Sven said. "They love us for ourselves. Isn't that sweet of them?"

"Don't be so cynical, Sven," Erna said.

"I'm not cynical. I'm realistic. I know that 'they like us as we are' means cheap binding from here on in."

"Two-color jackets," Jane Louise said.

"Really, I feel this is very inappropriate in front of an author," Erna said.

"Oh, don't mind me," Hugh Oswald-Murphy said. "I've been through this. My first book got caught in a takeover. That's when dear Erna rescued me and gave me that nice contract with the production clause."

"Production clause?" Sven said.

"It only means a sewn binding," Erna said demurely.

Sven groaned. "I'm going to have to find some early-nineteenth-century printer to sew it, Erna. Nobody sews anymore."

"They do!" Erna said primly. "It just costs more each book."

"Does this man agree to a reduction in royalties?" Sven said. "To cover the cost of sewing his book?"

"Hugh feels his books will last and ought not to fall apart when a reader of the future opens them," Erna said.

"Any writer would feel that way," Hugh said.

"I myself love notch binding," Jane Louise said. "If Erna and Sven would get out of here, I would show you the beauty of it. They cut little notches in the signature and glue it in. It's very elegant."

Hugh peered at her, a little hungrily, she felt. Erna looked agitated, the way she always looked after a few minutes with Sven. She looked as if she would like to have picked him up by the scruff of the neck, clenched in her teeth like a mother cat, and hauled him away somewhere. Sven, on the other hand, regarded her as an out-of-control, neurotic, runaway horse who needed expert handling. Jane Louise said she would be very happy to see their taillights and asked them both to leave.

"Marvelous woman," said Hugh as Erna closed the door. "All those children. That husband. This job."

"All those children. That husband. This job," repeated Jane Louise. "Yes, it's amazing. How does she do it?"

She looked into Hugh Oswald-Murphy's face. He was very large. His enormous head sat between two immense shoulders. You felt that had he been stripped of flesh, two medium-size women could have played gin rummy in his rib cage. His very face was enormous, and he had a big, mobile mouth with lots and lots of teeth. Jane Louise tried to imagine him eating and then stopped. At the moment, life seemed quite out of proportion. He was not that huge, and yet Jane Louise visualized him as rather a Gargantua, or Gulliver amongst the Lilliputians, nibbling on what to a normal person would be an entire side of beef. He gave her an appealing look, rather in the direction of her bra.

"Hey," she said. "Snap out of it."

"I do think, my dear, that you ought to have a little more respect for a famous writer."

"Really?" said Jane Louise. "Well, I think you ought to have a little more respect for the person who's going to design your book."

"My God, you're a snarky young person," Hugh Oswald-Murphy said.

"I am not young," Jane Louise said. "I'm old and I'm pregnant and I can say anything I want."

"You're not that old, my dear," Hugh said. "I was a very late baby. My mother was nearer to fifty than forty when I appeared. Oh, the power of women! Their internal depth. Their inner space. That procreative fire."

"It beats all hell out of me how we do it," Jane Louise said. "Frankly, I'm exhausted."

"And yet never used up," Hugh said, dreamily. Jane Louise wondered if he was drunk. "The replenishing source. The *ewig weibliche*."

"Oh that," Jane Louise said, trying to remember if this was some term from literary criticism or Nazism. "The Eternal Feminine."

"That's it in a nutshell," Hugh said enthusiastically. This was clearly a favorite topic.

Jane Louise wondered if she brought this sort of thing out in men, or if all men were really like this deep down inside and she was a kindly soul who didn't mind listening to them endlessly rabbit on about these things, or if she simply didn't know any normal men who dreamed about going fishing and did not fill up their minds with mush about the *ewig weibliche*.

But, on the other hand, it really *was* sort of amazing, all this procreative fire. The intricacy of all those dividing cells and chromosomal patterns, to say nothing of hormonal changes. When you were pregnant, your bones got softer in order to ensure a proper birth situation. This *was* a neat trick, especially when you were totally unaware of it. So maybe it was right and proper that men should be in awe of it. It was fairly awesome.

"One of my wives is an Eskimo," Hugh was saying, and Jane Louise realized that minutes had gone by and she had been in a daze. "Amazing people, really, when you come to think of it. A beautiful person and the mother of my son, Anguuleek."

"Uh-huh," Jane Louise said. "Hugh, don't you think we ought to have our nice little chat about the design of your book?"

"Of course, of course," Hugh said. He mopped his brow with a large yellow-and-red plaid handkerchief.

"Gee, that's pretty," Jane Louise said. "Where'd you get it?"

"Bradbury Hatters in London," Hugh said. "I'll send you a dozen. Is it hot in here?"

"It's procreative fire," Jane Louise said. "It gets the thermostat all out of whack. Now sit very quietly, Hugh, and I'll show you these sample pages. And then I want you very quietly to accept every little thing."

He gave her another unfocused look, and she knew he was not going to give her one single ounce of trouble. There was something to be said for the replenishing source. Before this minute she had had no idea how useful it could be in matters of business.

CHAPTER 28

After Christmas it became wet and sleety, and then it snowed. Teddy was at a conference in Germany, the headquarters of his company. Had he gone in for petrochemicals he could have avoided spending his life worrying about money, just as Jane Louise had missed her big chance to get into corporate graphic design, something in which she had no interest whatsoever. She liked book publishing and book design, and she was stuck with the sort of meager salary it brought her, just as Teddy loved to figure out the nontoxic, the noninvasive, the safe, and the benign. As a result, they never had very much money, and now that there would soon be three of them, their worry about money became more concrete.

Jane Louise lay under her down comforter, watching the snow-fall against the streetlight and reading Hugh Oswald-Murphy's Arctic masterpiece. She had now read it twice. On either side of her was a copy of Vilhjalmur Stefansson's *Arctic Manual* and Knud Rasmussen's *People of the Polar North,* which Mokie called *People of the Polish North.* She seemed to be unable to stop reading about snow houses, ice packs, seals, and people who left their elderly alone to starve when their number was up. This landscape, totally inhospitable and remote, held her in thrall. When Teddy had mentioned that someday when their unborn was a teen and if they had any money, they might take one of those Arctic tours, Jane Louise was horrified. "*Go* there?" she said. "Are you *kidding*? It's too cold!"

"Then why are you reading all this stuff?" he had asked, and Jane Louise had looked up from her nest of pillows, looking dewy and beautiful, and had given him a gaze of total confusion. "I don't know," she said.

She didn't know, except that in the Arctic no one worked for a publishing company that had just been sold, or for a small firm of do-good plant chemists who might go bankrupt at any minute. Furthermore, Jane Louise had a suspicion that her landlady, Mrs. Berger, was thinking of selling the building. This sort of thing did not happen in the Polar North.

The telephone rang her out of a doze. It was nine o'clock at night, and she could see that the sleety snow had turned into large, lacy flakes almost the size of Queen Anne's lace.

It was Teddy. "Hi," she said sleepily. "What time is it there?"

"It's afternoon and it's freezing. What's it doing there?"

"Beautiful snow," Jane Louise said. "Guess what? Hamish sold the press."

"Who to?"

"Bunch o' Brits," Jane Louise said. "I was very rude to Hugh Oswald-Murphy today."

"Good for you," Teddy said. "Did he behave?"

"I made him sit up and bark like a dog, and he was very good after that. How's the food?"

"Everything has talons or hooves," Teddy said. "These guys are very big on game with berries, and lots of meat for breakfast. I'm dying for a salad. Listen, things are not wonderful here."

"In what way?" Jane Louise said. A wave of anxiety was beginning to curl over her like a threatening wave.

"They may sell. They may refinance. They may go under. A Swiss company wants to buy them," Teddy said. "Anyway, there's a wage freeze."

"That's okay, isn't it?"

"No bonus," Teddy said.

"Well, that's okay, isn't it?"

"I was counting on it," Teddy said. "With the baby coming."

"It's all right," Jane Louise said. "We have insurance. We paid for the crib. It'll be all right, although Mrs. Berger has been nosing around."

"She's going to sell the building," Teddy said.

There was a long silence. The telephone was not Teddy's thing. He didn't much like being forced into a situation in which speech was necessary.

"It'll be okay," Jane Louise said. "She isn't going to sell it for a long time."

"You don't know that," Teddy said.

"Hey," Jane Louise said. "How about telling me how much you miss me, and we'll talk about our housing problems when you come home."

"I miss you," Teddy said.

"Well, I miss you," Jane Louise said. "Don't worry. We're not going to collapse."

These, of course, were the sort of consoling things Jane Louise often wished Teddy would say to her, but there was no reason in Teddy's mind to reassure Jane Louise that her dwelling space wasn't going to be sold out from under her, since Teddy had no way of knowing if this was going to happen or not, or when. He took things as they came and dealt with them, leaving Jane Louise in a state of anxiety.

It was hard for Teddy to believe her when she told him how anxious she often was. The Jane Louise he knew and loved was brazen. She had hopped right into bed with him and loved him from the first. She was open and aboveboard in her feelings: In fact, he thought of her as fearless. Furthermore, she was as snarky as Hugh Oswald-Murphy said she was, and she had never let any bully push her around.

Teddy was not romantic: He was direct. His hunger for Jane Louise was his testimony, his love letter, his poetry. In those moments she knew that for all his silence, he was hers.

Although she missed him, she admitted to herself that being pregnant and alone was very serene. In the mornings she lay in bed with her coffee and watched her unborn child cause her saucer to jiggle on her stomach.

She sighed and called up Edie. Teddy's call had made her lonesome.

"Mr. or Miss Edith Steinhaus," she began.

"Oh, shut up," Edie said. "I hate my husband."

"Trouble?" said Jane Louise.

"I love him, and he works hard," Edie said. "But I'm telling you, his mama treated him like an African prince. Did I tell you about the test shoe?"

"You didn't," Jane Louise said. "Is it funny?"

"It's tragic," Edie said. "I found one of Mokie's great big shoes in the bathroom, kicked behind the hamper. The other is missing, which is just as well because they're the sneakers with the holes in them that he wore to paint your mother-in-law's shed. Anyway, I put the sneaker on the top of the hamper, and it's been there for *six weeks!*"

"Cute," Jane Louise said. "Teddy's very neat, but only with his stuff. I could leave my coat lying on the floor for a year, and he would never pick it up because it's mine."

"It's because they don't see it."

"What is it about guys, anyway?" Jane Louise said. "Do you think they'll clean up after the babies?"

"Until the babies are five," Edie said. "Then we'll have to clean up after both of them."

"It's too bad we can't run away," Jane Louise said. "This is our last chance."

"It's too cold," Edie said. "I'm too tired."

"I'm exhausted," Jane Louise said. "Sometimes I feel as if I can barely crawl, and sometimes I feel I could leap over tall buildings with a single bound."

"Me, too," yawned Edie.

"Do you suppose our babies will grow up and hate us?"

"I don't see why," Edie said. "We're so terribly nice. We're so much nicer, more enlightened, and more self-examined than our mothers."

"Our mothers," Jane Louise said. "You know, the truth is, I never believe it when people tell me they liked their mothers. I always think to myself: You think you do. And now I'm going to be one myself, and I have no faith whatever that this unborn person will turn fifteen and not hate me."

"Mokie says we can't call a girl Ernestine," Edie said. "After his great-grandfather. I myself love it."

"Teddy says we can't call a boy Felix, after no one," Jane Louise said. "He says he'll get beaten up in school."

"We won't send them to that kind of school," Edie said. "We'll send them to a school where the name Felix will be honored."

"Edie," Jane Louise said. "Does Mokie ever reassure you that everything will be okay?"

"Don't be ridiculous," Edie said. "He knows everything will *not* be okay. His way of being reassuring is that he doesn't really care one way or another."

Jane Louise sighed. She was so tired she felt she would not even be able to crawl underneath her sheets.

"I'm fading," she said to Edie.

Edie said: "I hate to tell you, but I slept through most of this conversation, not that I don't find you extremely fascinating."

"See you in the future," said Jane Louise.

"In the Fullness of Time," said Edie, and they hung up.

CHAPTER 29

The baby, whoever it was in there, was now making itself known. In the bath Jane Louise saw what she thought were elbow-shaped bulges in her stomach. She felt her baby swimming and kicking and generally horsing around. It was the oddest and most bizarre sensation she had ever felt. Edie said she felt as if she were running the gymnasium of inner space. Her unborn liked to work out right before she went to sleep.

"Of course, I never sleep anymore," she said to Jane Louise one Saturday afternoon over lunch.

"Apparently we'll never sleep again," Jane Louise said. "Unless we get one of those gizmos that sounds like your heart."

"Her new toy arrived," Edie said of Mrs. Teagarden. "The one that replicates the birth environment. She played it for me. It sounds like being at the beach."

"I thought her child was about two," Jane Louise said.

"She says she likes to remind this child, whatever its name is, of what it was like inside. She feels it's an aid to bonding and that he or she will love her better for it. And also be so appreciative of the enormous birthday party they're having for it. They had Mokie over there the other night. They're searching for a theme, but they feel they haven't come up with quite the right thing yet."

"Oh, yeah? What did they reject?"

"Well, they thought birds might be a nice thing. They got a real Audubon for his or her room."

"What a nice present for a two-year-old," Jane Louise said. "I wish I were two."

"Then they thought they might have live doves, but then they were afraid they would shit all over their priceless curtains."

"To say nothing of the children," Jane Louise said.

"They didn't seem overly concerned about that," Edie said. "It's cheaper to clean a child than a curtain. They think they might buy a parrot because they live so long, he or she can have it all his life and take it to college, but then they thought parrots might bite small children, and they couldn't get one of those falconer's gloves in a small size and if the parrot wanted to sit on his arm, or her arm, it might hurt him or her with its claws."

"This woman thinks of everything!" Jane Louise said. "I'm so impressed. Falconer's gloves for children! Why don't we manufacture some and make a million dollars?"

"Now they're thinking trains," Edie said.

"It's hard to get one of those into your apartment," Jane Louise said.

"They may buy one of those child-size ones and put it in the room, and he or she can ride on it."

"Our children will be poor," Jane Louise said.

"They will be rich in values," Edie said.

"Oh, screw that!" Jane Louise said. "I want money."

"We all want money," Edie said. "One of these days Mokie is going to tell me how sick he is of catering and that he either wants to open a restaurant or go to divinity school, in which case we'll be totally broke. Honest, Janey, I don't think I can go on making five-tiered medieval cakes for these ghastly people."

"One of these days I'm going to be out of a job," Jane Louise said. "They'll hire one powerhouse to do all the design and get rid of me, probably while I'm on maternity leave, or they'll free-lance everything out, and I'll get a little job once in a while, and all those nice health benefits will vanish off the face of the earth, and Teddy's company will be sold."

"A pair of cheerful mothers-to-be," Edie said. "Mokie seems pretty cheerful for the moment."

"Teddy's cooking something up," Jane Louise said. "I can feel it. There's a small company right outside of West Minton that's only twenty-five minutes from Marshallsville. It's all about alter-native pesticides and household stuff. They've been nosing around him."

"Does that mean you'd live there?" Edie asked.

"It's something to think about."

"All right, Janey," Edie said. "Then we all have to think about it. We could open up a catering in Primrose Hill and do some-thing nice for all those rich matrons and their prep-school daugh-ters."

"And I could do design for the local paper. Wouldn't it be swell?"

"It would be something," Edie said. "It's unclear what."

"Edie," said Jane Louise. "Do you think we ever knew for one second what our lives would be like?"

"When I was little I felt certain that we would be in Mar-shallsville every summer," Edie said. "That's about it."

"How lucky you are," Jane Louise said. "I don't think I ever knew, and now it's worse—the whole world is going to change. I don't know what's what, and we don't have any money."

"Darling," Edie said. "We have each other."

"Yes, but when your parents do the right thing, you'll inherit, and I won't, because the only money my mother has is Charlie's, and he has three children."

"My parents are pretty young as parents go," Edie said. "You know what top shape they're in, what with skiing and sailing. And as for your mama, Charlie will predecease her, and you *will* inherit."

"I guess I ought to shut up," Jane Louise said. "This kind of agitation isn't probably any good for the unborn."

"It isn't great for the born, either," Edie said.

They were sitting in their favorite restaurant, a little Pakistani hole-in-the-wall with extremely fiery food. Both of them seemed to crave the hottest food they could find. The restaurant teemed with women in saris and babies in strollers. There were babies at almost every table being fed rice with a spoon, or being nursed while their mothers ate with their left hands, or they were half asleep in their buggies. There were a number of toddlers, whom Teddy referred to as "bipeds," walking around, several of whom found Jane Louise and Edie, with their fair skin and huge stomachs, totally irresistible.

"These mothers are young enough to be our daughters," Jane Louise said gloomily.

"Don't be ridiculous," Edie said. "Pass me some of that hot pickle."

"They're in their twenties," Jane Louise said. "Look at them."

"I'm looking. Who cares?"

"I care," Jane Louise said. "Poor Teddy. The guy married the president of the Withered Crone Society, who gets knocked up in her later years."

"I don't mean to be indelicate," Edie said, "but as you know, you decided to get pregnant and probably did on the first try."

"One shot to the moon," Jane Louise said.

"Not withered-crone behavior. Janey, will you cheer up, or do you think this is hormonal? You're a few weeks ahead of me. Is this what I have to look forward to?"

"Certainly not," Jane Louise said. "You're self-employed. Your company can't be sold."

"Yes, but," Edie said. "At least *your* baby has dropped, and you can breathe. I still have the stuffed nose of pregnancy, and this kid is pressing against my diaphragm. It must be nice to breathe again."

"Mine is sitting on my pelvic bone," Jane Louise said. "I feel so weird. It's like going into a dark wood. I'm scared."

"It's part of the process," Edie said.

"I guess I'll get over it," Jane Louise said. "By summer we'll be pushing these babies around in a conveyance."

Two weeks later Miranda Elizabeth Parker was born, and three weeks after that, Aaron Talbot Frazier, nicknamed Tallie, appeared on the scene, to the intense relief and exaltation of their exhausted mothers.

PART IV

CHAPTER 30

Motherhood is a storm, a seizure: It is like weather. Nights of high wind followed by calm mornings of dense fog or brilliant sunshine that gives way to tropical rain, or blinding snow. Jane Louise and Edie found themselves swept away, cast ashore, washed overboard. It was hard to keep anything straight. The days seemed to congeal like rubber cement, although moments stood out in clearest, starkest brilliance. You might string these together on the charm bracelet of your memory if you could keep your eyes open long enough to remember anything. Jane Louise had found herself asleep standing at her kitchen counter, and Edie reported that she had passed out on a park bench.

It was perfectly clear to Jane Louise, as soon as she held her baby in her arms, that she was not going to hire a nanny and go to work full-time when Miranda was three months old. It seemed to her that once you got your hands on these babies, you could not tear yourself away from them. She knew that the best thing she would be able to muster was some part-time arrangement. This made her feel torn in half. On the one hand, she and Teddy

225

needed the money, and Jane Louise did love to work. On the other hand, she was overcome and brought to her knees by what she felt for this tiny pink creature with her slaty, unfocused blue eyes. Perhaps it was raging hormones, but the depth of this love knocked Jane Louise out. She knew that she was not going anywhere for some time.

Naturally, as soon as Jane Louise felt she was up to being seen, Sven demanded an audience. He was preceded by Adele, who came bearing a little blanket knitted by her mother.

"Sven wants to see you," Adele said. "He really wants to. He seemed so excited about the baby."

"He wants to come and watch me nurse," Jane Louise said. "I know him."

"Well, of course," Adele said. "But he really got sort of gooey."

Jane Louise gazed at Adele, who was holding Miranda on her lap. Adele had dozens of nieces and nephews: She came from an enormous family with four brothers and three sisters. Therefore she was an old hand at babies. She did not come from the world of sex and romance but from the realms of family and stability. Her fiancé, Phil, was a perfectly nice person, yet it was not clear to Jane Louise whether he and Adele, who had been together since high school, slept together. It probably didn't matter a single whit. Adele and Phil would get married at Saint Patrick's Cathedral. She would wear a real white bride's dress. Their joint bank account would be appropriately safe. Her huge number of relatives would pour forth checks, small and medium-size, to get the young couple started. Passion did not really figure in all this, or if it did, it was of a lesser order compared to such things as family compatibility.

———

When Sven finally appeared, bringing a highly appropriate baby garment, Jane Louise ran this past him. Sven blinked his eyes, clearly wondering why anyone would have spent time considering Adele.

"Why would I ever think about her?" he asked.

"Because she is a fellow citizen and crawls around on the earth with the rest of us, Sven."

"Not with me," Sven said. "I don't have much of a taste for my species. I don't like the idea of crawling around on the earth with my fellow citizens. I can never keep her straight. She's a girl, right? She's getting married or something, right? She's my secretary, right?"

Jane Louise knew that people who held no attraction for Sven barely existed for him. He had two strategies for people who did: He either conquered them, or he came very close up to them and read their minds. Jane Louise had been rather terrified of the appropriate baby garment and asked Sven if Edwina had picked it out.

"I know a thing or two about baby clothes," Sven said. "Women don't know everything. Now, when is this baby going to wake up so I can check her out?"

"What exactly were you going to check out, Sven?"

"Oh, this and that," Sven said. "Number of fingers and toes, various configurations. Having a girl child is—" he broke off suddenly.

"Would you like to say what it is, Sven?"

"Not in front of *you,* Janey. You're much too prim."

Sven was wearing a pair of twill trousers and a blue-and-white-striped shirt. Jane Louise hardly knew what she was wearing: an old pair of jeans and a faded black T-shirt. Sven remarked that she appeared to have lost all her baby weight, and this was true. Both she and Edie had turned right back into beanpoles after a few weeks. Sven sat perched on the edge of his chair, his ear cocked for baby noises.

"So, Sven, why don't you tell me anything about the office?" Jane Louise said. "Or do you think that now I've had a baby my brain has turned into rice pudding?"

"There's nothing about the office," Sven said. "It's the same old same old. We'll just have to wait, but for now everything seems dandy."

Jane Louise looked glum. "When I come back will my office be bricked up? Or do you suppose they'll cut me during my maternity leave?"

"I thought you wanted to work part-time," Sven said.

"I guess I've lost my nice, sunny office," Jane Louise said.

"You'll have to share it with Peggy Resnick," Sven said. "It's only fair. You'll both be part-time. Besides, she doesn't take up much room."

Urgent baby squeals were suddenly heard. Sven's face brightened.

"So there really is a baby," he said. "Go fetch it."

His voice took on an intimate, caressing tone. Outside the sky was gray, and sleet occasionally clattered against the window. Inside it was warm and steamy. When Jane Louise returned with Miranda in her arms, Sven was settled comfortably on the sofa, waiting. Miranda began to squirm and fidget, and Jane Louise slipped her under her shirt.

"Just shut up in advance, Sven," Jane Louise said.

"I wasn't intending to say a word," Sven said. He sat comfortably in his chair and didn't utter a word. Jane Louise found his silence far more alarming than any comment he might have made. She could not read the expression on his face.

After a while, when she could stand it no longer, she said: "Has Dita married her Frenchman yet?"

"Ah, the beautiful former Mrs. Samuelovich," Sven said. "We are but flyspecks on her magnificent radar screen. Last heard she had finally divorced Nick, and it seems that she and her frog are one."

Jane Louise studied him. For the merest instant she thought she saw a look of true pain cross his features, but it might simply have been a leg cramp.

"She left us both in the dust," Jane Louise said. "She never even told me she was leaving."

"It was amazing," Sven said. "Little things always meant so little to her. I was sort of surprised when you two got friendly like that."

"I loved her. I thought she loved me," Jane Louise said. "Isn't that weird?"

"It's part of her charm," Sven said. "We all think our little Dita loved us. We see her for an instant, and then she vanishes. Maybe you knew too much or were about to find out."

"I didn't know anything," Jane Louise said. "Although she certainly had Grand Canyon–size emotions."

"She doesn't like those to be seen," Sven said. "She'll be so much happier living in the French language. Did you know that stutterers don't stutter in newly acquired languages? Not until they become fluent. Are you finished with that baby? I'd like her for a moment, if you don't mind."

Sven, without another word, took Miranda from Jane Louise's arms and set her on his shoulder.

"You'd better take this cloth," Jane Louise said. "She enjoys puking on quality shirts."

Sven took the cloth and rested Miranda's little head on it. It was hard to imagine what he was thinking. The room seemed suddenly very hot to Jane Louise.

Gently he stroked Miranda's back. "I haven't burped a baby in years," he said.

"I didn't peg you for a burping sort of guy," Jane Louise said.

"Isn't is strange, little Janey, that we all start out this way?" Sven said. "And look where we end up. Even Mrs. Samuelovich was a sweet little baby when she was a baby. This little baby's destiny will unfold right in front of us."

This thought brought stinging tears to Jane Louise's eyes. She gave Sven a steely look.

"Perhaps I ought to hire you as her nurse," Jane Louise said. "You seem very interested, and you're not bad at burping."

"I am the father of many," Sven said smugly.

"Several of whom you see once a year," Jane Louise said.

"I see motherhood has not made you any less good natured," Sven said. "Although you certainly are besotted. You might look at *me* for a minute."

"I am good natured," Jane Louise said. "I have one of the pleasantest little dispositions you'll ever find on an anxious person. I just like to see things as they are."

"And what is it you see?"

"Listen, Sven. You'll never be a mother. You guys can cut loose any time you want. You don't have to spend your days worrying about whether or not you're a good father. You have to worry about paying their school bills. You don't have to provide them with an appropriate home, a well-run household, decent cheer, religious upbringing, enjoyable holidays. The burden of their psychological development is not on your shoulder, so don't get smug with me."

"My, my," Sven said. "Touchy."

"Having a baby does that to you," Jane Louise said.

That afternoon the babies were napping in Miranda's crib, an accomplishment their mothers felt was a kind of miracle. It was the first time they had managed to get both asleep at the same time. They sat on Jane Louise's couch, on opposite ends, drinking decaffeinated coffee. Edie yawned.

"I'd love a cup of real coffee," she said. "But why should I feed him caffeine? He never sleeps as it is."

"He sleeps a little," Jane Louise said.

"I ought to hate you," Edie said. "Because Miranda sleeps through the night."

"Yes, darling," said Jane Louise, "if you consider eleven o'clock at night till four in the morning sleeping through the night. Oh, sleep! Don't you remember how wonderful it used to feel?"

"No," said Edie. "I'm too tired."

"Someday," Jane Louise said, "they'll be fifteen years old. Just think of it."

"You think of it," Edie said. "We'll be up all night wondering where they are. Then they'll be sixteen, and we'll lie in bed all night wondering if they cracked up the car. Then they'll be twenty, and we'll lie in bed terrified that they're taking drugs."

"Well, most of the people we knew did, and look at them now," said Jane Louise. "Didn't you tell me that Mrs. Teagarden wanted to give an old-fashioned hash party?"

"You look at them," Edie said glumly. "Oh, Christ. I'll never have a decent night's sleep for the rest of my life."

"Oh, well," Jane Louise said. "Anyone can sleep."

"Perhaps we're so old that our cells are way past the regeneration point, so maybe it doesn't matter if we never sleep again, since we probably don't have any cells left to repair."

"Hey," said Jane Louise, "why don't we just pass out quietly on the sofa while our little babies sleep?"

"Because they'll only wake up," Edie said. "Besides, I'm too tired."

"Sven was here today," Jane Louise said.

"Oh, yeah?" Edie said. "I bet he got an eyeful."

"Miranda and I were extremely discreet," Jane Louise said. "He just sat here very quietly for a long time. It sort of freaked me out."

"He just sat around and didn't speak?"

"I tell you, Edie. That guy scares me. He just sat here staring. He made me feel as if we had just gotten out of bed."

"I'm sorry, Mrs. Parker. You've left something out. I don't quite catch."

"Unspeakable intimacy," Jane Louise said. "You know, I've known him a long time. He told Adele that when women have babies they cross over some sacred line and change. And I felt he was sitting around observing me to see what I was like now."

Edie yawned. "I'm sure when he says change he's referring to our internal organs," she said.

"Maybe he does," Jane Louise said. "Maybe we've changed forever."

"There's no maybe," Edie said. "We have."

CHAPTER 31

The spring unfolded in a blur. Jane Louise woke up one morning to realize that the leaves had budded out on the trees. Miranda was now a baby, pink, round, and smiling. She began to coo and drool, a sign of eventual teething and talking.

A baby who talked! A baby with teeth! In the park Jane Louise saw mothers with toddlers. Next to her neat baby, they looked unformed and sloppy wearing an array of green, turquoise, scarlet, and dark yellow baby garments with T-shirts of purple, lime green, and hot pink. Now that Miranda could hold her head up, Jane Louise carried her around in a side pack.

Her darling baby wore a bright orange shirt and a pair of purple overalls with yellow stripes. Jane Louise wore green sandals, yellow shirt, and an azure-colored skirt. She had tied her lank hair back with azure ribbon. Miranda's hair stood straight up on her head.

She and Edie made quite a sight as they ambled around town, their napping babes in tow, looking for a place to sit and have coffee.

"Her first word will be cappuccino," Jane Louise said. "I'm too old for this. Other moms seem to be able to go for hours without constant infusions of caffeine."

"They have those pump devices," Edie said. "Hidden in their expensive handbags. It pours caffeine into their systems intravenously."

"Guess what?" Jane Louise said. "I finally got the Hugh Oswald-Murphy book finished, and he wants to take me for lunch this week."

"Shall I baby-sit?" Edie said.

"No," said Jane Louise. "He claims he has dozens of children. Miranda is very well behaved. I'm taking her with me."

Once a week Jane Louise went to her office, which she now shared with the impressively neat Peggy Resnick, who became extremely uneasy at the sight of Jane Louise and her baby. Peggy had taken a fairly commodious workspace and sat at it as if she were a tiny mouse. Her memos were handwritten in tiny, precise, crabbed script. Her own daughter was in college.

"They're so much nicer when they can talk," Peggy said.

"I think they're kind of nice now," Jane Louise said.

"You'll see," Peggy said. "You'll see."

On the day of her lunch with Hugh Oswald-Murphy, she put on a skimpy gray dress and a red jacket and decked Miranda out in fuchsia and olive. She found Hugh in her office, sweating slightly and wearing a rattled expression. "Two for lunch," he shouted into the telephone.

"And one baby," Jane Louise said.

"And one baby," Hugh said into the receiver. Jane Louise could hear squawking on the other end of the line.

Hugh turned to Jane Louise. "This woman wants to know will the baby cry."

"Tell her we'll stuff a sock down its throat," said Jane Louise.

"The mother says the baby will be muzzled," Hugh said. "No, madame, I assure you that was said in jest. This baby is extremely well behaved."

"It's a mute," Jane Louise said.

"It's a mute," Hugh said. "I do hope you don't have a no-baby policy, since we intend to spend an enormous amount of money."

He turned to Jane Louise. "She says dogs are allowed in handbags, but she's checking about babies."

"Tell her I'll put the baby in *my* handbag."

"Yes, yes," Hugh said into the phone. "Very good. Excellent. Thanks awfully." He turned to Jane Louise. "She says they don't really want babies, but it's okay."

"I hate other people," said Jane Louise.

Miranda sat on Jane Louise's lap during lunch, drooling happily and playing with the silverware. Hugh Oswald-Murphy ate in huge gusts, after which he stopped abruptly. Jane Louise, who was more along the lines of a delicate eater, watched him with interest. When he stopped, he fixed Miranda with an intent look and wagged his huge eyebrows at her. Since this made her giggle, he did it fairly often. Then he described Eskimo food.

"Now," he said. "*Giviak.* In bird season you spread nets and catch hundreds of birds, and what you don't eat on the spot you stuff with berries, and then you cram them into a seal bladder with lots of seal blubber, and then you bury it in your cache and let it mellow for a number of months."

Jane Louise looked at him with a kind of naked horror.

"What about the feathers?" she said.

"You eat them, too. It's rather delicious, my dear girl. Like artichokes. Explorers must not be ethnocentric."

"I'll try to keep that in mind."

"Your baby," Hugh said. "Your baby is very intelligent. She is also beautifully formed. Her fingers are quite long. She will be very tall. Is her father also tall?"

"Her father is a little taller than I am," Jane Louise said. "He has a beautiful disposition."

"Hmmm," Hugh Oswald-Murphy said. "Really, an excellent baby. I do love them—so small, so sweetly smelling, so fresh."

He went on at great length in this way. Jane Louise was reminded of his descriptions of musk-oxen, which she had found somewhat over the top. She felt a pleasant, dreamy warmth and realized that it was the result of hearing her baby praised. She put her lips to her baby's head and sniffed her warm, fragrant baby smell and rubbed her cheek against her small, hot, velvety head.

"The Eskimos are marvelous with children," Hugh was saying. "They are about the nicest babies in the world. Some nurse till they are four and will nurse from other mothers."

"Gee," Jane Louise said. She felt as if she were underwater. The things men said to one! Especially one who had only recently had a baby. You would have thought they would talk about money, the future, the appropriate type of schooling, and so forth, but instead they seemed to like to talk about such things as nursing and burping.

As they ate, a thin woman who seemed to be the maître d' buzzed by them. She had a heavy French accent, short hair, and the aspect of a whippet. The sight of Miranda seemed to make her nervous. Her eyes darted around the room and then back to the baby, as if the baby were some strange and awful thing that ought to have been concealed.

"Everything is all right, yes?" she asked.

"Everything is splendid!" boomed Hugh. "Such a nice place to bring a baby."

"Zis is your baby, yes?"

"This is my baby, no. The baby belongs to this enchanting young woman. But I would be proud if this were *my* baby. This baby is beautiful, intelligent, and beautifully behaved, don't you think?"

The woman's cheeks flushed, and she turned away in what seemed to be a combination of embarrassment and dread.

"Don't you think it's weird how much people hate babies?" Jane Louise said.

"This is not a baby-friendly culture," Hugh said. "But don't you remember before you entered your breeding years what a nuisance they were? Coming into restaurants and shrieking? Having one sitting behind you at the cinema yakking or yelling?"

"I don't think of myself as someone in my breeding years," Jane Louise said.

Hugh looked affrighted. "If you are breeding, my dear girl, then you are in your breeding years. How is the father taking this?"

"In a state of awe," Jane Louise said.

"Very appropriate," Hugh said. "Now, my oldest child is so old that when he was born, they didn't let fathers into the delivery room. It makes a big difference, to my mind. My youngest has just started school—a heroic little tyke. Very strong. And once a year I go up to Greenland to see my Eskimo son."

"And the others?" asked Jane Louise. "Aren't there dozens of others?"

"Five. Three in England and two in Argentina."

"How transcontinental," said Jane Louise.

"Quite," Hugh said. "Oh, look. Here comes that awful woman again."

"Everything is all right?" she asked.

"Madame," Hugh said. "Everything is perfectly lovely with us, but you seem troubled. Would you like to share your distress with us?"

"Zis baby when it cry."

"This baby has barely cooed," Hugh said. His voice was loud and cheerful. "This baby is a model baby. I personally feel, my dear woman, that this preoccupation of yours has to do with some deep, inner, psychic thing or other. Is there something you might like to reveal to us so we can understand this better?"

"We do not 'ave baby in this restaurant," the woman said.

"You do now," Jane Louise said. "And we made this reservation on the late side so that the place wouldn't be crowded. Now it's almost empty. Have you had complaints?"

"*Pas exactement,*" the woman whispered, and fled.

"A highly evolved urban type. Responsive only to things. No connection to the natural world. A person of the future," Hugh said. "Ah, for the Arctic wastes, those huge white spaces among which men are men and women are women."

"Aren't they men and women even near a fire hydrant, Hugh?"

"You know what I mean," Hugh said. "Anyone who has a baby understands elemental life."

He stared at Miranda, who had been given a tiny taste of Hugh's vanilla ice cream and had managed to get it all over her face.

"Yes," said Jane Louise. "Elemental life. It's highly elemental."

CHAPTER 32

The world had shrunk to the size of a pea, made up of such tiny things: the smell of a baby's feet, the fuzziness of its hard, hot little head, the amazing variety of expressions on its little face, the beguiling sounds it made. How it looked asleep in its crib, the intensity of its focus when it held something up in its hands to check it out, the way it wriggled with joy. These things were primal, vital, intoxicating. Here was a reality without peer through which Jane Louise felt she trudged, half beside herself with joy, half dead with exhaustion.

This life opened before her as if it had been a door, and when Jane Louise stepped through this door, it led into a secret room stuffed with a collection of strange objects, all of which produced odd, intense, and unexpected feelings.

These days Jane Louise read the morning paper after dinner and found herself half asleep on the couch. One night she found Teddy passed out at the other end. Their long legs were intertwined. He sat up with a start.

"Is it morning?" asked Jane Louise.

"It's nine-thirty," Teddy said.

"Hey," Jane Louise said. "Let's go dancing." She took off her socks and noticed that one was striped and one was polka-dotted. Had she worn two different socks all day? Of course, the only people she had seen all day were Miranda, who was too young to care, and Edie, who was too tired to notice.

Jane Louise's bony shoulders now ached constantly from hunching over a baby stroller or bending over to put a baby into a crib. There had been a time when she had gone bopping around town with only her money in her back pocket. Now she was a pack animal, battened down with diapers, blankets, changes of baby clothes, and bottles of water.

There were nights when she would happily have collapsed in a heap with her clothes on, but she was far too orderly to do that. Instead she laid her clothes on a chair, threw on her nightgown, and flung herself into bed.

Teddy said: "Mokie and I thought we would take the kids off your hands for a few hours on Saturday and give you and Edie a break."

Jane Louise had not been looking forward to having this conversation.

She instantly said: "But the weekends are our only time to be together."

Teddy said, "You say that every weekend, Janey. I have to prize my own child away from you. I can't even take her to the park without you having an anxiety attack."

"For God's sake, she's still nursing," Jane Louise said.

"Yes," said Teddy. "And she's also eating baby food. She can come out for an hour or two with her old man. I can't stand having this push-me-pull-you every time I want a little time alone with my own child. She is not exclusively yours. Besides, you *need* a break. You're wiped."

There was nothing Jane Louise could say. She had never had a baby-sitter, except at night after Miranda was already asleep. She did not have some nice woman to take Miranda to the park in the morning so she could get some work done: She got her work done while Miranda napped. She was so bound to her baby that she felt lost without her. What would she do with herself? She imagined Miranda out with Teddy and herself pacing around in the apartment like a caged cat, wondering where they were, what they were doing, picturing danger at every corner. She saw herself alone with the laundry folded, the dinner organized, waiting and waiting for them to come home, thinking that she would never see them again. She did not know how she could stand it. She began to cry.

Teddy propped himself on his elbow and regarded her. She hoped he would take her into his arms, but he didn't. He said: "Don't think I don't know how you feel. I do, but you have to know how I feel. You don't have exclusive rights. I'm her *father*. Do you think I would let anything bad happen to her? I arranged this all around you. You'll have Edie to calm you down, and I'll have Mokie to protect me from Tong warriors with guns, if they happen to come to the park. You really have to do this, Janey."

"I hope it rains," Jane Louise said. "Then you'll have to stay home."

Saturday was clear and sunny: a perfect May day. After the babies' lunch, Edie and Jane Louise left for their outing.

They walked to the corner and hailed a taxi. They had no idea where they were going.

"Do yoga breathing," Edie said. "Calm down."

"Why aren't *you* a nervous wreck?" Jane Louise said.

"I'm more of a slob," Edie said. "I worry about other things.

Miranda will be fine. It's you that misses her. She'll have a great time."

The driver looked around at them. "Do you two want to go someplace?" he said.

"We don't know," said Jane Louise. "Go south." She leaned back in her seat. On the one hand, it was thrilling to be free. On the other, she wanted to go home.

"Now, Janey," Edie said. "Take a deep breath and think lovely thoughts."

"The Chef's Bazaar," said Jane Louise. "The art supply store. The place that has the lamps with the paper shades. Or that place where what's her name got those beautiful red shoes. Isn't that lovely enough?"

"We could cruise some clothes," Edie said. "And then we can go to that new patisserie and have some coffee."

"Or we could go home!" said Jane Louise. "Besides, I don't have any money."

"Now, now," said Edie. "I'm supposed to keep you diverted and amused."

"Do you suppose everything is all right?" said Jane Louise.

"It is perfect and serene. The babies are on the swings. Then they will crawl around on the rat-poison-free grass. Then they will pass out, and Mokie and Teddy will read the sports page. You have to disconnect a little. You can love her wildly and not be so anxious."

"Uh-huh," said Jane Louise, who felt that her heart was not beating properly. "In Nigeria, babies ride on their mommies' backs until they're two."

"Don't waste a minute," Edie said. "Book your ticket now. Hey, driver! Let us out on this corner."

She took Jane Louise by the arm, and they went shopping. Edie bought an octagonal baking pan. Jane Louise bought some colored pencils. They ended up in a fancy baby clothing store where each bought a pair of tiny striped socks. Then they decided to go for a stroll, have coffee, and do nothing.

It was one of those gentle days in spring when the slight breeze has blown away the air pollution and the flowers are out on the ornamental cherry, crab apple, and mimosa trees. People smile at each other on the street and turn their faces up to the sun. Urban lovers wander arm in arm, drifting in and out of bookshops. At the outdoor cafés, people feed ice cream to their toddlers or sit happily, reading the Saturday paper. The doors to the shops are open. It is too mild for heat and too cool for air conditioning, the perfect weather for perambulating around a city.

A Tibetan monk in full saffron robes was walking down the street flanked by two well-dressed men. A man in a duck costume stood on the corner juggling what looked like eggs. At his feet was an open cigar box full of donations. Around the corner three Peruvians played flute, drum, and guitar. In front of the ceramic shop a beautiful redheaded girl was selling misshapen, multicol-ored teapots.

They strolled on. In the window of the patisserie they saw tiny boats made of short pastry filled with raspberry. Inside, people in wonderful-looking clothes sat at tiny tables, drinking cappuccino and talking intensely.

"Isn't the city ravishing?" Jane Louise said.

"I thought you were counting the minutes till you got to the country," Edie said.

"I am," said Jane Louise. "But sometimes, on days like this, you realize that you're living in a kind of treasure-house. I mean when you're not contemplating urban strife and social injustice."

"I'd like to contemplate these adorable hats," Edie said. "Look at that little charm-pot with the candy-striped ribbon."

"I think the one with the little cars hanging off it is very chic—

it's wearable sculpture," Jane Louise said. "Let's go find some-place to have our coffee outside. It's too nice to go in."

"This is really very nice," Jane Louise said. "It must be nice to have a baby and not be anxious, but I guess that only happens if you're rich."

"From my little bird perch as a caterer," Edie said, "what it looks like is, you bear children, and someone else raises them."

"Hmmm," said Jane Louise. "Tell more."

"They have huge living spaces, very neat," Edie said. "No baby toys around. They can have a house full of toddlers and never worry about their antique porcelain."

"How come?"

"Separate quarters for the children," Edie said. "They're also very big on stenciling. Many newborns have ABCs stenciled under the moldings on their wall so they can learn to read when they aren't sleeping."

"Timesaving," said Jane Louise.

"But don't think they don't have worries," Edie said. "They worry about lots of things. Out-of-season fruit and flowers are always a big worry."

"A vexing problem," Jane Louise said.

"Finding a source of unpasteurized cheese is another, and then, of course, there's always the agony of trying to find a conservato-rial cleaner who really does well by antique linen. Money does not buy everything, Janey."

"But *you* worry all the time," Jane Louise said. "Tell the truth."

"I have less imagination," Edie said. "You do art. I do food. I really and truly do not believe that someone is going to throw a bathtub out of a high window and that I'm going to be walking underneath it, but you do."

"Someone *might* throw a bathtub out a window. This is a big city. Anything could happen," Jane Louise said. "You just don't read the paper."

"I don't read the *lurid* parts of the paper. I don't worry about Tallie all the time. I think he'll be fine without me for a few hours."

"A few hours . . . " said Jane Louise.

"I'm not to bring you home before three-thirty," Edie said. "So let's get some more coffee. Oh, look! Speaking of things happening. Look down the street. Isn't that Sven?"

There, walking toward them, was Sven himself, his blond wife Edwina, and their little boy, Piers, who was five, a white-blond child with dark brown eyes. Piers was carrying a plastic sword with which he attempted to smack his mother, who wore impeccable clothes, a bright smile, and polished fingernails. Jane Louise was made to realize that she and Edie were wearing jeans, scuffed loafers, and that in certain lights the various baby stains on their blouses could easily be seen.

"Oh, Sven!" called Jane Louise. Sven spun around as if being seen with his family was some sort of naughty act.

"Ah, the young mothers," he said smoothly. "Edwina, come here and say hello to Jane Louise and her friend Edie." Edwina dragged her little boy over and said hello. Then Piers pulled her off down the street.

"How unusual to see you without your satellite," Sven said. "Where'd you stash the babies?"

"With their dads," Edie said.

"How nice for them," Sven said. "While you two laze away the time."

"We work hard," Jane Louise said.

"Hmmm," Sven said. He looked at Edie and Jane Louise in a

speculative way. The look on his face clearly said: I'll dump the wife and kid and we can go to a hotel. It was plain that he was seeing himself on a rumpled bed, surrounded by a pile of long limbs.

"Nice to see you together," he said. "And you, Janey. I haven't seen you since last week. The office is very tense these days. We need you."

"Your family is slipping away," Jane Louise said.

Sven gave her a hard look. "They tend to do that," he said. "Are you coming in next week? There's a huge amount of work. Oh, by the way, did you get a baronial-looking card from the former Mrs. Samuelovich?"

"We got a card and a little baby hat that's too small," Jane Louise said.

"I hope she's happy with her rich French bore," Sven said. "A nice change from a down-at-the-heels Russian bore!"

"I thought Nick was sort of funny," Jane Louise said.

"Really?" Sven said. "She didn't. I think little Mrs. Samuelovich had many interesting plans when she was married to him. What a girl." He looked at Jane Louise in a kind of sultry way. "You have baby marks on your shoulder," he said. "Drool—very attractive on you. You really must come in next week, Janey. I miss you."

This made Jane Louise's heart thump. How nice it would be if her life were seamless—if she were sealed, almost like a mummy, into what she ought to be: the wife and mother—a smooth, integrated being without strange feelings, loose ends, and no unwanted twinges of doubts of any kind.

"Your family has disappeared," Edie remarked to him.

"Oh, them," Sven said. He stared at Jane Louise and Edie. "Good-bye, girls," he said. "What an enchanting encounter."

"He's sort of a devil," Edie said.

"Yes, but he's my devil."

"It's amazing," Edie said. "He has a really and truly dirty look."

"But it isn't smutty," Jane Louise said. "There's nothing furtive about it. It's straight up front. He's some kind of elemental force with nothing mitigating it. It's pure sex. Sometimes I wish he would disappear and I wouldn't have to be reminded that although I am a happily married woman, my extremely weak flesh can still be made to creep."

"Huh," Edie said. "You want everything to be pure. You think everything ought to be just one way, and that if it isn't, it's wrong."

"Well, I do feel that," Jane Louise said. "I tell you, Edie, just when you believe you're turning into a drudge or a mindless dispenser of liquids, Sven comes around and lets a person know that there's only one thing really interesting after all. I hate to admit this about myself, but it cheers me up."

"Don't be so ridiculous. Motherhood swallows a person. The other day I went to talk to this corporate guy about a party, and I realized he was staring at me. I was wearing my big hat with the flowers on it. I was in ecstasy—all alone with a *grown-up!*"

"Life is too complicated," Jane Louise said. "I don't like to be complicated. It makes me nervous."

"It's been complicated, and you've been nervous, since the first day I ever met you," Edie said. "You've managed to have a pretty good time. Let's go home."

They walked for a while in the warm spring air, and then they parted. Both of them had errands to do. They had been instructed to go home and not meet the babies in the park—this was their afternoon off, after all.

Jane Louise walked slowly through Washington Square. All along the east side of the park were parents with little children.

There were children everywhere, like swarms of birds. On the west side college students held hands, and unsavory types attempted to sell drugs.

Her anxiety came and went in little waves. She felt curious and light-headed with nothing to carry.

It was nearing the end of the academic year. Everywhere she looked students were lugging boxes of books, clothes, and standing lamps out of their dorms. She stood on the sidewalk and watched a serious young boy haul two duffel bags into the trunk of his father's car and dash into a building. His father, a gray-haired man with a wide chest and a linen sports jacket, was loading the trunk. Jane Louise stood perfectly still, blinded by the sunny glare. Hazy light poured down around her.

Someday Miranda would grow up and go to college. Day would follow day: She would lose her baby teeth. Her adult teeth would come in. She would go to school, learn to read, go to high school, have boyfriends, leave home. To her amazement, Jane Louise found herself in tears. Her throat got hot, and tears poured down her cheeks. She felt powerless to brush them away or to move.

The gray-haired man walked past her, carrying a pair of suitcases. When he saw her, he stopped and set his cases down.

"Are you okay?" he said.

"I was just thinking about my child going to college," Jane Louise said.

"How old is your child?" the man asked gently.

"Just five months old," said Jane Louise, and she began to sob. "You must think I'm a nut."

The man looked at her thoughtfully. "When my kid went to sleep-away camp for the first time, I wanted to lie down in the driveway and eat dirt," he said.

Jane Louise looked up at him. He filled her vision entirely. The hazy sunshine swirled around them. She grabbed his wrist and kissed his hand. He was wearing a beautiful gold watch.

"Thank you," she said. "Oh, thank you."

Then she collected herself. The man picked up the suitcases.

"It'll be all right," he said. "You'll grow into it."

"Thank you," said Jane Louise again, and she began almost to run in the direction of home.

CHAPTER 33

At the end of June they went to Marshallsville. Eleanor had found
a crib at a rummage, which she put into a shady, underused room
at the back of the house near the guest room where Teddy and
Jane Louise slept in the ornamental bed. Jane Louise packed
one large case of crib blankets, bumpers, crib sheets, and stuffed
animals.

Teddy, who had bought a secondhand car from a colleague,
drove up one afternoon with Mokie, drove down again, and then
he and Jane Louise packed. They strapped Miranda into her
infant seat and took off. A few days later, Mokie, Edie, and Tallie
would appear to stay in the rented house of the appalling Paul
and Helene Schreck.

Jane Louise sat in the car looking out the window and dreaming. This would be her first summer as a mother. She would take
Miranda to the lake in the afternoon, when the sun was not so
fierce, and she would hold her tight and walk her into the water.
She would nurse Miranda in Eleanor's old rocking chair.

Having a baby in a small town made all the difference. She was no longer some transient friend of Edie's, or Eleanor's daughter-in-law: She was the mother of a child—a Marshallsville child. She had gained citizenship. People who had never spoken to her before now spoke to her: A baby provided a common language. If Jeanne Pugh at the hardware store had never said more than hello, she now quizzed Jane Louise on Miranda's development, and compared notes with her. People she barely knew now began to say things like: "Why don't you and Teddy start thinking about moving up here? Old Mrs. Burner's house is for sale, and the Phillips want to sell, and there's that nice house on the river—it's a little damp, but it has that view."

Down at the beach, the lifeguards—all college girls—greeted her warmly and cooed over Miranda. Late in the afternoon Peter, who was Miranda's godfather, would stop by, pluck her from Jane Louise, and dip her tenderly in the water. It often seemed to Jane Louise that this life, so orderly and well arranged, had parted just an inch and let her in.

Her companion on the beach was Teddy's godchild, Harriet, who said she did not want to be called Birdie anymore. She was now nine, still skinny, freckled, and somewhat clumsy, although Jane Louise could see that she would develop into a great beauty. Her deep hazel eyes were framed by very dark lashes. Her mouth, for such a young child, was soulful. Her years of struggle were written all over her. She had finally learned to read, slowly and painfully. She loved Jane Louise because Jane Louise so openly adored her, and because Jane Louise seemed genuinely not to care whether she read or not. When Miranda was asleep in the shade, covered with a little net tent Teddy had rigged up, Jane Louise and Harriet sat side by side at the picnic table sketching.

———

At ten o'clock three mornings a week, Harriet was delivered to Jane Louise. Beth and Peter's enormous van drove up, and out jumped Beth, who even in the morning looked pulled together, cheerful, and eager to meet the day. Laura and Geneva, in white shorts and blue shirts, their brilliant hair pulled back by black headbands, jumped out with her. They were pink and gold, blooming, with rosy cheeks and bright brown eyes. Jane Louise, who never slept through the night even if Miranda didn't wake up, felt old, wrecked, exhausted.

Last of all was Harriet, still called Birdie by her mother, who was constantly saying: "I'm sorry, Harriet, I forgot."

Harriet was a bit disheveled and barefoot. Her eyes were cast down, and her sisters appeared to be glad to off-load her. They were going to Heathfield to buy shoes and to go to the library.

Jane Louise's heart opened like a flower. Going to the library had always filled Harriet's heart with dread. Even her little sister had been able to read when she could not. She had been sur- passed on every side. Jane Louise knew that feeling of exclusion, of being weird and odd, of never quite fitting in. When she saw it in Harriet, it brought out a fierce, protective streak—the same fierce love she felt for Teddy and Miranda. She wanted to hurt anyone who had hurt them, and when she saw Beth, Laura, and Geneva, so effortless, so fitting, she wanted to take bony, beloved Harriet into her arms and cover her with kisses. She put her arms around her husband's goddaughter.

"You two look alike," said Laura, who was twelve. "Don't they, Mom?"

"Our Birdie is a little changeling," Beth said with a tender smile.

It never ceased to amaze Jane Louise what people said out loud.

"I think she looks like her daddy," Jane Louise said, pulling her close. "She has those beautiful hazel eyes."

Laura peered at her sister, whose eye color had never been of much concern to her. Harriet was not much fun for Laura, who had a red-blooded competitive spirit and found Harriet useless to compete with. Instead she fought with Geneva, who was very advanced for six.

They drove off, leaving Jane Louise alone with Harriet and Miranda. The day was hers. She breathed in the clean air. In front of her was a long stretch of almost peaceful time, even if the house she was living in had never been hers, and this countryside was hers on loan. She could actually say: "This is my daughter and my goddaughter."

She would lend Harriet her straw hat, and Miranda would wear her tiny piqué sun hat. Together they would go down to the beach. With Miranda in her arms and Harriet by her side, Jane Louise might even feel—if just for a second—that she was here by some sort of right.

CHAPTER 34

On the Fourth of July, Edie and Mokie served a big celebratory lunch on the unstable, wrecked, splinter-strewn porch of Paul and Helene Schreck's house. Edie's brother Fred, his wife Stephanie, and their two perfect boys had threatened to come up and then changed their minds. Jane Louise could never figure out why Edie still never got to stay at her parents' house: Fred and Sam had first dibs. Even though Edie was far better off renting, it made Jane Louise angry that Edie so easily submitted to putting up with being just a girl, but that was Edie's style, and the form her rebellion took was never to ask for a thing.

Fred was tall and bony, with a big political agenda. He had been in the district attorney's office and had then run successfully for Congress. It seemed to Jane Louise that the entire family had run for Congress. Even the small Steinhaus children seemed preternaturally well behaved.

It was Mokie's opinion that these children, too, had had speechwriters hired for them. He particularly detested Fred, whom he considered an unreconstructed racist. Nevertheless, he forbore him and tried in the gentlest possible way to make him very uncomfortable. He had found that any allusions to himself and Edie sharing the same bed caused Fred to squirm and his flesh to creep.

As for Edie, her present preoccupation was the unabated dire state of the Schrecks' housekeeping. Their kitchen was most unsanitary. She had found moldering vegetables in the refrigerator and fetid potholders that had been torn to shreds by mice. It was clear that only the most cursory cleaning job had been done before they arrived. Helene Schreck had told Edie more than a dozen times how wonderful it was that Paul would, at great peril to his back, bring down the crib for them. Naturally, when they arrived, the crib was in the attic, and a note had been left saying that Paul's back had gone out at the last minute.

No complaints could be lodged against the Schrecks, however, since their son was Fred's congressional assistant. As for Beth and Peter Peering, they had only a bare idea who the Schrecks were: The Schrecks belonged to that segment of Marshallsville life that had no interaction whatsoever with the locals, but lived in a kind of bucolic, hermetic jar in which they saw and socialized with other weekenders and only knew the locals as tradespeople.

After lunch the babies took their naps at the lake, and the adults went swimming. It was the perfect Fourth of July: hot, breezy, and clear. The sky was a deep, deep azure.

At six o'clock everyone collected on the town green for a chicken barbecue, and then began the exodus to Ford Bridge Racetrack for the annual fireworks. Jane Louise and Edie had packed cupcakes and a thermos of iced tea. Mokie brought a six-pack of beer, and Teddy toted several enormous bags of potato chips.

They spread their blankets on a hill overlooking the racecourse.

From where she sat Jane Louise could easily see a dozen people she knew. Teddy probably could identify everyone from Marshallsville. He explained that even the seating was traditional. The Marshallsville contingent usually occupied the hill and slope. The people from Heath seemed to prefer the meadow near the track. The Avesbury crowd sat on the plain opposite the hill, and the rowdy teenage boys from Gloucester milled around on the racetrack itself, setting off squibs and roman candles. Slowly, slowly the light began to fade.

Teddy sat with one arm around Harriet and the other around Jane Louise, who held their drowsing baby in her arms. Next to her sat Edie with Tallie in her lap, then Mokie. The Peerings sat behind them.

"I hope the noise won't wake them up," Edie said.

"These babies would sleep through a hydrogen bomb attack," Teddy said. "It's the little things that wake them up, like telephones ringing, and sneezing."

It seemed that it would never be dark enough—the light failed so slowly.

"If it doesn't start soon, I'm going to pass out," Edie said.

"I think it's nice just to sit here," said Jane Louise.

"You're transparent," Edie said. "I can read your mind. You're sitting here thinking how steady it all is, and that you really don't belong here."

"I married in," Jane Louise said. "I'm just a poor wayfaring stranger."

"Oh, *please*," Edie said.

"It's easy for you to say," Jane Louise said. "You grew up here."

"I was a weekender, honey doll. A summer person. A snappy New Yorker from a private school."

"Don't I wish," Jane Louise said.

"No, you don't," Edie said. "You just be happy being your own moved-around, anxious self. The world isn't going to fly apart."

"Really?" Jane Louise said.

"What are you two muttering about?" Mokie said.

"Anxiety," Edie said.

"Oh, *that*," said Teddy. "Look alive! It's about to start."

A great boom echoed over the hill, and a point of light burst into a shower of green sparkles, which then burst into tiny silver stars. Jane Louise held her breath. These things never lost their charm for her. She gasped.

Fireworks, in Sven's opinion, were exactly like sex. "First there's the waiting, right?" he had said. "Lead-up, tension, a brilliant release. Just like the act itself."

As she sat next to Teddy, her leg pressed close to his and their baby breathing softly on her lap, on the same hill from which Teddy had seen these fireworks almost every year of his life, Jane Louise contemplated this.

Around her the dark sky hung like a curtain. In back of her Lynn Hellman's children were making rude noises. Under the tree, the Paulings, a couple in their late seventies, sat peacefully, holding hands. They were Marshallsville's great love story: married to others, madly in love for years and years, they had been widowed around the same time and had finally married in the Congregational Church and were now never seen apart. They seemed perfectly happy; everyone said how patiently they had waited for each other. He was tall, gray haired, and smoked a pipe. She was willowy, gray haired, and languid. For years he had been the headmaster of the Heath School. It was not hard to imagine them as lovers.

Jane Louise leaned her head against Teddy's shoulder. She had heard about the Paulings for years. She did not find this story sweet. She thought about the years and years in which the Paulings were not married to each other but suffered in secret. How fraught their lives must have been, but now the world had settled down and made for them—for an instant—a kind of peaceful sense.

She watched the sky light up and flash. She watched the sparkling drops that burst into brilliant sprinkles and disappeared into the velvety sky. It was magical: that deep, echoing noise, that glowing tension, that unexpected, magnificent, beautiful release, like the unexpected joy that swept you away, like life itself.